MAD BOYS

MAD BOYS

A NOVEL BY ERNEST HEBERT

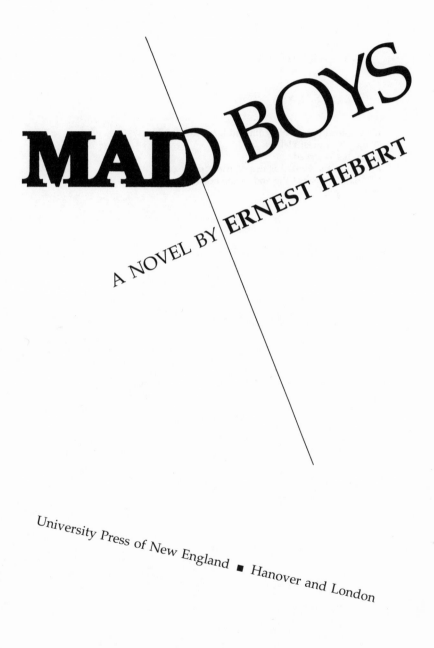

University Press of New England ■ Hanover and London

University Press of New England, Hanover, NH 03755
© 1993 by Ernest Hebert
Printed in the United States of America 5 4 3 2 1
CIP data appear at the end of the book

CONTENTS

ACKNOWLEDGMENTS

I'd like to thank Audrey Lyle, Dayton Duncan, Annie Proulx, and Jim Schley for critiquing earlier crude drafts of this work, with special thanks to Terry Pindell, who read two drafts and made several key suggestions that helped get this project rolling. Michael Lowenthal deserves tremendous credit for his editing job of *Mad Boys*. I couldn't have done it without you, Mike. To Medora Hebert, Lael Hebert, Nicole Hebert, Barbara Cunningham, Kathy Harp, Lou Renza, Cleopatra Mathis, Cynthia Huntingtom, Tom Sleigh, William Spengemenn, Nat Sobel, and Ted Timreck: bless you all for keeping up my spirits. I'd like to thank Dartmouth College for sabbatical time and for some money to help cover the travel expenses for the research on this project. To Mary Jane McCord: a special thanks for your kindness and hospitality on the road.

AUTHOR'S NOTE

I grew up in Keene, New Hampshire, with two brothers, no sisters. Lived in a neighborhood with no girls my age. Went to a Catholic school where boys were segregated from girls. In short, I grew up with boys. They had a tremendous effect upon my life, so this book is dedicated to the boys who enriched my childhood and especially to: the memories of Dick Doherty and Michael Patnode, who left us too soon; my brothers, Omer and Paul; and my "best" friends, Gordon McCollester, Bill Sullivan, Dennis Patnode, and John Westcott, who taught me the A-Y-G language.

The character Royal Durocher in *Mad Boys* is named after Royal Desrosier, a boy I idolized when I was a kid. The real Royal, who was kind and warm, is nothing like the fictional Royal. The characters of Mary Jane and Marla are named after my Texas cousins; the real Mary Jane McCord and Marla Norman are not to be confused with their fictional namesakes in personality, or in any other way.

The inspiration for *Mad Boys* came from photograph I saw of a boy who had been raped and murdered. I thought: this is the Huck Finn of our time; what if he got away?

MAD BOYS

Journal Entry 627: On the TV a bearded man speaks of the child within, distracting me from writing my essay on Virtual Realism. There is not much room in a van for two, and the TV definitely takes up room. I gave the van an exciting name, the Green Hornet, in hopes of keeping up the boy's interest. He went along with the name for a while, but lately he's been calling our home on wheels the mother ship. I'm afraid he has mother on the mind, but at the moment he sleeps at my feet on the mattress. I have installed the TV to keep him occupied and to provide myself with company. Sometimes I do not need the TV; sometimes the boy is company enough. He's bright and inquisitive, but there are moments when a man needs someone his own age to talk to, to listen to. The TV neither speaks nor listens, but it does alleviate loneliness by exciting the emotion of belonging and by simulating engagement with another. The TV is a virtual companion. Which returns me to my ruminations regarding Virtual Realism.

"Virtual Reality" was brought into the language as a computer term. It means merely that one can electronically simulate conditions in the real world; for example, train a pilot by having him react to a virtual moving world on a video monitor. The first time I heard the term "virtual reality," I was, like many people with an intellectual turn of mind, suddenly, completely, complicatedly, and inexplicably captivated. I felt like a man digging in a garden whose spade hits metal and in the vibration, shuddering through the shovel handle to his hands, thinks "buried treasure." In other words, my elation at the phrase was far greater than its given meaning. The term suggested something grander than a computer-aided simulation. But what? For a long time, I struggled to unearth this "treasure." Now I think I have found it. The virtual life we humans create through an artistic rendering of experience is more vivid, meaningful, and profound than the ordinary life of our day-to-day existence. What defines us as a species is our ability to create virtual worlds, as in art, religion, ideology, and values, and then not only to exist in but to thrive in the virtual reality of these virtual worlds.

To explain further, let us say that I am not the essayist Henri Scratch, but a more intuitive soul, the fiction writer Ernest Hebert. For breakfast, Hebert eats a boxed cereal, virtual corn (flakes) or virtual (puffed) wheat or virtual (rolled) oats. In Hebert's office, incandescent light bulbs provide virtual sunlight to illuminate the virtual wood grain of his metal and plastic desk. He telephones his agent, a virtual friend. He shops at the local mall, a virtual village. In a bar (a virtual living room), Hebert reads the virtual news in *USA Today* over a drink, which supplies virtual relaxation. Hebert's virtual world is not one of substance, but of style; not of fairness, but of *Vanity Fair*; not of speech, but of spin; not of the chicken, but of the McNugget.

In Hebert's virtual world, events are enhanced by human imagination and technology. For example, let us say this bachelor author of long standing marries. The ceremony is submerged in a murky sea of conflicting emotions and the tick-talk of time and ritual. The marriage only comes round as a vivid, felt reality later when the bride and groom view the videotape of the wedding ceremony. For a truer, more profound experience, viewing is superior to participation.

Not Hebert, but another anguished Catholic author, Jack Kerouac, was the first blatantly obvious virtual reality sensibility. According to his biographer, Anne Charters, young Jack remembered a flood in his hometown of Lowell, Massachusetts, "as something in 'The News of the Day' on the screen of the Royal Theater." Kerouac enhanced the reality of the flood on a virtual movie screen in his mind. The author's adult life had three aspects:

(1) the day-to-day drone of ordinary existence; (2) the meticulous record-keeping of that existence in hand-written notes; (3) the presentation of his life, highly romanticized, in prose fiction. It couldn't have been a good life for the creator. He died of drug and alcohol abuse before he was fifty. How can a man be real at the same time that he is recording the event of his reality? Which of the two acts is real, the living or the note-taking? Or is it the third act, the artistic rendering of the notes into fiction, that is real?

I am distracted again by the bearded man on the television and his talk about the child within. I shut off the TV, and now it is quiet in the van. The silence is more oppressive than the noise. I cannot gather my thoughts. . . . Once there was a child within me but he is gone, a virtual dead boy. Perhaps that is why I took a living boy off the Indian plateau. Five years now we have criss-crossed the country, avoiding pursuit. The first years were full of adventure. We took in the sights—the giant redwoods of California, the Badlands, the Grand Canyon, the Tetons, and Yellowstone. The boy liked the Carlsbad Caverns best of all. I eked out a living by writing magazine articles and book reviews. I was happy; the boy was happy. But as he turns the corner into adolescence, he is getting harder to handle. I think he's losing respect for me. I have to do something about this situation.

Journal Entry 635: Somebody on my trail. Boy becoming disruptive. Can't find the peace of mind to work on my essay.

Journal Entry 638: I've identified my pursuers, the boy's half-brother, Royal Durocher, and my darling wife, Marla. I was the one who first recognized Royal's genius; I had his IQ tested; I galvanized him with a detailed account of his father's suicide. When Marla married me she was just another marginally talented visual artist. I was the inspiration for her bizarre sculptures. Now they mean to kill me. The ingratitude.

Journal Entry 641: The boy is becoming a burden. He's losing his appeal. Traveling alone, I would be less conspicuous. I would be free.

Journal Entry 642: Night. I am in a New Hampshire community of perhaps 25,000 people. I have parked the van in a cemetery. Below are some trees, brush, and a swamp. The boy sensed what was in the offing and tried to get away. But I caught him, carried him down to the swamp, and drowned him in black, sticky muck. As frogs croaked in mating calls, I knelt on the moist ground and cleansed myself in a fit of weeping. Now I can get back to work on my essay. May God—if, as I once believed, there is one—have mercy on my soul, if there is one.

BAPTIZED

First memory: A series of still frames in a movie. Me, running up a long, slippery ramp leading to the mother ship suspended in space. Studio lights in my eyes. The ramp, so steep. "Faster! Faster! You're not going fast enough," yells the Director. He's got a carrot-colored beard, black cat-burglar suit, a hunched back, and he speaks through a device that disguises his voice, so that he sounds like a drowning man about to go down for the last time. I slip. Reach for a rail—there is no rail. I fall and start sliding down, head first, on my back. I come right out of the screen in two dimensions. Last frame: ramp, hovering mother ship, the stars, me outside the screen, in a zone between dimensions.

I can't remember my actual birth, but I know the feeling from the second memory: squeezed out, new, empty, choking, wanting so bad just to get a breath. I coughed and coughed and spat mud out of my mouth and throat. After I'd finished and began to breathe, I saw trees, one tree, branches, one bare branch, bugs, one bug, grid-eyes of a fly, one cell staring at me as it would stare at a turd: with hunger.

I struggled to escape. It was hard going. A big suck kept drawing me down. But I finally pulled free. I didn't have any clothes on, but I hadn't realized that yet. My nakedness was covered by a thick paste of mud.

At the sight of me a startled bird up a tree screeched and flew off. I didn't see it, but I heard the thwip-thwip of its wings and the noise turned my thoughts to the sound of my own breath. It came fast, in troubled pants. Thoughts, dreams, events, and breaths flowed together like streams making a river, so I couldn't judge how long I lay there. It must have been a while because the mud had dried on my skin. I didn't think "dry"—I thought alligator scales; alligator: great big jaw. The mind picture didn't scare me, but the sound the alligator made in my head, an echoing roar, did, and brought me to. I realized I was laying on my side on prickly ground. In the offing were hemlocks, their weepy branches and, in the spaces between, gloom. A snake of light slithered through the trees and beckoned to me. I rose up on my feet, not sure whether to run toward or away from the light. I tottered, fell, rose again, and staggered forward.

The land edged up and when I came out of the swamp and forest I was in a cemetery. Faded flags. Faded flowers. Freshly turned earth. Dark, dank earth. Kiss the flags. Kiss the flowers. Kiss the earth. Read the "the ends" on the tombstones. Elman. The end. Jordan. The end. LaChance. The end. Jordan again. The End. Salmon. The end. I tried to think of my own "the end." The image of a tombstone appeared in my mind, but instead of a name carved in rock there was a question mark. I tried to recall the face of a loved one. Nothing. My own face. Nobody. I searched my memory for something, anything. Everything in my head: gone. I tried to will myself aboard the mother ship of my first memory. I couldn't see the beginning or the end of the ship. Nor did I see doors or windows, but it was fraught with hatches barely two feet high. Locked. I conjured burglary tools, and imagined myself cracking open a hatch. Crawled in. Dark inside. I turned on the lights and found myself standing in a video library where the shelves went on as far the eye could see. I grabbed a tape. The cover was a plain, dull black upon which was a figure silhouetted in white. No details, just the slim shape of a boy running. I jammed the tape into the VCR and pressed "play." The tape was blank.

I moved on, out of the cemetery onto a street, hot on my bare feet. Two-story, wood-frame houses crowded together. Lawns. Gardens brimming with vegetables. Hedges. Sandboxes. Shade trees. The weather kindly. Must be late summer.

I heard the echo of a scared holler. Somebody had seen me, a kid probably.

A minivan approached, slowed; woman inside gave me a funny look; in response I gave her a funny look, or so I think she thought. In fact, I was trying to catch my reflection in her window to see what I looked like, but I missed it because she sped off.

Someone had been washing a car in a yard. Garden hose draped over a tree branch where it threw down a fine spray. Nobody in sight. The car wet under the sun and shiny as a gun barrel. I thought I might look at myself in its glass. Rainbows made by the hose spray against the sun. I forgot about me. Walk into the rainbows. Smell the rainbows. Touch the colors. I stepped into the spray, and the rainbow disappeared but the colors fawned over me.

After the water had washed the muck from my skin, I stepped out of the spray and looked at myself in the side mirror of the car. I saw a boy twelve or thirteen, dark skin, eyes of green and gold, stiff, shaggy hair the color of hardtop, body immature. Naked as the day he was born.

Then something really strange happened. I saw another boy in the mirror. He wore a silvery space suit. Although he had the features and build of a boy, he seemed very old and wise. He wore a tight-fitting cap, so I couldn't see the color of his hair, but his skin was pale, as if it had never seen the sun. Eyes like black dimes looked at me with pity and spite, and I was afraid. As the light stroked his suit, colors flashed and disappeared. It was like looking at the belly of a trout. It was like looking at the back of a mallard duck. It was like looking into the mind of God. I turned around to where he should have been. Gone. I looked again at the mirror. Nobody there, not even me.

Next thing I knew I was in a speeding ambulance, while a brawny-armed woman attendant checked me over. Another attendant, a man, drove the vehicle. The siren wailed, and we tore through the streets. I was in a small city in a broad river valley surrounded by wooded hills. Main Street was wide and dead-ended into a town square with a white church at its head. I wondered if this town was home.

"Where am I?" I asked the attendant.

"He's perking up," the attendant said to the driver, who relayed the information to the hospital on a microphone he held in his hand.

"This is Keene, New Hampshire," the attendant said to me.

"Keen?" I said.

"Yah, Keene."

"Have I been here before?"

"I wouldn't know," she said, then barked at the driver. "Pulse fast and uneven, can't give you a number; blood pressure one-fifteen over sixty." She turned back to me. "What do *you* think? Have you been here before?"

I was suddenly suspicious because of the way she asked me that question. "I'm the thousand-year-old boy, and I've spent these last 999 years and 364 days and 23 hours on a spaceship." I didn't know why I said that; the words just spilled out.

"Is that so? A flying saucer?"

"We call it the mother ship."

"We?"

"Yah, we."

"Who are the others?"

"Boys. They study boys from Earth on the mother ship." I was amazed, wondering as I spoke these words where they came from and whether they were true. They certainly felt true, but they did not seem to be my words, and I could tell that the attendant didn't believe them.

"That's real interesting, who is they?" the ambulance attendant asked.

"I can't say. I promised. You'll have to torture me to get me to talk."

"I see. What did you say your name was?"

I tried to create a name by voicing it, but the sound came out horrible and twisted, "Xiphi." I thought I would cry, but I held back.

"What's that? I didn't get it. Now tell me your name."

She was trying to get information out of me, and I knew I had to deliberately throw her off the track. "We didn't have names on the mother ship," I said. "They gave us numbers. Mine was 29868836462323."

"You have a nickname?"

"We didn't have nicknames. They called us by our number."

The attendant said to the driver, "Possible concussion. Possibly hallucinating."

I closed my eyes and tried to think of my name. Or maybe my number, which I had already forgotten. I concentrated so hard I blacked out.

When I came to I was in the hospital. A nurse who looked like a female Santa Claus gave me a little smile and then stuck a needle in my arm. I wanted to pull away, but I could barely manage a mumble of protest. Didn't realize how weak I was. Arms limp. Legs limp. Maybe I didn't have any bones. Maybe I was a snake disguised as a boy. I could see the snake in my mind now, a slithery body with the face of a man. The image disappeared when the nurse spoke.

"Going to pump some sugar and spice into your veins to rehydrate you." The nurse stroked my forehead. I liked the gentle touch of her hand, and I shut my eyes to feel it better.

An hour later I was awake and alert but still weak. My nurse introduced herself as Nurse Wilder. In her white uniform, white cap that swept down over her ears, and white cape, she looked like a tank in a wedding gown. She held my hand in her own big, dry hands, and she whispered, "As long as you're my patient, I'm going to take good care of you. You can cooperate by not giving me any guano." She screwed her face up into a fake glower. I knew I was going to like her.

My room was on the third floor. It had a television set equipped with cable, a bed, a dresser, a bathroom, a window with a view of the tops of pine trees partially blocking distant hills. There was also another bed (unoccupied) and a funny-shaped bowl on the floor.

"What's that?" I asked.

"A bedpan. For people who can't get out of bed to go to the bathroom. Now you rest up until Doctor Hitchcock comes." Nurse Wilder tucked me in and left the room.

As soon as the door shut, I jumped out of bed, grabbed the bedpan, and put it on my head. It was a little shaky, but if you added foam for a lining it would make a good helmet. I went into the bathroom to admire myself in the mirror. I looked like a soldier in an army of maniacs. I pranced around holding it squared away on my head. When I was bored with this act, I removed the "helmet" from my head and dropped it on the floor. I lifted my johnny gown and used the bedpan for the reason it was designed. It sounded a little bit like a ringing door bell. Then my aim went bad and I dribbled on my foot. I put the bedpan in the bathtub and went back to bed.

I clicked on the TV with the remote. Reception was great. For a while I didn't watch anything in particular, just flipped through the channels until I stopped at a reel of the Earth from outer space. It was blue with wisps of clouds. Seen from the darkness, above and far away and maybe in a spaceship, the earth looked like an inviting place.

A minute later Doctor Hitchcock walked in. He was a big man with reddish-brown hair. I could tell it was dyed by the flecky gray beard stubble on his face. I was scared of him, because he reminded me a little of the Director in my imagination.

"How are we this afternoon?" he said. "What are we watching on television?"

"Program about the sky," I said.

The doctor gave the TV a puckered look for a few seconds. "Oh, the depletion of our ozone layer," he said.

"In the mother ship, they called it the Old Zone," I said.

"Tell me about this Old Zone," Doctor Hitchcock said. He started to poke and prod me, and I could see he didn't really want to hear about the Old Zone or anything else I had to say. His friendly talk was just politeness. And he was in a rush. I wanted to apologize for putting him behind in his work. But the way he went about his business, as if I wasn't really there, made me bashful, so I shut up.

After he left, Nurse Wilder brought me a plate of food. I asked her about my loss of memory. She said that in cases like mine the patients either got their memories back a little bit at a time over the course of a few weeks, or they didn't get them back for months or even years. Sometimes never.

"How did I lose it?" I asked.

"A shock to your system." She wouldn't look at me; she stared out the window to the hill behind the pines.

"Oh," I nodded and nodded again, as anybody does when they don't want to let on that they don't know what's being said.

She turned and looked at me. "For a while, maybe, you were the devil's child."

"The devil." A shiver of pleasure and terror shot through me. I asked Nurse Wilder to tell me about the devil.

"He changes to any shape he wants. Your fears. Your desires. Your dreams. Your guesses. But his touch is always the same. Like slimy fire." She rolled her eyes and breathed like a hurrying hound. "Do you know Jesus?"

"I know the name. Religion. God, right?"

"Right. Jesus is the son of God. Jesus is God. And the Holy Ghost. The same. Three persons in one God."

A picture appeared in my mind of a cranky, three-headed man with his three toothbrushes, three combs, and three toupees. I must have flinched, because Nurse Wilder brushed her hand against my forehead. "Are you all right? Did I scare you?"

"No," I answered, "I was just thinking: There's a God, and he comes in a three?"

"Yes. Have you been baptized?"

"I don't know."

"To be on the safe side, you should be baptized," she said. "I will go to my priest. I will confess to him my sins. He will give me absolution, and I will be a child of God. Then I will return and baptize you, and you will be a child of God."

"Baptize me? Will that get my memory back?"

"Not likely."

"What good is it then?"

"Baptism qualifies you for heaven. Without it you either burn in the everlasting fires of hell or go to limbo."

"Limbo?"

"A state of being where nothing happens."

An image appeared in my mind: a sign off a multi-lane highway. "Like the weather forecast for San Diego, California." The words just came out of me, as if spoken by someone else.

"See, you knew that. You know a lot of things. You just can't remember why you know them." She took my hands into her own. "Another benefit of baptism is heaven assigns you your own guardian angel. He's always there, looking over you. Now pray with me."

I liked that idea of a guardian angel. Nurse Wilder raised her eyes to heaven, and she prayed, "Man makes bad seem good, good seem bad." Then she stopped and said, "Well?"

"Well, what?"

"Repeat the words."

So, I repeated the words—"Man makes bad seem good, good seem bad." And she went on and I went on, line by line.

"We trust not good in man. So in God we trust."

"I think I've heard that one before," I whispered.

"Don't think; thinking doesn't go well with prayer."

"In God we trust," I prayed, then spoke, "Maybe you could clue me in a little, I'm not quite following what this prayer is all about."

"Suppose I have a date," she said.

"Aren't you too old for that?"

"When you're too old for that, you're too old." She squeezed my hands so hard they hurt. "Fact is I don't have a date. My husband is in this very building at this very moment eaten up with cancer. But suppose I do have a date. His name is Mister Good. There he is. Job with benefits. Good intentions. Etcetera. Mister

Good looks at me and tells me with his eyes what he sees. Older woman. Lines in her face. Fat in her cheeks—both upper and lower. Too much craftiness in her eyes. You think that's going to make me happy?''

I shook my head no.

"Suppose Mister Bad shows up.'' Nurse Wilder let go of my hands. "His eyes and his lips feed me apple-pie lies to make me swoon and forget my troubles. You see what I'm saying?''

As softly and as kindly as I could, I said, "No.''

"You must only trust in God, because in man, good makes bad and bad makes good.''

I still didn't get it, but I wanted to move on to something else, so I said, "Now I understand.''

"That's because God's grace is already spreading through you. Have a good meal. Get a good night's rest. Keep God's gentle flame burning.'' Nurse Wilder yawned. She was tired; a few seconds later she was gone.

I dug into the tray of food, some kind of meat in gravy, mashed potatoes, salad, carrots, slices of nice soft white bread with pads of margarine. I ate everything. I hadn't realized how hungry I was.

After the meal, Doctor Hitchcock came to my room with four men and two women in white uniforms and badges on their lapels. Later Nurse Wilder told me they were beginner doctors. I was poked, pinched, prodded, squeezed, and punctured by needles. Quite an experience. Lights shined in my eyes, mouth, and even my . . . you know. Blood taken from my arm. Pee in a special plastic container, please. Move the elbow joint, please. Stand on tiptoes, please. I grew sick of pleases. As the examination progressed, I began to feel creepy and a little scared. A camera flash went off in my mind. In the afterimage of that light, it was as if I wasn't there. As if I was drawing away from my body. "Hold still,'' said Doctor Hitchcock, "we're doing this for your own good.'' I could see then, as Nurse Wilder had taught, that good makes bad.

Finally, they left. It was dark outside. I went to sleep with a single idea in mind: escape.

It was noon the next day before I woke up. Nurse Wilder brought me lunch—tuna salad, potato chips, extra pickles (because she liked me), and two glasses of milk. With each bite I could feel my strength returning.

Late in the morning a reporter and photographer from the *Keene Sentinel* newspaper arrived with Doctor Hitchcock. The doctor said that once my picture was in the paper, my parents would discover where I was and come and fetch me and take me home. I tried to picture these parents and this home in my mind, but drew a blank. It occurred to me that I had never had parents or a home; I was created out of nothing, for mysterious purposes, by Nurse Wilder's three-headed God. He/She/It/Them thought things over and said to themselves, let's make a boy. Let's not worry about giving him parents and a childhood. Let's just get him going and see what he does. They were up there in heaven, watching, and it was my job to put on a good show.

The reporter had a beard and doughy eyes. He typed what I said on a portable computer. "Have you really lost your memory?" he asked.

"I did lose it, but it's back," I said. "I remember plain as day what's happened to me."

"This is an important development." Doctor Hitchcock pushed the buzzer to the nurse station. "This is Doctor H. Send for the psych interns, and tell them to come to the amnesiac's room on the double." Then he looked at me. "When did your memory return?"

"Middle of last night, I started to remember. The rest came back this morning while I was using the bedpan."

"Can you tell us your name?" said the reporter.

"May we wait for the interns? He's part of their training," said Doctor Hitchcock.

"Makes no difference to me," said the reporter.

A few minutes later the rookie doctors arrived, and I was allowed to talk. "I was kidnapped," I said. "Stolen. Put in a cage. Starved."

"Who did this to you?" the reporter said.

"A doctor," I said.

"What?" said Doctor Hitchcock.

"A doctor from another planet, an alien. He took me aboard his space ship to study me."

The reporter stopped typing, but the young doctors started furiously taking notes.

"Oh, no, a schizoid," said Doctor Hitchcock, as much to himself as to the rest of us. "Can't they think of anything better than little green men from outer space?"

"Can we tape this?" asked one of the rookie doctors.

"Not important enough. Let him continue while his steam is up," said Doctor Hitchcock, and he turned to me and smiled with his mouth only. "A flying saucer. Tell us all about it."

"That's what the attendant in the ambulance called it—she saw it plain as day," I said. "But it was only the transfer shuttle. The mother ship is not a flying saucer, but a flying sausage. A hundred-mile-long hot dog. They keep it parked behind the moon, so human spy satellites won't pick it up. I was playing alone in the orphanage when the Alien came and got me. I was beamed to the transfer shuttle, and then taken to the laboratory behind the moon. The whole trip took only a few seconds."

"What was this alien being like?" the reporter asked.

"He was more than a being. He was my doctor," I said. "He looked like a snake with a human face. He wrapped his coils around me, and my eyes bugged out of my head and I couldn't breathe. Then he'd let me go. 'Just kidding,' he said, and slithered away."

I had started with the idea of telling a big lie, and a lie, I suppose it was, but the more I talked the truer the story sounded to me. I wondered if maybe just talking, talking, talking, talking helped a person find the truth. I didn't know, so I just kept on. The more I talked, the more marvelous the experience of talking grew.

"Inside the ship were big rooms full of Earth plants and animals, for study," I said. "I was allowed to go anywhere I wanted, except behind hatches that said 'Danger. No Earth Atmosphere Behind This Point.' I opened one of the hatches anyway, but it only led to an air lock where the atmosphere could be changed. The hatches were barely big enough for me to crawl through. After all, the Alien didn't need tall doors. I tried to open one of the hatches, but it was wired and gave me a shock. I left, realizing that I didn't really have the run of the ship. The Alien was watching my every move."

"Can you describe your own personal living accommodations?" the reporter said.

"I had my own room and television. We all did. We could watch TV programs and monitor first-run movies from Earth. Reception was much better than on this pitiful planet. The actors left the screen and came out and played with us. For meals, we would squat on the floor of our tree house and put in our order: 'A Graphic Burger with the works, fries, and a chocolate shake.' The food would be served by robots. They were built like the snake doctors, but they didn't have the smell."

"The smell?" said the reporter.

"Oh, I didn't tell you about the smell of my doctor?" I stared hard at Doctor Hitchcock. "It was like something musty and dirty. Like laundry that's been laying around for ten years beyond the door in the bathroom. Like the puke of sick people. Like the hiney breath of dragons."

"I think we get the point," said Doctor Hitchcock.

And on and on I talked, ending with my escape. I told them that they were bringing me on a transfer shuttle back to Earth to pick up some more captives. I was supposed to welcome the new subjects on board, but as the vehicle hovered over Keene I jumped into the transfer beam and ended up in the swamp behind Greenlawn Cemetery.

Middle of the night, my room almost pitch black. A hand on my shoulder and I woke up. I wasn't scared. I could tell by the whiff of powder it was Nurse Wilder.

"I have the holy water," she whispered.

I sat up in bed and stretched, and Nurse Wilder flipped on the television, turned the sound down but left the picture on. Colors flickered in the dust molts around us like our own private northern lights.

"Next best thing to a holy candle," Nurse Wilder said. She took my hand and pulled me gently out of bed. We knelt on the hard floor. It wasn't until afterward that I realized she cheated by resting her butt on her calves.

"Now we are in our church," she whispered.

"Yes," I said in a return whisper, in awe.

"Tip your head back." I did as I was told and she poured water from a vial on my forehead. It dripped down into my eyes, and I blinked and my nose itched. Nurse Wilder whispered the sacred words, "I baptize thee in the name of the Father and of the Son and of the Holy Ghost."

She put the vial in her breast pocket and took my hands in her own. "Now pray with me. Oh, God in heaven, welcome this soul into your realm. We trust in your goodness." Nurse Wilder paused, then added in a lower, sidelong whisper to yours truly, "Say amen."

"Amen," I said.

She let go of my hands, stood, and put on the light. "I've got to go down to ICU and look in on my husband. He's dropped into a coma." She took a deep breath. "I'm so tired, I could join him. If only I could shut my eyes. If only. . . ."

"Where's my guardian angel?" I looked around.

"You can't see him, but he's here. Now that you're baptized, he will help you when you are in trouble. Now pray with me. Repeat these words from the good book: 'See first the kingdom of God and everything else will be added unto you.'"

I spoke the holy words, as I tried to "see first the kingdom of God." But I didn't *see* anything. I did, however, hear the voice/ voices of the three-headed God, arguing with Himself/Herself/ Themselves. *He's made, but he's not doing much. Give him time, he's just a kid. Brand new, they squeak.*

Nurse Wilder kissed me on the forehead, shut off the TV, and was gone. I lay in bed and I tried to pray, but I had nothing to say to any of the three persons of the one God. I wasn't worthy. I called for my guardian angel, but he was a no show.

WEB

The next day another nurse came in with some good news, some bad news, and some middling news. Nurse Wilder's husband had passed away, and she was taking a few days off to make the burial arrangements. That was the bad news. The good news was that I was given some clothes. The nurse opened a bundle, and dumped out jockey shorts, blue jeans, a T-shirt, and track shoes. The middling news was that I was scheduled to talk to a psychiatrist who was supposed to help me remember.

"I need some exercise," I said to the nurse.

"I guess it's all right for you to walk up and down the corridor," the nurse said. "Get dressed and go ahead."

After I put the clothes on, I felt more like a boy, less like a hospital patient. I cruised the hallways of the hospital, pretending to be woozier than I was. The exits were clearly marked. You didn't have to be Houdini to get out of this place.

Doctor Thatcher, the psychiatrist, showed up while I was wearing the bedpan on my head. She was a dark woman, square-built as a toy dump truck with dark eyes for headlights, and gray hair over her cab and a few white chin whiskers where the bumper would be, and she dressed like a guy. She said I should ramble on about whatever was on my mind. I asked if it was all right to wear the bedpan when I talked, and she said okay. That relaxed me a little.

"Do you want to lay on the bed or sit on a chair?" she asked.

I was thinking that I wanted to sit on the window sill and pretend I was on a ledge, but I said, "I want to pace around."

"All right, I will sit in the chair and you pace around," she said.

"Do I have to tell the truth?" I started pacing.

"Do you know what the truth is?"

"Maybe. Maybe not."

"Say what is on your mind." Her voice was soft and dry, almost friendly. She wasn't a know-it-all like Doctor Hitchcock, but close.

"I'm an orphan," I said. "An alien infected my mother with a disease while she was pregnant with me. Luckily, she had a huge inheritance, so she could afford to give me nothing but the best. For an infected boy, that meant a world without germs. I was brought up in a plastic bubble."

"A plastic bubble, that's interesting," said Doctor Thatcher. "Tell me some more about this environment."

"I had my own bedroom and bathroom. All the comforts. Radio, TV, video games, trucks, cars, baseball glove, basketball, hockey puck, football, bowling ball, golf ball, tennis ball, skateboard, bicycle, knives, and hundreds of toy guns. But I had no direct contact with the outside world. My food and everything else came to me through a series of chambers, where the germs were killed with radiation."

"And what were your feelings toward this environment?"

"I didn't have feelings."

"No feelings? You must have felt something."

"No, nothing."

"If you didn't have feelings what did you have inside of yourself?"

That was a good question, and I had to stop and think for a second before I could make up a good answer. "I was full of imagination," I said.

"And what did you imagine?"

"I used to imagine I was on the Alien's spaceship. Actually, maybe I really was on a spaceship, and the Alien left a false memory of that bubble in my mind to cover up what really happened." Now I was beginning to make sense.

"Intriguing hypothesis. What else about this plastic bubble? If it wasn't on the spaceship, where was it located?"

"In an exposition," I said, not sure where I'd gotten that word from.

"Exposition? Like a fair?"

"That's right. The Exposition of the Uncanny. Everybody there was insane, but I was the only one with his own plastic bubble, left to him by his loving mother."

"Were you happy in the bubble?"

"Miserable. Absolutely miserable."

"So you did have feelings."

"Maybe I did, but they were private."

"I can respect that. Something that you didn't have in this bubble was access to parents. Isn't that so?" said the Doctor.

I didn't say anything. Her words squeezed me like the coils of the Alien. I listened to the short pants of my breath. Doctor Thatcher said something.

"What?" I said.

"I said tell me where your parents were while you were in the bubble."

"Both dead." Saying that relieved the squeezed feeling. "I've never seen my father. He was a brave soldier, killed in the line of duty in a faraway country. I can't tell you which one, because it's classified information. My mother died when I was six. I barely remember her. She was beautiful and kind, but I could never feel her arms around me. You know, because of the plastic bubble? If I left the bubble, germs would make me sick. I would waste away like my mother and die.

"One day I decided I'd had enough. I was going to see the world. I broke out of the bubble and ran away, but I was disappointed. The world was dirty and smelly. I tried to get back to the bubble, but there was a swamp in the way and I was sucked down into its muck. I remember a choking feeling. Next thing I knew I was coming out of the muck. And here I am. I've got a year, maybe two, to live before the disease takes hold and kills me. Which is all I want, really. All I deserve." Suddenly I could say no more. I wanted to cry; I wanted my mother; but I didn't want the doctor to think I was a wimp so I held back.

I hadn't noticed, but I'd stopped pacing, and I was standing stock still and stiff. Doctor Thatcher stood and removed the bedpan from my head.

"Today's session is over," she said. Up close she smelled like a woman, all fine powders. I wanted her to put her arms around me, but she left without touching me.

A week went by. I watched television and ate huge amounts of food.

My talks with Doctor Thatcher went on morning and afternoon. I told her nothing but wild stories. She knew I was lying but she never complained, which made me wonder about her. We only had one outstanding session. I asked her what was wrong with me besides losing my memory. She said it was too early to tell, and then she asked me a question: "What do you think about to make your penis get hard?"

"My penis doesn't get hard," I said.

"You don't become excited down there?"

I blinked at her, not knowing what she was talking about. "You mean, peeing?" I said.

"No, I do not mean peeing," she said. "You're telling the truth for a change, aren't you?"

"No, I'm lying."

"Do you know the facts of life?" she asked.

That question was like opening a door to a pit of screaming demons. "Don't tell me!" I said. "I don't want to hear." I blocked my ears.

"Okay, session's over. Relax," she said.

But tongues of light lashed my eyes, and the deep moans of the damned echoed in my head. I hugged myself and jumped up and down. Doctor Thatcher ran to the intercom, calling the desk for help. I screamed at her, "Xiphi! Xiphi! Xiphi!"

A minute later an orderly held me down, while Doctor Thatcher gave me a shot. Somewhere behind the blue sky in black space, the mother ship pulsated like a living thing.

I wiled away my free time thinking about escape. It was during one of those moments when, lying in my bed, TV on but the sound down, I had a visitor, a handsome boy about fifteen. He slipped into my room, closed the door behind him, and looked around, greedy-eyed as a cat in a bird cage. He was well dressed, in an ascot, sunglasses, and an orange baseball cap with the black letters A-Y-G on the visor. He put a finger to his lips. "If somebody comes to the door, I'll duck under the bed, and you don't tell I'm here. Gayget aygit?"

"What?"

"Get it equals gayget aygit. Stupid equals staygupaygid." He pointed to the A-Y-G on his cap. "Secret language."

"Okay equals aygokaygay," I said.

"Raygight," he said.

I felt an instant hero-worship for this boy. He seemed to throw off light from within; his voice was full of command, without being bossy. He had my full attention.

"Who are you? And how did you find me here?" I asked.

"Your picture was in the newspaper. Lost boy. Amnesia. Flying saucer stories. They've got an APB out on you. You better get out of here, or pretty soon your so-called loved ones are going to be on your trail."

"What do you care?"

"I don't, really. I don't care about anybody but me. But I always follow my instincts, and when I read the news account about you, my instincts brought me here. I knew you were one of my own kind."

"You mean we're related?" I said.

"We're virtual brothers. I mean that like me you got away."

"You think I ran away from home."

"Exactly. Life was so bad there you had to bug out. I know that routine. Once they find you, all they're going to do is bring you back to the life you hate."

"Actually, an alien being from outer space . . ." I started to tell my story over again, wondering how I was going keep the details straight. I'd forgotten half the stuff I'd said to the doctors. But it didn't matter. The boy cut me off before I got started.

"I hear 'spaceship,' and I want to yawn. When you find one that can make some money, give me a call."

"You saying I'm a liar," I challenged him.

"I'm saying you're a sicko," he said.

I suppose he should have made me angry, but instead he relaxed me. I couldn't fool this teenage whiz bomb, so why should I try? "Tell me who you are," I said.

"Royal Durocher. My associates call me Royal. Notice that I said associates, not friends. I don't believe in friendship. There's no profit in it. I believe in partnership. I do something for you, you do something for me. Want to know the secret of my power?"

"Sure do."

"There's no love in my heart. That's my power. It's the power of Satan himself."

"I don't believe you."

"I'm the son of a rich record producer who lost everything in the 1987 stock market crash. My mother abandoned me when I was an infant, so I hated her. If you won't love your mother, why should you love anybody?"

"That's sad."

"Don't you pity me. There's no reason for it. You see, I'm not discouraged. I'm completely undiscouragable. I'm infuriatingly upbeat; I'm a positive thinker; I'm more gifted than a cross between a porpoise and a parrot. To sum it up, I am the proud possessor of 'the gift.'"

"'The gift'—what gift?"

"The entrepreneurial gift. Enough about me. We have to get you out of this joint," he said.

Though I'd been bent on escape, now that it was put to me that I ought to leave, I wasn't so sure I wanted to go. "Maybe I don't want to escape. Maybe I just want to find out who I am. And if you're so smart, you show me how to get my memory back."

"Okay. Sometimes drastic measures are called for." Royal picked up the bedpan and knocked me on the head with it. I saw stars, saw a green and gold frog, saw a dark, oily shadow, saw a grinning fat man, then blacked out for about a ten-second count. When I came to, I was fingering a lump the size of a tomcat's hairball on my right temple.

"Remember anything?" Royal said.

I thought and thought. Blank tape. "No. You're not going to hit me again, are you?"

"Why should I? It didn't work. One more blow and I might kill you, and that would help neither one of us. I'll think of something else."

"I don't know," I said, rubbing my head.

"Look," he said, "if you want to stay here and wait for your loved ones, go ahead. Know what grown-ups do? Make you suffer in your heart." Royal thumped his chest.

I thought about that for a minute. As far as I knew, I had no loved ones. What I did have, though, was a hollow place inside that needed to be filled with memories of people, events, and feelings. At the least, I wanted to know my name.

"Do you know who I am?"

Royal looked me up and down, real serious. "You're nobody," he said.

"Wha—?"

"Follow me. You're about to be tested." We went into the bathroom.

"Look in the mirror. What do you see?" he asked.

I saw the face of a kid. Black hair. Twist in the mouth. "I see a tough kid," I said.

"Look again. Look at the eyes."

The eyes were scared. I wondered why, and the brashness disappeared from my expression.

"What you see is a frog," Royal said.

Sure enough, as I looked closer I saw bulging eyes, a wide, sarcastic grin, and smooth, shiny, mottled skin the same color as the eyes, green and gold. "I'm not a frog," I screamed. "You're making fun of me."

Royal just laughed.

"You're mean," I said.

"I'm not mean, I'm cruel. All great men are cruel. I'll show you. Ask me where your mother is."

"My mother? You know her?" I was frantic.

Royal gave me a nasty smile.

I snarled at him, "Where is my mother?"

He chuckled in an exaggerated way designed to get my goat, "How much will you pay me to tell you?"

I doubled my fist and held it up in front of his face.

"You couldn't lick a stamp," he said.

"I'll kill you," I said.

He sneered, "Your mom choked to death on a fish bone."

I threw a punch, but Royal just grabbed my arm and twisted it behind my back until I yelled in pain. He let go of me, and said, "Stay calm, it was just a joke. I'll tell you what I've figured out. You don't have suburban swagger. You don't have street smarts.

You're not a country boy. You aren't spoiled. I know spoiled, because I was spoiled, so that means you aren't rich. I'd say you've done some time on the roads of America, because you got a little bit of this and little bit of that in your accent. Deep down you're mixed up. All mixed up."

I felt the intelligence of his words. Royal Durocher had told me more about myself than Nurse Wilder on my platoon of doctors.

We left the bathroom and returned to my room and hopped on the bed. I sat at the tail end, Royal at the head end.

"Take me with you," I said.

"In my car?" he teased.

"You have your own car?" I said.

"Not just a car, a white limo. It was the one thing my father protected from bankruptcy. Last month I was old enough to get my junior license. I claimed my old man's car and moved out."

"Where do you live?"

"In the car, dummy."

"How do you get money for food and movies and stuff?"

"Look at this." Royal pulled out his wallet and showed me a wad of bills. "I've been selling steroids to high school athletes. It's a pretty good business. But I've got other plans, plans for making big money, really big money."

"What's that?"

"Number One: Gun running. Everybody wants guns. Number Two: Development of new forms of entertainment. Number Three: Start my own empire. The adults haven't done anything for the country. It's time the kids took over, with me as the king kid, the czar of adventure and synthetic violence, the emperor of ice cream, the duke of vice, the dauphin of mean."

At that moment Nurse Wilder's voice came across the intercom, "Get dressed, young stranger. Flush your toilet and turn off your TV. We've got big news for you."

"This may be the end for you," said Royal. "Your loved ones could be coming to drag you away. I'd better go."

"I'll go with you; I won't be any trouble," I said.

"Back there when I was being cruel, irritating you with that stuff about your mother? Well, that was the test, and you flunked. You're not ready to face up to the world. You're just a baby." He slipped out of my room, and I was suddenly alone, a white nothing swirling in a blinding light.

A minute later in came Doctor Hitchcock, Doctor Thatcher, and Nurse Wilder. Nurse Wilder had lost a few pounds since her husband had died.

"We've been able to identify you," said Doctor Hitchcock. "Your name is Langdon Webster."

I don't know why, but I exploded, saying strange things, my body writhing as I spoke, "Xiphi elphege alcid vaccarressi flora."

"He's having a seizure," said Doctor Hitchcock.

"He's trying not to feel, not to remember," said Doctor Thatcher.

"He's speaking in tongues," said Nurse Wilder. "Langdon? Langdon?"

"Don't you call me Langdon." I was suddenly clear in my speech, if not my thinking. "That's the dead boy. He's not me. Understand? I'm him. We're me. He's us."

"He's going to need more therapy," said Doctor Thatcher.

"For now, let's make do with information," said Doctor Hitchcock sarcastically. "Your father, a gentleman named Joseph Webster, reported you missing as a possible runaway five years ago when you were seven years old."

"Is my father going to come and get me?" I asked.

"Mister Webster is not in, how shall I say, a financial position to support a young boy," said Doctor Hitchcock.

"The plain fact is your father is an old hippie from the 1960s, a drifter, an alcoholic, and possibly a drug addict," said Nurse Wilder. "It's a shame that he's going to be allowed to claim you."

I tried to picture this father in my mind, but couldn't.

"Nurse Wilder is right," said Doctor Thatcher. "But, to give the devil his due, your father has vowed to start a new life now that you've been found. He's coming to get you."

At that point, something dawned on me. "And my mother?" I blurted out.

Nurse Wilder dabbed at a tear, and I felt a shudder pass through me. Doctor Thatcher said, "I'm afraid that the whereabouts of your mother are unknown."

That night I couldn't sleep, and Nurse Wilder prayed over me. I tried to join her, but I couldn't get the words out. I just babbled, "Xiphi, exlibo, sanskrew, lyxpyks." After she left, I switched on my television. Just when I was dozing off, a white light filled the room, and the boy in the iridescent space suit who I had seen the first day out of the swamp appeared on the TV screen.

"Now I know who you are. You're my guardian angel," I said.

"That is correct. I'm an angel."

"Help me."

"I'm afraid that my abilities in this world are severely limited."

"Is it true that there are three persons in one God?"

"At least three."

Maybe there were four-headed and five-headed gods. Too many to deal with. I changed the subject. "What is your name?"

"My name is Langdon."

"They say my name is Langdon."

"No, Langdon is the dead boy, and I am his spirit."

"I want. . . ."

"I know what you want. I can read your mind. You want to feel your mother's arms around you."

"I can't. . . . I don't know. I have a need, an empty." I couldn't translate my deep feelings into English; I was choking on my own words. Langdon helped.

"I will tell you this: there is such a thing as the search for truth. Truth is what you seek."

The search for truth: I thought that was about the most noble idea I'd heard since coming out of the muck.

"Where is my mother?"

"Not today. That is not on today's list of things to say. Today I will inoculate you with your, with your, with your. . . . Oh, oh, stuck-record syndrome. Your name. My name. Our name. His name. The dead boy . . . the dead boy . . . the dead . . . Scratch . . . Scratch . . . Web . . . Web . . . Web."

I opened my eyes, the program was back on the screen, my guardian angel was gone, I was alone, awake, ignorant as ever.

The next morning I was released into the custody of my father. Nurse Wilder made me sit in a wheelchair, even though I didn't need one. I was a little embarrassed, but I have to say I enjoyed the ride down the hall, to the elevator, into the lobby, and out into the open air. In the parking lot, I spotted Royal's white limousine, but the glass was tinted and I couldn't see inside.

Less than a minute later, I heard a noise like a ruptured lawn mower. Out of nowhere a battered pickup truck, backfiring and roaring from a hole in the muffler, pulled right up on the grass beside the hospital gate. The next thing I knew, the passenger side door was flung open, and a voice called out, "Get in!"

I froze. Behind the wheel sat about the scroungiest human being I could imagine, a man with a scraggly beard and dark, greasy, shoulder-length hair. I thought the devil had come to take me away.

"It's him," said Nurse Wilder.

I got out of my wheelchair, and Nurse Wilder gave me a big, strangling hug. Next thing I knew, a hand grabbed my wrist and jerked me into the cab at the same time that the truck ripped out of the hospital lawn, tearing up divots.

Rock music pounded on a tape deck as we sped out of the parking lot. The man wore filthy blue jeans, a flannel shirt, scuffed leather boots. From his clothes, I smelled wood smoke and b.o.; from his breath, I smelled alcohol and pizza with everything on it, including anchovies, and something else I couldn't identify. Later I found out that the smell was marijuana.

"You're . . . you're my father," I said, trembling.

"Joe Webster, your old man. I got custody of you."

"I'm . . . I'm . . . Web," I said.

"Of course, you're Web—we always called you Web."

MOTHER/FATHER

Father had been a homeless man on the streets of Seattle, Washington, when he'd received a telephone call at the shelter where he was staying. An unidentified man had informed Father that I'd been found in New Hampshire, and then hung up. Father had hitchhiked back East, not sure how he was going to take care of himself, let alone take care of a son he hadn't seen in five years. But I'd brought him luck, he said. He had bumped into an old hippie friend, fellow with a sick liver who had offered to let Father squat on his property ten miles west of Keene if Father promised to watch over the place while he was convalescing. The fellow never did convalesce; he died. Father and I moved onto the land and started acting like we owned it. Father figured that if he paid the property taxes nobody would bother us.

The land was deep in forested hills, on an unmaintained dirt road one mile up slope from the town road. The place soon began to feel like home. Father taught me about the woods, and soon the knowledge spread through me almost as warmly as Nurse Wilder's blessing. Fluttering leaves: poplar. Sticky bark, soft, white wood: pine. Winter green smell in raw wounds: black birch. Reddish bark and roots that hug granite: hemlock. Tough wood, good to burn: red oak. Sweet sap, good to lick: hard maple.

Most of the trees were about fifty years old, having grown up after a hurricane ripped through in 1938, but some sugar maples four and five feet in diameter had survived the storm, and down slope was a sugar shack. One of the maples, which must have been two hundred years old or more, had been hit by lightning maybe around the time I was born or before. The strike hadn't killed the tree, but had weakened it, and it had fallen shortly before Father and I moved onto the property. You could still see the black gash from the lightning hit. The trunk of the tree was huge and twisted with cavities big enough for someone my size to hide in. I loved sitting on the trunk, feeling the sunlight which squeezed through the space in the forest created when the maple had fallen.

In this twenty-acre forest lot, scores of transit hippies had lived in yurts, tents, log huts, and the hulks of vehicles. The hippies were gone; the tents were gone; the yurts and log huts had fallen into themselves because of bad roofs; the hulks of vehicles had hunkered down and become part of the landscape. Small trees and bushes grew out of them. They added a lot to the beauty of the scenery. The property was on the dark north side of the hill. (Other places our "hill" would have been a mountain, but in this part of the country they liked to exaggerate in reverse.) Not a neighbor in sight. We preferred it that way. Behind a screen of trees was Father's garden. Here he planned to grow some table vegetables next year. Meanwhile, he'd found a stash of marijuana harvested by previous occupants.

Father and I lived in a school bus with no engine and no wheels. We didn't have indoor plumbing or electricity in the school bus home, but there was a wood stove, a couple of mattresses, chairs, a propane-gas refrigerator, and tie-dyed curtains on the windows. We had a generator to run lights and the water pump, but Father shut off the juice at bedtime and we made do with flashlights, candles, and the moon. Father never got on my case for lack of neatness.

He wangled a way to keep me out of school, not for my benefit but so he could put me to work. Still, as far as I was concerned, the benefit was mine. Father petitioned the school board for the right to educate me himself, because (he swore) organized education was against his religion. Which was almost true. He signed a paper saying he'd teach me at home. He talked a lot about education, how good it could be "outside the system," but he never actually taught me anything by way of formal learning. Actually, I already had a pretty good handle on the basics of reading and writing, so apparently I'd learned something in the five years that we'd been separated. The main thing Father taught me was cigarette smoking. He bought me a pack every day or so, even later when we were low on cash. I thought this was a very progressive action for a parent. Father believed that nothing was more important to an individual than his addictions.

Early on I asked Father about Mother, and he whacked me. He said he didn't want to talk about her, about family, or anybody from the old days. He had his reasons, and that was that. I figured eventually he'd have to say something more. I just had to bide my time. Meanwhile, I waited for Langdon, my guardian angel, to appear. I had a plan; the angel would tell me where to find my mother. Father and I would track her down. Father would forgive her for hurting him; she would forgive him for whatever he needed to be forgiven for; they would both forgive me for whatever I needed to be forgiven for. I didn't need to forgive them for anything. They just needed to forgive me and each other. Once that was done, the three of us would live together happily ever after. I told Father about Langdon, but he said he was only a figment of my imagination. Maybe so, but I still remembered his visit and the wonderful idea he'd left me with: the search for truth.

I also asked Father about the facts of life that Doctor Thatcher had referred to. He explained to me the whole business about putting it in and squirting that stuff inside and babies growing up. This was information I already should have known about, Father said. He thought I was faking interest just to embarrass him, but it was all news to me. He asked me if I had the feeling yet. I asked him what he meant by the feeling. He said the feeling that you feel when you feel yourself down there. I told him I didn't have the feeling. He said he'd lost the feeling after he'd gotten into heavy drinking. Maybe it was all for the best, he said, that neither one of us, for whatever reason, had the feeling. He surprised me, then, by crying and taking a swing at me, but I saw it coming and he missed.

The leaves exploded with colors. Late fall after the leaves were down was even better. No bugs. No humidity. No leaves blocking the sun. No tourists.

Father and I hunted, fished, and trapped for many of our meals, and sometimes just for the fun of it. Once in a while Father cooked on the wood stove and, during a spell of Indian summer, outdoors on a stone fireplace; more often, we ate our meals cold right out of cans. Local people called Father Dirty Joe; I didn't care. I missed Nurse Wilder, but getting away from the hospital, getting away from doctors, getting away from politeness was like cutting a good fart: a big relief. For a while I was happy in the woods.

During the daytime I helped Father with his business as a free-lance firewood dealer. He would hook up with a contractor who was, say, building a house or a condo. Loggers would cut down the trees and take the good sawlogs. Father would be in charge of clean-up. He'd cut the rest of the wood with his chain saw, and I would toss the sticks in the bed of the pickup. We sold the wood to a wholesaler, who split it with a hydraulic machine and sea-soned it a year before selling it to homeowners for firewood. After we moved out the salable wood, we'd stack the slash on the con-struction site and burn it. Cutting firewood, loading it, unloading it was hard work. But burning brush, that was no work at all. Fa-ther and I would get the fires going with the help of kerosene and old tires, sit back, and smoke cigarettes. Sometimes Father drank a six-pack of beer. I didn't like it when he started in that early, be-cause he wouldn't stop, and by nighttime he'd be in an ugly mood.

Father drank beer and/or smoked marijuana every night. He let me try them both, but something told me to lay off. Nicotine became my vice.

I don't want to give the impression that everything was blissful. The problem was Father's personality. He used to beat me up. He never punished me; he never corrected me for bad habits such as public spitting, farting, nose-picking, rudeness, back talk, or bird-flipping; he never criticized my manners or my posture or my oc-casional swearing. It was never anything I did that triggered his anger. It was all in him. He started out cuffing me with the flats of his hands, but he sprained a thumb and after that he used a stick (except when he was being spontaneous). He was careful never to hit me in the belly, because I think he wanted to avoid any internal injuries. I was grateful for that. I had black eyes, cut lips, puffy cheeks, and bruised arms and shoulders from trying to protect my-self; to this day I have a ringing in my left ear from getting whacked.

I don't want to exaggerate. At the time I didn't mind too much getting whipped by my old man. I thought it was just part of growing up. He handled his frustration by getting stoned and drunk, waffling the bejesus out of me, and pretending the next morning that nothing had happened. Father would never have thought of pounding on a stranger. I felt kind of exalted, knowing that if he hurt me he might feel a little less stress and frustration. If there was one thing that kept me going it was that Father needed me. He said as much: "Without you, Web, I'd be back on the streets and dead in a year."

When Father was sober, he more or less ignored me, but when he was stoned he liked to giggle and listen to music on his battery-operated boom box. He'd talk about the 1960s and early 1970s when he was hot stuff. He'd scoff at both conservatives and liberals. They were all part of "the system." Not Father—he was part of "the revolution"; he loved that word "revolution." Sometimes he'd say it just to excite himself. The revolutionaries had set the country on fire. They showed what people could do living together, loving together, playing music together, planting crops together, making home brew together, discovering new highs together.

When Father was drinking, he would criticize the government and the country, which he said was rigged so that only certain people got ahead. The system was responsible for lobotomizing the brains of young people. Talking about the system got him to talking about his own father, who was "straight" and who had died without ever getting stoned. Sometimes Father's anger would turn to sadness, and he would become weepy. It was during one of those moments, on a gray December day on a wood-cutting job, that I dared spring the subject of my mother again.

Other boys my age were buying Christmas trees with their families. Father and I were delivering a load of firewood at 19 Oak Street in the neighborhood near Greenlawn Cemetery. Snow had fallen, melted, and frozen up solid, leaving the land hard and drab in color. Our client was paying us extra to stack the wood neatly. Father was in the bed of the truck tossing me sticks, and I was on the ground stacking the wood in rows four feet tall. It was a pretty good background for a touchy conversation, because Father and I didn't have to look at each other. At the same time, I felt energized because I was so close to the muck, the place of my second birth. I sensed it was time to pop the question that had been on my mind since the day Father had taken me from the hospital.

"I want to know more about my mother," I said

He stopped work for a second. "Why?"

"Because she's my mother."

Father didn't say anything, just kept working as if he hadn't heard me. But I knew I'd caught him in a weak moment, so I didn't let up.

"I want to think about her," I said, "but I don't know what to think about because I can't remember her."

"So I have to draw you a picture."

"Do you have a picture? Can I see it?"

"I had a snapshot, but I lost it."

"Lost it?"

"Actually, I threw it away. I got sick of remembering her."

All I could think to say was, "Oh."

"I suppose you deserve to know something," Father said, and he went back to work, tossing a stick at my feet. "She looked like you, a lean body, not an ounce of fat on her. Both of you, Websters all the way."

Something didn't add up. "Was her maiden name Webster, too?"

Father didn't say anything, and he wouldn't look at me as he worked faster and faster, fast work being a rare occurrence for him.

"You weren't related to her, were you?" I said. "She wasn't your sister, or something weird like that?"

"No, nothing that far out. Webster is not my real last name," he said.

"Well, what is it?"

"Can't say."

"Why not?"

"Back in the good old days of the revolution, I blew up a building. A couple of people accidentally bought the farm from flying debris."

"You're a wanted man!" I said, impressed.

"That's right. By the FBI. I took your mother's name to salvage my freedom. You ever tell anybody and I'll deny you're my son and kill you."

"You'd really kill me?"

"Probably not, but I'd want to. See when a man feels boxed in, like his freedom's going to be taken away, that's when he starts killing his loved ones."

"I won't tell. I promise. Cross my heart. Don't I have any Webster relatives?"

"She was the last Webster, claimed Daniel Webster as an ancestor, claimed also some Indian blood, Ompompanoosuc tribe. Also, French-Canadian. Total American, she bragged. She'd say, 'The Webster line dies with me.' But of course she was wrong, because now you got the name, and you might just pass it on."

"Did she love me?"

Father didn't answer that question right away. He tossed wood at my feet, and I stacked it. We raced to see who could out-work the other. He had the advantage. It's easier to throw wood from a truck than to stack it nice and neat. Finally when I couldn't keep up and Father knew he had bested me, he slowed down and said, "She had some problems—booze, LSD, anything you can ingest. Maybe that's why you're a little coo-coo. I don't know if she loved you or me or anybody. I know this: I loved her.

"We used to go around together. We'd split up, get back together, split up, get back together. This went on for years. She ran with other guys, but I always forgave her. We went from commune to commune. You could do that in those days. All you had to do was be skinny and carry a guitar. We made plans. We were going to start a homestead. Then you came along. It was an accident. Everything in those days was an accident. Explosions, music, love, everything. We thought accidental was the way to go. She didn't know what to do with a baby. If the truth be told . . ." He paused, then went on. "I'm one that thinks truth's overrated."

I was thinking about the search for truth, that noble idea which Langdon, my guardian angel, had given me. I caught one of the sticks Father tossed down in mid-air, and I shook it at him. Fiercely, I screamed, "I want to know. The truth. All of it."

Father thought for a moment, and then he said, "The truth is children interfered with her life-style. The truth is she didn't want you, I didn't want you, nobody wanted you."

The air went right out of my balloon. "Oh," I said.

"After you were born, she become morose. There was more LSD; there was heroin. Real heavy. Want more truth?"

"Absolutely," I said, but my determination was only stubbornness. In my heart, I was hoping for a soothing lie.

"She and I pretty much neglected you. Sometimes we wouldn't see you for months at a time. You'd stayed with this or that group. In those days we thought we were a tribe, a great big American tribe. The idea was everybody took care of everybody else. There was no such thing as family or country."

"Seems like everybody in those days was just wishing," I said.

Father got down from the truck. He put his arm around my shoulder. "That's what it was, ten years of wishing. I don't regret being part of it, though. It couldn't have been any other way. But it's hard today to make people respect that every once in a while, folks need a time for wishing." Father removed his arm from my shoulder. "We used to have an expression back in the revolution. Never trust anyone over thirty." He wiped away a tear, and then his face grew hard. I knew that look, so what happened next was my own fault.

"Father," I said, "you're over thirty."

He hit me with the flat of his hand, and my nose started to bleed. But I didn't care. I just wiped the blood on my pants. A couple minutes went by when neither one of us said anything, and then Father said, "Let's go," and we got into the truck and went. We were out of Keene, on Route 12 headed home when I decided to find out everything else I could about my mother. What could he do but hit me again?

"Do you know where she is?" I said.

Father reached down into his crotch, where he kept a 16-ounce beer bottle as he drove, and took a drink. He put the bottle back and said, "Who?" I could tell he was still mad after hitting me, mad at me for making him mad at himself.

"You know who. My mother," I said.

Father laughed. "I was a little out of my head at the time of your disappearance, actually a lot out of my head, so I can't tell you exactly what's what. But I know where you can find out. There's a remnant commune, actually a cult. They called themselves Children of the Cacti in the desert town of Sorrows, New Mexico. They were into the Dead and entertainment, but nothing political. They wouldn't have anything to do with a revolutionary like me. Maybe she's still with them."

"I'd like to find her," I said.

"Why? She doesn't want to find you."

"How do you know?"

Father gave me a dirty look. "Would you like me to crack you across the head?"

"No, Father."

"Then show a little respect." His beer was almost empty.

"Okay, Father. I respect you," I said, but I didn't mean it. "What was her first name? She had a first name, didn't she?"

"Not really. She was christened with a name, but she gave it up. We rejected everything that was part of the system in those days. Like the name they gave you."

"What did you call each other?"

"I called her Woman."

"What did she call you?"

"She called me Man. Whoever we were with at the time, we called The People. Everyone else we called 'them' or 'the system.'"

"Then you must have called me Boy."

"Uh, that's right," Father said, but I could tell by the way he looked away from me that he was hiding something.

"What did she call me? Tell me the truth," I yelled; I didn't care if he hit me or not.

"It."

I didn't understand. "What?" I said.

"That was what she called you. She'd say, 'It's hungry.' Or 'it's got a dirty diaper.' Had enough truth for today?"

"Yes, Father."

The next day I was working in our woods behind our school bus home, cutting some maple saplings. They'd grown up and shaded part of Father's marijuana patch. It was awkward to cut such small stuff with a chain saw, so he sent me out to do the work with the bow saw. It's a wonderful tool for cutting skinny wood and totally useless for fat wood. I liked it. It was quiet and simple.

Father was gone, having driven into town for "supplies." Translation: booze. I had etched a mark on my saw to measure each piece sixteen inches long for our wood stove. I would cut enough pieces to fill a fabric wood carrier and then I'd bring the load to our "woodshed." Translation: plastic over a pole lean-to. After five or six hours, I was tired but content from my labors. I was a little worried that Father hadn't returned. The longer he was away, the drunker he'd be when he got back.

I decided to take a break, sit on the big maple trunk and feel the sunshine. I bushwhacked through saplings so when I came upon the carcass of the fallen tree it was all of a sudden. Side-saddle on the butt log, in the light, was Langdon, my guardian angel. The colors in his suit were like concentrated wild flowers.

He smiled at me, and held out his hands. As Nurse Wilder had taught me, I knelt on both knees in front of him on the hard, frozen ground.

"I'm with you all the time, even when you can't see me." Langdon's words didn't come through the air, but were spoken directly into my mind.

"God sent you to take care of me," I said.

"Not exactly. I'm not even real in the way people think of as real. I'm just part of your mind. I have been sent by the Alien. I can only do so much here on Xi."

"Xi?"

"Yes, Xi. You call this planet Earth. We call it Xi."

"Like the name I made up, Xiphi."

"Exactly. Xi, roughly translated, means strife."

"Can't God fix it?"

"Of course, but God does not interfere, because except in the most unusual of circumstances he refuses to override the free-will rule. The Alien who captured you and doctored you was trying to find a way of bringing Xi back into the communion of planets. That is why he studied you for five years."

"I see," I said.

Langdon verified my observations about God and the three persons within Him/Her/Them. God had a body somewhat like a human being, but with three heads. God the Father-head had a beard, and looked like a cleaned up Dirty Joe; God the son-head was a boy, just like me only without the nicotine vice and without fear; God the Holy Ghost-head was just what you'd expect, white-sheeted, eyeless, noseless, mouthless, faceless. I didn't say anything to Langdon, but I knew that the Holy Ghost was really the female part of God. I knew that to fill in the features of that blank face I had to find my own mother.

I told Langdon that I didn't have the feeling that a boy is supposed to have about the facts of life.

"That's because you're part angel," Langdon said. "People have to do it to create more people, but angels don't make more angels. Angels just are."

"I see," I said, but actually I didn't see. Finally, I got the courage up to ask Langdon about what was really on my mind.

"Where is my mother?" I whispered.

"It has not been revealed to me."

"I don't believe you. Where is she?" I trembled as I spoke. I was suddenly aware of the forest, encircling me.

"The reason Xi exists is . . . the being. . . ."

A new presence. The Director, my first demon, dropped down out of a tree, fell, picked himself up, brushed off his hump, and then said to Langdon, "Cut! Cut! You got the line wrong. It's too early for that."

And the forest was silent. No birds sang, no branches clacked in the wind, no car tires whined on distant highways. I bowed my head so low that I could smell the ground, raw mung of dirty ice. When I looked up, no Langdon, no Director. I didn't know any more now about my mother than before.

BURGLARS

The winter dragged on, and finances started to get tight. At first I was a little confused, because the firewood business was fairly steady and we didn't need much money. Most of the meat we ate was available from the forest. There was no rent to pay for our housing. Beer was cheap in New Hampshire, and Father's supply of home-grown marijuana would last well into the flowering of the next crop. The only major household expense we had was the upkeep on the truck. Eventually I figured out that what drained the budget was that Father had discovered a new drug, cocaine. Suddenly there was never enough money around. Father wouldn't buy me new mittens—I had to get them from the Salvation Army. Father made do with an old chain on his saw, until there was no metal left to sharpen. We drove the truck on a bad tire until, worn to canvas, it just popped. Any income we had coming in just disappeared, down his throat and up his nose. Father had moments when he believed I was trying to kill him. He'd beat me, realize his own madness, and break down and cry. I would bring him a beer, and that would calm him down. Father said we were both hopeless cases, and I was inclined to agree with him.

Things took a turn for the better one day in early March. It had been a cold night, but during the day the sun was strong and the temperature had inched up into the forties. That meant something very important to Father and me: the maple sap was running. We'd hooked plastic tubing to spouts in our maple trees, and the sweet juice flowed down into a big tank in the sugar house. From there, I dumped it into Father's evaporator, an aluminum jobber that we'd inherited from the hippies who abandoned this land. We burned slabs of hardwood to boil off the sap into syrup and maple sugar. Father loved this kind of work, because there was plenty of time to get drunked up. I liked it because of the sweets.

Father was complaining about the property taxes that he hadn't paid when I heard the echo of a voice come cascading down the hill, "Langdon! Langdon Webster! Laygangdaygon Waygeb-stayger!"

I whipped my head around to see a kid dressed in an orange topcoat, striped, gray business suit, white shirt, black tie, and sunglasses sauntering toward us.

Father, who was screened a little by some hemlock boughs, hollered in a menacing tone, "Who goes there? Jehovah's Witness? Mormon?"

"You old dope fiend! Royal Durocher goes there." Royal's voice had changed; he sounded almost like a grown-up.

"What do you want?" Father sounded mean and suspicious, but he didn't scare Royal.

"I came to see you, Dirty Joe, because you are the man in our dreams." Royal blew Father a kiss, then turned to me, "Daygeth taygo aygall aygadaygults."

"I've seen you before," Father said.

"Long time ago, Dirty Joe; long time ago when I was just a little boy."

I turned to Father, "He's my friend. He can help with the sugaring."

"I'll do more that. I'll make you rich," Royal said.

Father was confused, but he didn't do anything but glower. Royal just ignored him.

A couple minutes later Royal and I were wrestling on the hard-crusted snow. Royal had grown a couple of inches since I'd last seen him, and he pinned me quicker than you can say Attila the Hun. "I give," I said. Royal rubbed my face in the smashed bits of snow we'd made tumbling about, and then he let me up. I was glad to see him even if my vision was a little blurry from the beating. We lolled around the evaporator, talking, while we fed the fire and boiled off sap. Royal and I ate bananas dipped in maple syrup, and we smoked cigarettes. Father sucked down his brew. It was a relaxing time.

"How'd you get here?" I asked Royal.

"Parked my limo on the blacktop and hoofed it up your nasty hill," Royal said. "I wouldn't risk my dream mobile on your pitiful excuse for a road."

"Town won't plow it," Father said.

"When it snows we just keep rolling our pickup over and over it to keep it packed down," I said.

"It's hell when it storms in the middle of the night," Father said. Actually, in the middle of the night, driving to pack down the snow was my job.

"I pity you when mud season comes," Royal said.

"It's only a mile to the town road," I said.

"Web's an optimist. Reminds me of his mother," Father said.

"Yes, his mother, quite the hot ticket, I bet," Royal said.

"Where you staying?" I asked Royal.

"I don't have an address at the moment," Royal said.

"You can move in here," I said.

"No, he can't because I won't allow it," Father said.

"I'd die before I'd pollute my noble self by living in this hole." Royal stared through his dark glasses into the reflection of Father's eyes and fiddled with the knot in his tie. Then he stepped back and said, "I am currently residing in my vehicle. Unlike the squalor you live in, my condition is not permanent, and I want you to know that I have plenty of money. I'm putting the profits I make selling steroids into my gun-running business. Eventually, it'll pay off, but right now I'm living like a pauper. This is called investment by some, sacrifice by others, but it amounts to the same thing: the future. It's a lesson I learned from my old man that he never learned from himself, the bastard."

The words "gun" and "running" got father's attention, which was just what Royal had intended, and a few minutes later Royal proposed a deal. Royal was collecting handguns for the black market. He'd pay Father good money for burglarizing houses of people who owned firearms.

"So I'm supposed to break into somebody's house in the off chance they might have a gun, preferably a handgun?" Father was sarcastic.

"I'm going to make it easy for you. With lists," Royal said.

"What lists?"

"Lists of gun owners. Lists of vacationers. Lists of Bingo nights and recent winners. Let me show you." He took out some papers from his inside jacket pocket. "These are the names and addresses of people in Cheshire County who subscribe to gun magazines. You follow me? There's a ninety-percent chance a person on this list will own a gun. It's only common sense. On this other list, procured with great cunning from a certain computer database, are the names of all people in the county with flight reservations. Lists—I have lists. You understand what I'm saying?"

Father nodded. "They're out of town, they got guns; all you need is a man brave enough to break into the house. You're a smart one, Durocher; I'll say that much," Father said with a sneer. He was just sick with envy, but he was willing to swallow his pride to make some money.

Royal gave Father a few names and the prices he'd pay for guns. Father tried to dicker for more money and more names, but Royal played it stingy.

"Dirty Joe needs Royal Durocher—I know about your drug habit—but Royal Durocher doesn't need Dirty Joe," Royal hissed. "I have a whole network of thieves working for me, people more reliable than you. I'm only doing this to help out Web. If you have a better deal lined up, well good luck, good-bye, and good riddance."

That called Father's bluff. He agreed to do business Royal's way. Royal didn't bother to shake Father's hand. He said, "See you later Dirty Joe," jammed his hands in the orange topcoat, and started up the hill. I watched him walk away wishing he'd take me with him. But he kept going and never looked back.

And so Father and I found ourselves in a new business—residential burglary. City neighborhoods were pretty risky for break-ins. For one thing, our truck was conspicuous, and if neighbors saw you prowling around a house in the middle of the night, they'd likely call the cops; for another thing, there wasn't much cover to hide in; and anyway, Royal had given over those neighborhoods to other burglars. So Father and I stuck pretty much to rural routes. For a short while the good times returned. Or, as Father would say, "rolled."

Royal would send us his lists. He called this information "referrals" and the victims "clients." Father picked right up on this way of talking. "Web," he'd say, his voice full of importance, "we have a referral from young Durocher. The clients are on vacation in Bermuda."

I remember one particular burglary. The clients lived in a year-round house on Spofford Lake, one of the many lakes in south-western New Hampshire. It was a big house surrounded by smaller, seasonal cottages empty at this time of the year. During the day, a few ice fishermen sat by their tip-ups but at night the lake was deserted. The clients, a family of five, were visiting Disney World.

As per our usual procedure, Father dropped me off nearby with a pair of wire cutters, a flashlight, and a hand-held walkie-talkie radio, and drove away. No wind tonight. The air felt almost warm. Bob houses frozen in the ice from the last thaw looked cozy. I had an urge to haul one of these tiny buildings to the lake's island. Set up a camp. Live like a hermit. Build outdoor fires. Howl at the moon. I howled anyway. The sound came back full of grief. I wanted to tell the speaker to take it easy and look at the moon. So I looked up at the moon. A spy prod from the mother ship twinkled like a star.

I'd almost reached the client's place when a roaring sound startled me. The lake was making ice. A crack ran between my feet loud as thunder. The three-headed God was clearing His/Her/Their throat(s).

The dock had been pulled in on the beach, and I climbed on top of it for a better look at the house. I spotted the telephone line and cut it. I ran back on the ice, seeking protection in a vacant bob house. If the police came, it would mean there was a burglar alarm in the house. No police, no burglar alarm. I called Father on the walkie-talkie. We conversed in code.

"If the blue fish are biting, we'll eat them for supper," Father said. (Translation: If the police come, walk to the end of the lake and meet me in front of the restaurant.)

"Yo, Tarzan." (Translation: Yes, Father.)

Half an hour later, I called again. "The fish aren't biting," I said. (Translation: No police, and therefore no activated burglar alarm.)

Ten minutes later, Father arrived in his pickup. He parked it on the road in front of the house. It was a risk, but not a big one. According to Royal's informants, the lake road had almost no traffic in the middle of the night, and the police were not scheduled to make a round for another couple of hours.

Father smashed a window, and we went in. Father didn't bother to use his flashlight. He just snapped on the house lights.

"I'm going up in the bedrooms," Father said. "Remember our plan in case the cops come."

If the police showed up, I was to pretend that I was a runaway and that I had hidden in this house and freaked out and called Father, who had come after me. If there was any damage, I was to take the blame.

I could hear Father ransacking the upstairs rooms. Father was not a quiet burglar. He talked to himself, and he almost always found some reason to get angry with the clients. They were too middle class, or too rich, or their tastes were uptight. This particular night, he was in a bad mood. I knew if he didn't find the guns right away, he'd take it out on this poor house.

I started making a mental inventory, and decided I liked the people who lived here. They favored solid wood furniture. They hung paintings on the walls, and they were neat. I found letters smelling of perfume. A daughter in college had written home. She seemed to like her parents. "Dear mom and dad, it's warm on campus, and sometimes I can hear the monkeys at the zoo from the dorm room. But I miss the lake—the water here is sooo scummy; I even miss you getting after me about my hair. . . ." From the way the parents kept her letters, wrapped in rubber bands and neatly filed, I guessed they liked her, too. I put the letters back real careful and thought about writing a letter of my own. "Dear Mother, I am no longer an it. I am me, dark and on the skinny side, and, like you, full of personality (Father says) and wanting to make it all up to you for whatever I did that made you unhappy. Or maybe Father lied to me about you. If so, forgive me for doubting you. Yours truly, your son, Web." I never actually wrote the letter. I got too choked up just thinking about it. I found some boy toys—dump trucks, a Storm'n' Norm'n doll, Lincoln logs. I never damaged or stole toys. In fact, I never stole anything for myself, and I never enjoyed stealing from strangers.

Downstairs, in a den with sliding glass doors that opened toward the shore of the lake, I found a setup for an electric train. I pushed a lever, and the train started to move. It passed through covered bridges spanning rivers, went up grades, went through mountain tunnels, entered a little village with a church, a library, a school, some stores and houses, stopped at a station, and took on passengers. A feeling of rapture came over me, then died away, like the morning dew under the gun of the sun.

A minute later I was jarred by a roaring sound even louder than the lake making ice.

I ran upstairs. Father stood grinning in the bedroom with his chain saw. He had carved open a locked oak roll-top desk in an office off the master bedroom; he'd found two pistols in the desk, plus a rifle and a shotgun in a case. The pistols were stuffed in his pants, and we should have beat it out of there, but Father was enjoying himself. He spent the next couple of minutes sawing his way through the dresser bureau, some paintings on the wall, and the wall itself. He shut the saw off, laughed, sang "Twilight of Destruction," and danced all the way to the pickup truck.

The day after the burglary we celebrated, meeting Royal in a crowded shopping-plaza parking lot. Father gave him the guns, and Royal gave Father an envelope with some money. Royal talked to me in the A-Y-G language, and that, as always, got Father angry, which was the whole point. Royal's attitude toward grown-ups was, maygake thaygem sayguffayger.

Father raced off to Miranda's Bar, and Royal and I drove around in his limo. We did a lot of talking. Actually, I did most of the talking. Royal liked to listen to my dreams and fantasies.

"You want to hear the one about the three-headed God?" I said.

"I know that one cold. Tell me some more about the guy with the head of a man and the body of a snake."

"The Alien," I said.

"That's the one."

So, I did. I rambled on about the Alien, The Director, Langdon and the counter-earth, Xi—everything.

"You know what your main quality is?" Royal said.

"I'm loyal," I said.

"No, your main quality is you're an entertaining nut case."

Afterward Royal dropped me off at the bar where Father was drinking. Royal said to Father, "Hey, Dirty Joe, I got a joke for you. A horse walks into a bar. Bartender says, 'Why the long face?'" But Father's sense of humor had deteriorated, and he didn't laugh. Royal left, and I ate some Slim-Jims and potato chips for supper while Father had another beer. Then he drove me home. This was scarier than burglarizing the house. Father was not a good drunken driver.

The good times ended when Royal said his work was done in New Hampshire and it was time for him to take his wares to the big city and make a profit. When father picked up the last envelope of cash, I asked Royal where he'd be staying. He said, "Saygouth Braygonx, Naygew Yaygork. Laygook faygor ayga-aygy-aygee, Daygalaygi Straygeet. Come on, let's go for a last drive."

While Father went off to the bar, Royal drove to the cemetery. We got out of the car and looked around. The place was quiet and restful, which of course is what a cemetery is supposed to be.

"This is the place, right?" Royal said.

"Right."

"And you still can't remember."

"No," I said.

"Listen, Web, I'm ambitious. I want more. More of everything. Glory. Money. Power. I need a right-hand man. I believe you're ready, and I want you to come with me to New York."

I thought about Royal's offer for a minute, and then I said, "I want to go with you, but I can't."

"What do you mean, you can't?" For the first time since I'd known him, I saw disappointment and hurt in Royal's face.

"It's Father. If I go, he'll just chew himself to death with his own character flaws."

"Saygo fayguckayging whaygat?"

"I got a plan, Royal. When we have enough saved, and Father's outgrown his drug habit, I figure him and me will strike out for New Mexico. We'll find my mother and reunite the family."

"Maybe she's dead."

"Maybe she's alive," I countered.

"What about me? I thought we were tight as brothers."

"You can come and live with us, Royal."

Royal burst into laughter, and then he sneak-punched me in the mouth, cutting my lip.

"You frog," he said, choking back tears. "You betrayed me."

"Did not."

"Did so. Betrayer! Betrayer!"

"I'm just doing what I can for my old man," I said.

Royal pulled himself together real fast. "You're right. I lost my head. I was starting to care. When you care, you're dead. I have no love in my heart."

"No love in your heart, right," I said.

He raised his hand suddenly, as if to hit me. I flinched, and he slapped me on the back on in a friendly way. "Don't let Dirty Joe push you around, and if things get desperate, come to Dali Street." Then he gave me the finger, turned his back on me, hopped in his car, and drove away. I had to walk a mile to the bar. By then Father was almost passed out.

Father and I were both broken up. I'd lost my only friend, and Father had lost his meal ticket. We went back into the firewood business, but the money wasn't enough to support Father's drug habit.

March ground into April. What passed for spring in New Hampshire was really another version of winter. Wet, rainy, dull—mud season. Father's four-wheel drive just barely made it on our road, and some days we got stuck and had to winch ourselves out. Father got grouchier and more selfish and kind of wild. He'd shout at nobody in particular that the revolution was coming. He rambled on. The country was going to hell because the rich people had said screw you to everybody, and a fellow couldn't buy land to homestead anymore, and women just couldn't seem to stop having babies, and nobody understood anybody else. The country was going to be turned upside down, inside out, ass backward, and bottoms up. Start over with the scratch of a match. I concluded that Father was spinning out of control. I began to feel scared. Something terrible was coming on, something like bad weather.

Item. After father had gone on the lam in the late 1960s, he gave up not only friends but relatives. Since I was lonesome most of the time, it would have been natural for me to want to get to know Father's people, but I couldn't seem to warm to the idea. Maybe I was afraid they'd be too much like him.

Item. Father as Joe Webster used to be on mailing lists having to do with subjects like homesteading, wood-burning for heat, organic agriculture, goat-raising, solar energy, and weird building construction, such as houses of logs, stones, dirt, beer cans, or car tires. But most of the old-time hippie companies had gone out of business and no longer sent out their catalogs and magazines.

Item roundup. Because father had no family, no friends, and no catalog outlets we didn't get much mail. Even so, it was a treat to go down to the post office, because Father would be full of anticipation, the meanness gone out of him for a while. You see, Father had a dream. Royal had got a big laugh when I had told him about it, but I thought it was a pretty good dream.

When he was growing up, Father used to watch a program on television called "The Millionaire." Every week some lucky person would be given $1 million by a billionaire named John Baresford Tipton. Father loved that program, and throughout his life, especially after the 60s turned turtle on him, he used to soothe himself by imagining that a billionaire was watching over him, waiting for the right moment to give him a million.

Wouldn't you know it, but one day somebody really did send Father some money, although it wasn't anywhere near a million. I know he was surprised, or else he never would have opened the package in front of me. "What's this?" Father said, a little excited as he tore into a book-mailer and reached inside. There it was, in his hand before he even knew it, a fistful of bills. No note, no writing of any kind in the bundle. No return address. Just money. Not a million, but enough for a couple weeks of high-on-the-hog living, at least by our standards. Father gave me a big hug, and he started to cry with joy. I cried too; but I don't know if it was for joy.

That night Father took me with him when he bought his drugs.

He made a telephone call from a pay phone, and then there was a switcheroo in the parking lot of a supermarket. A van pulled up beside Father's truck, a hand reached from the window. Father put an envelope in the hand. The hand disappeared for a moment and then emerged again with another envelope. Father took it and drove off. The whole thing took less than a minute.

Later Father got drunk and stoned in our school bus home. He was content as a pig in you know what. His good mood rubbed off on me. For a couple of hours, I thought things might work out.

Next day, Father practically ran to the post office. No mail that day. Day after that, no mail. And so on for a couple of weeks, right into May. By then, the cash Father had was gone, the drugs were used up, the booze was drunk. Father was in a grumpy mood again. But just when he figured that things weren't going to get any better, there was another package with money in it. This time there was a note. Father didn't tell me what the note said, but I could see right away that it didn't make him happy. He spent hours deep in thought, a very rare activity for Father. And he had some orders for me. Stay close to him. Don't go anywhere alone.

This went on for a couple of days. I asked Father what he was thinking about, and out of nowhere he cracked me against the side of the head with the flat of his hand. The blow didn't draw blood, but it did leave my ear ringing for a couple of hours.

"Get the message?" he said.

I knew the right answer and gave it to him. "Yah, don't ask questions."

Father then did something real strange, so strange that I knew something had gone terribly wrong between us: he apologized for striking me.

The days passed. The cash came in dribs, drabs, and dispatches. Father read the notes, burned them so I wouldn't see them, and spent the money on his addictions. But he was not happy. He was morose.

One day we drove to Keene, and he bought a Polaroid camera.

"What are you going to do with that?" I asked him on the ride on the way back.

"Take your picture," he said.

"My what?" I was suddenly shivering, as if in an icy wind, although the air was still and warm.

"Your picture. It's no big deal."

"You're lying to me."

Father wound up to knock me, but I didn't flinch and he didn't throw the blow. I knew right then and there that he didn't love me anymore. I wanted to beg him to beat me, but I knew it wouldn't do any good.

When we got home in the woods, he made me take off my shirt, and he took a whole bunch of pictures of me outside. I stood amidst ferns. I sat on rocks. I swung from branches. Finally, we ended up at the huge, fallen maple. "Strip to your shorts," Father said. I stripped to my shorts. "Straddle the maple." I straddled the maple. "Look wistful." I looked wistful. "Good." He took my picture. I didn't feel cold. I didn't feel anything. There was a great silence within me, a great stillness, a huge nothingness, an immensity of white light taking up the space of a limitless void. From the light emerged a figure, walking toward me.

"Langdon?" I wasn't sure it was him.

"Stop mumbling!" shouted father.

Kill him in his sleep! Kill him in his drunken sleep! Kill him in his stoned sleep.

"What? What did you say?" I said.

"I didn't say anything," Father said. "Stop mumbling and be still."

Langdon tore off his cap. It vanished after a noiseless explosion. His dark hair was on fire. He unzipped his magnificent suit. A second later: fireworks. When they faded, I saw a boy covered with black, slimy mud.

"Langdon?" I whispered.

"Langdon is gone," said the boy as muck dripped from him. "I am the real dead boy, I am Xiphi."

A second later he was gone, and Father was yelling at me to stop babbling.

The next day, Father went out of his way to make it seem as if nothing unusual had happened. He didn't yell at me, didn't hit me, hardly even talked to me. He wasn't my father; I wasn't his son; I was just a boarder who was staying with him, and he didn't have any strong feelings about me one way or another. I felt like an android. In a way, everything was easier. For several days, we walked through our routines, cold to each other, cold to our own feelings, cold to the world outside.

One afternoon after Father had bought a case of beer and we were driving back to the land he said, "Web, I've got some business that's going to keep me on the move for quite a while."

I could tell that he'd chosen to talk to me while he drove because that way he didn't have to look at me.

"Where we going?" I said.

"Not we. Me. I can't take you along. You'll be staying with a friend."

"Who? The one who sends you the money. Is it the Alien?"

"I don't know who it is. But I've heard his voice. He's a friend, I'm sure of that. I can't take care of you anymore, Web."

"When is he going to come?"

"I'll let you know. It's not decided yet."

I could tell it was decided. "When?" I said. I was trying to work up some anger, some fear, some alarm, but all I could feel was a clamminess.

"Tomorrow, first thing in the morning."

"What if I don't want to go?"

"You don't have to go if you don't want to go, but you do want to go. I know you do."

"Okay, I want to go. But what if I didn't?"

"I can't take care of you anymore. I just don't have the . . . where-withal. You just do what he says and everything is going to be all right. He's going to take care of you. Good care, he promised. I have his solemn word, and I believe it."

Father never looked at me when he delivered this speech.

"Okay, no problem," I said, kind of cheerfullike.

That night in our school bus home, Father got even more drunk and stoned than usual. It was way past midnight, and he was on his bed about to pass out when he called me over. It was real dark.

"Listen," he said in a wet whisper, "I'm far out, far out."

"I know," I said, and I could just barely see his face in the darkness.

"I should tie you up. You'll run away, won't you?"

"No, Father." I tried to see his face. The barest of moon glow coming in through the tie-dyed curtains reflected off his sweat. "Father, if we could find Mother, maybe she'd take care of both of us."

Father laughed a little, a tiny heh-heh.

"She's in Sorrows, New Mexico, right?" I said.

But Father wasn't listening to me. "You wouldn't do your father a favor and tie yourself up, would you?"

"No, Father, I won't tie myself up."

He took my hand and gripped it hard. I thought he was going to tie me up, but he only said, "I tried to live free. Put it on my gravestone, will you? He lived free and died."

It occurred to me that Father and Royal had the same motto. "Please don't die," I said.

"We died a long time ago, your mother and me. We died at Woodstock. We died at Altamont. We died far out. Far out. Far out." His grip on my hand slowly loosened. "We were already dead when we had you—the son of the dead." He shuddered, just vibrated as if in an earthquake. After that his hand went limp and I slipped free. I stayed with him, kneeling beside his bed; I think I dozed off, half-waking to Xiphi's voice, "Kill him in his sleep! Kill him in his drunken sleep! Kill him in his stoned sleep!"

Father was dead asleep. Why not just plain dead? I could kill him right now. I put my hands around his throat. If he woke up, he would kill me. Or maybe we would kill each other. That would be perfect. Peace. Together in hell. I squeezed, cutting off his air for maybe two or three minutes. Then I let him go and fetched a flashlight and shined it into his face. It was sweaty and pale. I lifted open an eyelid. The eye looked at me, not seeing. I dribbled some spit in the eye. No reaction. Maybe he was already dead. But no, I could smell his breath, like radioactive flowers.

I started to squeeze again, determined to continue until the life was far out. But I couldn't do it. I relaxed my grip. I had to face the fact that I was too much of a coward to kill anyone. Father picked that moment to wake up. He grabbed his throat, and his eyes opened wide.

"You're trying to kill me, my own son." He jumped up and made a grab for me, but I was too quick for him. He came after me. I opened the door to the school bus and ran out. Father lunged for me, missed, fell, and cracked his head on a rock. From out of nowhere, Xiphi leaped between us. He picked up a stone and brought it crashing down on Father's head. I heard a squashing sound. I stopped, watching Xiphi run off into the woods. Father lay on the ground. I knelt beside him, and put my arm around him and just held him.

Maybe I fell asleep or maybe I was out of my mind, frozen in place by madness. Anyway, the next thing I knew there was a wall of kingdom-come white light. I threw my hand across my face to protect my eyes from the light until I realized it was only the dawn. Father didn't move. I figured he'd be knocked out for quite a while, three or four hours before he'd wake up and come after me. I went through his pockets and took all the bills from his wallet: about enough money for a pizza and ten video games.

The weather was cool but I could feel warm temperatures coming on. It was going to be a nice day, maybe even a summer's day. That's spring in New Hampshire, jumping back and forth between raw winter and cooked summer, rarely behaving like spring. I wondered what the weather was doing in Sorrows, New Mexico, as I started down our hill.

THE AUTODIDACT

I didn't take any changes of clothes or a coat or anything. I even forgot my cigarettes. When I reached the town road I stuck my thumb out for a ride, and a few cars went by but nobody stopped. Local people wouldn't give me a ride, because they wanted nothing to do with Dirty Joe Webster's son. Once I reached the state highway, the traffic would thicken and I'd stand a better chance of getting a ride. I calmed myself down by running a mental video of a good Sam who'd pick me up. A feeble, little old man. "Hop in, son," he says. I can tell that he's not very strong. I could rob him if I felt like it. But I don't want to. I give him the money I took from Father, and he brings me home to his feeble, old wife who feeds me a hot meal. They're farmers. I work with them in the fields. We're happy together. The day I turn twenty-one, they die in each other's arms, me kneeling at their deathbed. I inherit the farm. I open an orphanage for lost boys. Royal shows up, and establishes his empire. After that I couldn't create clear images in my head, so I rewound the mental video of the old folks and ran it again.

Three or four miles went by and I began to feel the fatigue of the long night, plus I was hungry. Half a mile before the main highway, I came upon a pickup truck hauling a trailer home pulled over to the side of the road. The vanity plate was memorable. In big letters it said FREE over the New Hampshire motto in little letters, "Live Free or Die." The driver was outside, a pale-skinned, dark-eyed man. He was gazing off into the valley like any gooney tourist. Which was strange, considering the New Hampshire plates. I crept toward him until I reached the trailer, and peeked through a window. Amazing! Books lined every wall of dark wood. The furnishings included a cherry wood desk, a stuffed leather easy chair, a wooden table holding magazines and yet more books. It was as if somebody had built a motor home around a library. At that point, the man sensed my presence and slowly turned around.

He took a long look at me, the way you'd look at the clock on a time bomb, then in a voice rich as hot chocolate, he said, "Good day."

I liked his greeting and answered back with it myself, "Good day to you."

He came toward me, and I got a good look at him in the morning sun. He was fifty-five or sixty but husky with a shiny head shaved smooth as a bowling ball, a gigantic salt and pepper mustache, waxed and curled up at the ends, white teeth, basset-hound eyes, sly full mouth in a half-smile.

"Beautiful, isn't it?" He seemed to be looking past the valley into the heart of the country.

"I wouldn't know," I said. "I'm near-sighted as a bat, and anyway I like it better at home."

The man broke out in a grin. "Is that so? Well, where are you from?"

"I'm from a little western town called Yonder, Arizona," I answered.

"I suppose one way or another we all come from yonder. Your family with you?"

"Oh sure, I was just taking a walk. My family's around the corner, collecting firewood and fiddlehead ferns, my brothers, Craig, John, Howard, Frank, Russell, and young Robert, my sisters, Cathy, Carolyn, Annie, Cleopatra, Cynthia, and my mother, Grace, and my father, Tom. My dad's got tattoos and he's a gunner on an F-16 fighter plane and a Congressman. My mom's a school teacher, a lawyer, a singer, and she bakes pies."

"Splendid performance. I don't have a family, unless you count a thousand or so books."

"So, you're a bookworm."

"Yes, a bookworm. The way a silkworm spins a web of silk, a bookworm restructures the very web of mind. The result: . . ." He

let the answer hang for a minute, tapped his bald head, just above
a cliff-overhang brow, and said in a voice full of importance, "an
autodidact."

I was about floored by the word, but I didn't show it. "You don't
look like one."

"And what do I look like?"

"A retired boxer."

"I'll take that. And how would you describe yourself?"

"I'm a spy for the Xi government of the Fourth Dimension," I
said.

"You spell that the way it sounds? Zy, z-y?"

"Sorry, I can't say. The spelling is a secret."

"You must have a code name."

"Xiphi. But my friends call me Web."

"I am known as Professor John LeFauve, Professor Emeritus,
Department of Autodidactism, Harvard University."

"I guess I can call you the Autodidact, then," I said.

"Done deal," he said, and we shook hands. I smelled something
that made my mouth water.

"What's that?" I sniffed the air.

"Breakfast. I suppose you'll want some."

The next thing I knew I found myself sitting down for victuals
with the Autodidact. He'd set up a camp about fifty feet into the
woods, with cooking gear, a small fire, a log to sit upon, and, in-
evitably, a book. We ate bacon, eggs, and toast off paper plates.

"Why don't you eat in your trailer?" I said, and shooed away
bugs.

"I like to be among the birds and the bees."

"Don't forget the black flies and the mosquitoes."

"And the snakes in the grass. And the hawks above. Enemies
everywhere. Even in the midst of beauty. It's nature's way. I will-
ingly submit myself to it."

"Is that so?" I dug into the food. A minute passed with no conversation, just eating. Then I took a break from chewing, and just
to be polite I asked him about the book he'd been reading.

"I'm glad you're interested. In this book, you'll find example
after example of how nature mediates against necessary violence

with elegance." The Autodidact picked up the book and showed me a picture of an orange and black butterfly. "Do you know what this is?"

"Sure, it's a monarch."

"That's correct. It's marked so vividly to warn off birds. You see, it's poisonous."

I thought about Royal, whose colors were orange and black. The Autodidact showed me a picture of another orange and black butterfly. "What's this?" he asked me.

"Trick question," I said. "I'm supposed to say it's a monarch and you're going to call me a liar."

"I can see that you have some experience in the world of deception. This is a viceroy, which is not poisonous and which therefore is a fine meal for a bird. But the viceroy, like the monarch, is orange and black and good-sized. It's a deceiver. It fools the birds into thinking that it's a monarch."

The Autodidact talked on. Father and I used to finish our food quicker than you can say oink oink. With this fellow, eating was different. It was dining. That meant food for thought as well as belly. It took forever to get through the meal, though, and I was anxious to put some miles between New Hampshire and me.

"There's another butterfly whose name escapes me at the moment, but which I find even more intriguing than the monarch and the viceroy." The Autodidact flipped through the pages of the book, and showed me a picture of a drab bug with wings. "In its caterpillar state, this creature crawls down into an ant hole."

"And the ants kill it and eat it," I said.

"No, the ants bring eggs from their queen for the caterpillar to feast upon. You see, the caterpillar gives off an essence which intoxicates the ants."

"It gets the ants stoned?"

"That's correct. You are worldly indeed. This creature is a like an entertainer. As long as it intoxicates its audience, it's loved and revered. The minute its charm wears off it's attacked and destroyed by its audience. With luck, the caterpillar pupates."

"What?"

"Pupates. It means transformation. Its body is transformed

from a caterpillar to a butterfly. It crawls out of the ant hole, spreads its wings, and flies away."

If a caterpillar could pupate, why not me? Maybe it had already happened. Maybe before coming out of the mud, I had not been a boy at all, but some other kind of being. I thought about the Alien. The Autodidact sounded like a robot at times—maybe he *was* a robot!—and the Alien had sent him to confound me. I mulled all this over and concluded I had not yet pupated.

"Where you from?" I said.

"Native of New Hampshire, via French Canada. When I was a kid, the Yankees and the Irish called us Frogs. That made me mad, and I got into a lot of trouble."

"Are you still mad?"

"At times, yes, but I am no longer violent. My people came here to earn enough money to return to the farm in Quebec. It didn't work out that way. Temporary became permanent. Destination became destiny."

I liked that word "destiny." It meant headed not for a place, but for a position in the universe, like a star in the heavens. Father had taken a wrong turn and missed his destiny. Royal was pursuing his destiny like a shark after a swimmer. Me? I was waiting to pupate. Was that enough for destiny?

"So are you a monarch or a viceroy?" I asked the Autodidact.

My question caught him off guard. The half-smile disappeared, and his mouth turned mean. "You do have a meddling little mind, don't you, young man?" I thought for a second he might hit me, but the smile returned, and he said, "You make me stop and think. Perhaps I'm so happy being free that I'm not suffering enough to write. Perhaps thirty-nine years is insufficient atonement. I can't say."

I should have guessed from his ramblings that something was unusual about the Autodidact, but I was so satisfied by the food in my gut that my guard was down. I cleaned my plate and drank three glasses of milk. I would have had a fourth, but the milk carton was empty.

A breeze tiptoed through the trees and kissed our faces, and the

Autodidact said, "I'm thinking about trading the trailer for a sail-boat. Have you ever been sailing?"

"No, my dad preferred to fly his jet plane," I said, "but he did take me fishing when he was home from a war or when the Congress was let out. We would catch perch in the daytime and hornpout at night." As I rattled off this lie, it reminded me of a true-life experience, and I related it to the Autodidact. "Once Father saw a Fish and Game truck stocking brookies in a stream. Father and I showed up an hour later. We cleaned out the hole, took a hundred of the state's trout."

"As a boy, I too fished, but for thirty-nine years I never saw water except in toilets and faucets. I contented myself with dreaming and reading. Joshua Slocum, Francis Chichester—wonderful writers, wonderful adventurers. Now it's my turn, and I find myself excited but also a little hesitant, a little befuddled by the world on the outside. A little afraid."

"Afraid of losing your life?"

"No, most of my life is already lost."

"Lost? Where?" I was thinking: lost destiny.

"Back there." The Autodidact pointed behind him.

"What's back there?"

"Time."

"Oh, I get it. You're old."

He laughed suddenly, roaring loud as a waterfall. The laugh, the force in it, scared me a little. I thought about Father, how mad he'd be when he woke and found me gone. He wouldn't be laughing. He might be waking at this very moment. A little frantic, I said, "I have to go."

"Have to get back to your family, I suppose."

"That's right." I got up from my seat in the woods.

The Autodidact stood, took my hand into his own, and shook it. "Have a good trip."

"Thanks." I pulled away. He looked at me for a moment in pity or disgust, I couldn't say which, and started breaking camp. I hurried off, planning to start hitchhiking. Instead, when I reached the trailer, I paused. Maybe I could stow away in this rolling library.

The door was ajar, and I walked in. A kitchen flowed into a living area. Beyond was a narrow hall, a bath, then the bedroom. Everywhere, on shelves, on tables, on the floor, were books. I couldn't imagine what one person would want with all that reading matter.

A minute or so passed when I heard the Autodidact coming. A split second before the door opened, I slipped into what seemed like a linen drawer under the living room couch built into the wall. I dropped down with a thump. It was surprisingly roomy in this compartment. I could hear the Autodidact humming and strumming to himself and putting away dishes and the like. Happy in his solitude.

I lit a match and saw that I was in a storage space built underneath the floor. There were a couple of suitcases and yet more books, but I still had room to wiggle around. My match went out. I lit another. Now I could see a side entry that must have led to the outdoors. Just then the engine in the pickup started, and the rig jerked forward, rolling me into some luggage. The transmission yowled like a treed cat. The Autodidact wasn't much of a driver. For all his problems, Father never had trouble shifting gears.

I worked my way forward to the hatch under the couch and came out of my hole. In the living room, in the light, I felt safe, and I launched a serious search to look for cigarettes and just to be nosy. But it was difficult to concentrate on criminal behavior, because there were so many books to draw my attention. The old paper in the books gave the place a pleasant, dank smell.

I sat down by a window in a big easy chair, feeling blank and silly and almost happy for a minute or so. In that relaxation, I spotted a notebook on the table beside me. Folded inside was a map of the United States. I thought about my mother and looked up Sorrows, New Mexico. It wasn't on the map. Maybe it was just too small and insignificant a town to put on a road map. Or maybe Father had lied to me. How could I find my mother if the town she was supposed to be in didn't even exist? I folded the map, returned it to the notebook, and looked out the window, reading bumper stickers as they flashed by: "Too Old to Be a Yuppie, Too Young to Die"; "Cree Dance Music"; "Rework Norman Mailer for

Movies and You Get Danny Divito"; "Rush Limbaugh and Willard Scott in '96"; "Kids Leave Home So They Don't Have to Lie to Their Parents"; "Why Would Anybody Want to Make a Computer That Thinks Like a Human Being?"; "The EPA Should Regulate Nocturnal Emission Standards;" "If You Can Fool Yourself, You Can Fool Anybody"; "Work Hard—Hard Is Good"; "For a Better World, Put Women with Small Children in Charge"; "A Waist Is a Terrible Thing To Mind"; "If You Were Always Nice I Couldn't Love You." I grew bored, picked up a pencil, and doodled on the Autodidact's notepad. I drew a picture of the sausage-shaped mother ship; I wrote "Daygalaygi Straygreet, Saygouth Braygonx."

Soon I started to feel drowsy. Trailer wall opens, the Alien, backed by white light, wiggles his forked tongue. "Follow me," he hisses. I float through the opening and on slippery feet ski on a long, silvery ramp slick as ice, swooping up into the sky to the mother ship.

When I woke up, I was sweating from the heat in the trailer. I yawned, stretched, stood, and stared out the window. We were on I-95. A sign said: "Housatonic, NY—5 Miles." I glanced at the clock on the desk. I'd been out cold for four hours, and it was already midafternoon.

I had some energy now and I had the urge to do something. I knelt on the floor and just let my imagination run wild. I pictured an avalanche of books burying me in knowledge, me waking in heaven knowing everything. I pictured myself back in the forest behind Father's place except Father was gone. Out of the nowhere of my imagination appeared a woman in blue robes. She wasn't Mother, though. She was bossier. *Maybe she's a Witch.* That was it: she was a Witch. She had a book. *I will teach you the ways of evil.* I grabbed the Autodidact's notebook and held it to my chest, bending my neck so my nose was in the pages smelling the paper. I absorbed the powers of evil.

Bored with this game, I decided to read the Autodidact's notebook. The story of his life, he'd said. I wondered why he'd waited so long to tell it. I only had to read the first sentence to get my answer. At the same time, the rig slowed and pulled off the highway.

The words on the title page said BOOKS AND PRISON BARS: *The Autobiography of John LeFauve*. I flipped to page 1. "After thirty-nine years in the New Hampshire State Prison, following my conviction of murdering a young boy, I am now a free man." Murdering a young boy!

I stared out through curtain slits in the window while the rig came to a stop in front of a gas pump. I figured I'd stowed away long enough; it was time to get out of here. I watched the Autodidact come around and put the gas nozzle in the hole. It took forever to fill that tank, and I started to pace. Finally, I peeked through the window again. The nozzle was hung up, and no sign of the Autodidact. Maybe he'd gone to pay. Now was my chance to escape. I threw open the door. And there he was. Right in front of my nose, the Autodidact. For a split second I looked at his face: cliff-overhang brow, black-white mustache twitching, basset-hound eyes wide open with surprise. I bolted past him, and he reached out a hand that grabbed the back flap of one of the hip pockets on my jeans. "Hey, boy!" he bellowed. I twisted away, leaving him holding fabric. The Autodidact's shout drew the attention of a woman pushing a baby carriage and a mailman wearing shorts.

I screamed, "He kidnapped me! He kidnapped me!" And then I ran, almost knocking over the baby carriage.

I must have run for half an hour straight at top speed. I ran through streets, across people's yards, and finally into some woods. I never looked back, and I never slowed until the brush was thick and slapped my face. Finally, I stumbled upon a trail amidst tall trees that ended at the bank of a big, sluggish river. Exhausted, I paused. The river made a gentle breathing sound.

I relaxed. A minute later, I felt a thump on my shoulder. What looked like blood stained my shirt, although I didn't feel any pain. A second later, another thump, this time on my head. The "blood" was blue.

"You're dead!" I heard the voice of a boy about my own age from above. I looked up. I couldn't see the boy who had challenged me, but I did see the nose of his paint gun sticking out of the tree house sprawling across the branches of a huge oak. Something about the structure looked familiar. And then I realized where I'd seen it before: in my daydreams, my home aboard the mother ship.

"You got me, I'm dead," I said.

"Who goes there?" shouted another boy.

What should I answer? "Langdon Webster"? "Xiphi"? "Some unknown person"?

"Web goes there," I said.

"Friend or foe?"

"Friend."

"What are you doing in our territory?"

"Am escaping pursuit by an autodidact," I answered.

I could hear two or three boys argue for a minute, and then a voice said, "So what?"

"So, how about a cigarette?" I yelled.

A moment later a rope ladder dropped down from the tree house.

RIVER RATS

There were five of them, Terry (handsome as a movie star), Ronnie (built like a stump), Dunc (fat), Chuck (blond and quick), and Aristotle (a geek), and they all carried paint guns. They called themselves the River Rats, and they had taken over the tree house, built over the last twenty or thirty years by who knows who. It sprawled through the giant oak, and you had to scramble along branches to get from one section to another. The rooms included the "dungeon," which had a solid floor and a roof that didn't leak; the "hole," which was full of rot and stank like the armpit of a sweaty giant; and the "torture chamber," which was almost as big as the dungeon, but leaked like a punctured bladder.

I told the Rats about the man who wanted to kill me. I said he was seven feet tall and that he looked just like a river carp, and I pursed my mouth to show them. They laughed, even Chuck, who didn't believe me. Terry gave me a cigarette and we smoked. I asked if I could join their club. Dunc, whose father was a trooper for the highway patrol, said I might have AIDS and that the boys should call the Po and turn me in.

"Shut up, Dunc," said Ronnie.

Dunc bumped Ronnie with his big belly, and the two boys wrestled briefly until Terry put his foot between them.

Chuck tried to stare me down, but I beat him at that game.

"Let's burn his eyeballs with lighted cigarettes until he tells us the truth," said Chuck.

"You're so gross," said Aristotle.

And then there was just the slightest "umm" sound from Terry. I could see that it didn't matter what the rest of the boys said, because Terry was the leader. In the time I spent in the tree house with the Rats I rarely saw Terry smile or laugh. He was not happy, but he lived to make his friends happy. That was why the Rats had made him their leader.

"Speak," commanded Terry, and I knew it was time for me to perform.

I told the Rats that my real father was the exiled king of French Canada. Once he was restored to power he would come and take me home, and I would be a prince. When I was eighteen I would rejoin him in the underground and fight the evil cartel of Eskimos and drug runners that had taken over the country and made it cold.

Ronnie slurped his own snot and laughed like a hyena.

"Don't interrupt him," said Aristotle to Ronnie, and then he turned to me and said very seriously, "You dreamed up this father, didn't you?"

"I'll say he dreamed it up. He's a suck-shit liar," said Chuck.

"If a person of great intelligence, such as myself, dreams hard enough, it comes true, and that's no lie," Aristotle said.

"What does this father-king look like?" Dunc asked me.

"Tall, dark, and handsome," I said. "Strong and carries guns and several knives hidden in his sleeves and in his boots. Not that he needs them, because he's good with his fists and his feet. He can even butt a man to death with his head."

"Get serious," said Chuck.

"Get real," said Ronnie.

"Get bent," said Dunc, and bumped me with his belly.

I asked Dunc if he wanted to fight me. He said, no; he admired me. He said I was such a good liar I might one day become a lawyer, which was what he wanted to be when he grew up, because lawyers had even more power than the Po.

"Suck my snot," said Ronnie, and flipped a bunch of runny mucus at me. I spat on my finger and flipped the spit at him.

Everybody laughed like maniacs. Ten minutes later I was elected as a member of the Rats. The boys, even Dunc, took a solemn oath not to turn me in unless I betrayed them, in which case they'd torture and kill me. They issued me my own paint gun, with my own color—green.

During the next week, the Rats brought me junk food, gum, and cigarettes. The domain of the River Rats became my home. Terry always got things going. Usually he never said a word, just started doing something and the rest of us would follow. For example, Terry would start taking off his clothes, and everybody would know it was time to go swimming. Or he'd say, "Let's get rich," and we'd search for coins with Dunc's metal detector. Or Terry would start us in playing Instant Death with our paint guns. Or tree climbing. Or fishing. We caught a lot of perch. I wanted to eat the fish, but the boys told me the river was polluted and if we ate the fish we would all end up looking like Freddy Kruger.

The other boys went home to bed at night, but I stayed at the tree house, sleeping in the dungeon. Now and then I would be attacked by mosquitoes. Otherwise, I didn't have any problems with weather or animals, although I did worry that a snake might drop down from the tree and wrap its coils around me in a grim hug. Once in a while, some older boys would meander through at night, drinking beer and carrying on and even invading the tree house to party. I would scramble further up the tree and hide in the crotch of a branch. Nobody ever saw me, and the Rats never betrayed me and I never betrayed them.

After a while, I began to understand why the Rats were so close. They each had secret wounds. Terry's father used to beat him up with a strap, and he also beat Terry's mother. Part of the problem was Terry's older brother. He had run away and had done something that shamed the family. He had branded his buns with the word "dad," and mailed home a polaroid picture. Later, Terry had learned that his brother had taken up with a black sugar Daddy. I didn't know exactly what that meant, but I knew this much: Terry hated black people and dreamed of killing them.

I often thought about this brother of Terry. Like me, he was a runaway. Like me, he was separated from his parents. Like me, he was polaroided. Unlike me, he had branded himself: I thought that was about the bravest, most brazen thing a boy could do. I wondered what kind of life he lived, what his future might be. I told Terry I wanted to meet this brother, for he seemed almost like my own brother. Terry said if the River Rats could get guns, they could kill the sugar daddy and rescue his brother, and then the brother could move in with me in the tree house. I asked Terry why he wouldn't live with us, too. Terry said he wanted to run away, but he had to stay home and protect his mother from his father.

Ronnie's problem was that his parents had divorced and his mother had remarried an idiot who had moved him and his sister to the 'burbs. His real father had moved to California in disgust, and Ronnie hadn't seen him in two years. Ronnie had a motto for living: The world as reams of snot. You suck it in, blow it out, wipe it away for relief. You don't like it, but you can stand it, and when it's dry, you pick at it until the blood flows.

Chuck's father had been sick for a number of years and had lost his job. His mother was an elementary school teacher and she was grouchy. The family had a lot of bills; the truth was they were poor. Chuck might have had it the worst of all the boys because, living in a 'burb neighborhood, his family was supposed to look well off. As far as Chuck was concerned, the faking around made for more misery than the poverty.

Dunc's mother was a drinker and pill popper and she had been committed a couple of times to a mental hospital. Dunc didn't like to talk about her; in fact, he couldn't talk about her, because he got all choked up.

Aristotle had been adopted by some cousins after his parents and sister were killed in a car wreck. His guardians were old. They didn't allow television in the house or video games or anything. They made him take piano lessons and go to church. They nagged him. They disapproved of the Rats. When school was in session, he had to sit up straight at meals and study two hours a night.

As for me, well, I was happy. Life with the Rats was so much more relaxing than life with Father. I hardly ever had morose thoughts. I didn't forget about looking for my mother, but I didn't know where to look. I was waiting for a clue. Meanwhile, I figured I might as well enjoy myself. I did exactly what I pleased, whenever I pleased, and there was always somebody to play with except after dark. At dusk, the boys would leave and I would lie down alone in the dungeon room.

It was only in those few minutes before I drifted off to sleep that I was at all uncertain about anything. A weakness would come over me. And a loneliness. I knew I was living on borrowed time. At any minute I'd be discovered and returned to Dirty Joe. At the same time, I missed him. Father may have had some bad points, but he was my father. Maybe if I'd been a better son, he would have been a better father. Maybe Mother could straighten all these problems out. Some day. These boys who watched over me in the day were gone now, gone to loved ones who watched over them. More or less. They had something I didn't have and would never have—family—but I had something they didn't have and likely, because of their families, would never have: freedom.

As the days went by, I became closest to Aristotle, the geek. He was all glasses and nose, very tall, as tall as most grown men, but he was thin and weak as a straw sheath. Aristotle and I had a secret which we had discovered in conversation after the other boys had been talking about doing it. Like myself, Aristotle didn't like sex talk. He said sex was disgusting. Aristotle was such a pitiful wreck that he had nothing better to do with his life but think. Which was another reason I liked hanging around him. He called his thoughts "my great ideas." He claimed they came from deep inside his mind.

I remember one particular discussion. The other boys were

swimming, washing off the paint bullets, and I had just come in and gotten dressed. Aristotle refused to go in. He wasn't very athletic and he couldn't swim, and anyway he got embarrassed when he had to take his clothes off. We sat on a limb looking out at the river as we talked.

"See those rocks on the far side?" Aristotle said.

"Sure do."

"They're not rocks. They aren't even real."

"Are so real. I barked my shin on one of them," I said.

"Nothing is real. Everything is made of atoms and molecules, nothing more than clumps of energy. Your blood only *looks* red. You only *think* you hurt. Rocks only *look* solid."

"If a rock can't be real, and it's more solid than I am, then I can't be real," I said.

"That's right. You're not real. I'm not real. This conversation is not real."

"Then, what is?"

"It—*it* is real."

"What is it?"

"The great force."

"The great farce," I said.

"No, I'm serious. There's a great force out there, a final force, and we are only thoughts in its brain."

"You mean this force could accidentally forget, and I would just disappear." I was thinking about my mother, Langdon, the planet Xi.

"You would cease to exist or even to have existed."

"I don't believe you."

"I have thought it out, and when I think something out, it's true."

"If we're just thoughts in this being's mind, then how can we have thoughts that it doesn't have? How could a person think what he thinks if he's not real?"

"Because we've taken over from it."

I gave him a you-dummy look.

"It's like a dream," he said. "You don't control your dreams. You don't even remember them. They happen in your head without you thinking about them. They take over every night for a while. That's what's going on with Earth at this very moment. The characters in the dream are taking control of the dreamer, their creator. You know what I'm going to do when I grow up? I will take over the force completely. I will become the force myself."

"Prove it."

"Sometimes people's dreams take over their personalities. Right?"

"They do?" I was getting wonderfully scared.

"Absolutely. That's why people go psycho. The characters in their dreams come to life. Through my great powers of concentration, I plan to do the same thing, take over the headquarters of this force. It created me, I'm just a thought, but a thought is a powerful thing, and pretty soon the thought is going to assume command of the thinker. And then . . . and then . . . and then. . . ."

"What?" I yelled, exasperated.

"I'm going to become ruler of the solar system."

"Wow," I said softly.

"Admit it. You never heard ideas as great as my ideas."

I had to agree.

Everything went along fine for a couple weeks. I was so busy playing guns, eating, talking, swimming, fishing that I had no time for time. I didn't care what hour it was or what day or what week or what season.

One sunset after a perfect summer day, five of us, all but Dunc, were sitting on the river bank talking and fishing and smoking. I'd just finished eating. The boys always brought more food than I could eat, and we used the leftovers for bait. We all smoked like fiends except for Aristotle, who wouldn't touch a cigarette because he was such a geek. We knew that cigarettes eventually killed a person, but none of us expected to live that long anyway. After we smoked we'd flick our butts into the river; we called it the Cigarso Sea. We weren't talking about anything in particular, and the Rats were about to leave because they weren't allowed to be out after dark, when Dunc showed up out of breath from running.

He'd been home, grounded for telling off his sister, when he'd heard something over his father's scanner. There had been a murder on board a yacht at the River Marina, and the Po had made an arrest. It was the first murder in the suburb that the boys had ever heard about, and it had happened only a half mile downstream from the tree house. My mind began to fill with pictures of dead bodies—shot bodies, stabbed bodies, strangled bodies, poisoned bodies, smashed bodies, blown-up bodies. The boys were excited, but they were supposed to go home and get ready for bed. You'd think I'd want to do the same thing. Not so. I wanted to check out the murder scene. I wanted to see the body. I told the River Rats they were chicken. Ronnie turned to Terry, who said, "What do you think, fool?" That was the okay sign.

A minute later we were on our way to the marina. We walked through the brush and woods along the river bank, and by the time we reached the marina it was almost dark.

"I'm going to get killed when I get home," Aristotle said.

"No loss to the world," said Ronnie.

A couple of police cars were parked near a fancy cabin cruiser, and we could see figures moving to and fro. It wasn't going to be easy to approach the scene of the crime, because the murder boat had already been cordoned off.

Looking around, we spotted a little dinghy tied to a wooden post in the water. Anchored out a ways was a sailing sloop, a forty-footer. Apparently, the people in the yacht had rowed in.

There wasn't room for everybody in the boat, and the boys were arguing in whispers about who should go. Finally, Terry took over. He said, "Me and Web are going. Everybody else wait here." Terry and I slipped into the dinghy and pushed off from shore. I heard a muted protest from Ronnie, and then all was silent as we started downstream and the boys receded in the darkness. The water smelled like dead fish and rotten weeds. There was a barely perceptible current, and I noticed now that the marina was built in a cove off the main channel of the river.

When we reached the murder craft, we saw a uniformed police officer and an inspector in civilian clothes. I knew he was an inspector because the water carried the voices of the men just as clear as can be.

"I'm going back to headquarters. Don't let anybody on board until the lab people check for prints."

"Okay, Inspector."

"And, DeGraccio?"

"Yes, Inspector?"

"Stay out of the cabin where the murder was committed. We don't want to disturb anything."

"Yes, Inspector."

The inspector left, got into his cruiser.

After he drove off DeGraccio said to nobody, "Fuck you, Inspector."

Officer DeGraccio stationed himself at the narrow dock that led from the yacht onto the main wharf. A minute later I almost swallowed my tongue when a flash of light startled me. It was only a newspaper photographer taking pictures of the yacht. After he'd finished, he approached Officer DeGraccio. Terry and I took that opportunity to tie the dinghy to the boat ladder on the stern of the murder yacht and to climb on board. We crawled on our bellies, staying below the gunwales. Terry went first, and I was right behind.

"Can I get a few frames of the body?" I heard the photographer say.

"It's up to the Inspector, and he ain't here," DeGraccio said.

"How does she look?" the photographer asked.

"She?" DeGraccio broke into some sarcastic laughter. "She's not in too bad shape for your page one, but she is dead."

"Perfect," said the photographer.

We crept down into the only lighted cabin in the yacht. I was really curious about what the murder scene would look like. Whether there would be blood everywhere. Whether the eyes of the victim would be open or closed. Whether the skin would be blue. I'd heard somewhere about dying people turning blue. Maybe blue was the race of the dead. Maybe the body would be an entirely different color, like orange or aqua.

The door to the cabin was open and we just walked in, if you can count motoring on all fours as walking, because we were on our hands and knees. There in front of us was the victim, a girl about sixteen. The fact that she was so young knocked me sideways a little. It bothered Terry, too. He stopped dead in his tracks, and his eyes bugged out of his head; I crawled past him. The girl's skin was very pale. I wondered whether that was her natural color. It was interesting to me that a person who was as white as white can be was dead. Was white the race of the dead?

The victim wore a short, lacy gown and high-heel shoes. She was laying on her side, arms outstretched. Her face was very heavily made up with shiny red lipstick, rouge on the cheeks, and black stuff around the eyes, which were closed. I could smell her perfume. Stinky and chemically—I didn't like it. I didn't see any blood. That was disappointing. I wanted to touch the body, and I even had it in the back of my mind to roll open the eyes.

Meanwhile, Terry had gone chicken on me. He had crawled to a corner of the room and curled up into a human granny knot. I lost respect for him. I knew I had to get him out of there before we got caught, but first I wanted to get a good look at the dead body.

I got down on my belly, lower than a worm, and inched forward. As I got closer I could see how the girl had been killed. There was a bruise around her throat, like a purple necklace. Somebody had strangled her, probably with a belt. When I got to her, I saw that her cleavage was open and that she was wearing a black bra. Inside the bra was a pack of Marlboro cigarettes. I helped myself to a cigarette. When I replaced the pack in the bra, I noticed that she was wearing falsies.

The sound of the water lapping against the boat caught my attention for a second, and I listened. I heard a ship's horn far away, car traffic nearby, no voices, and an eerie sound, a sustained hush. It took me a moment to realize I was listening to the river. I was starting to feel fairly secure. I decided to try to get a look at the victim's eyes, and I flipped back an eyelid. All I saw was bloodshot whites, no pupils. Apparently, the seeing part of the eyes had meandered to the back side of the eye socket.

Then something strange caught my attention. The gown the victim was wearing was of a dark, see-through material, and something underneath didn't make sense. I didn't want to disturb the body because, really, I didn't want mess up the investigation. So what I did was look up the gown from the feet end. The toenails were painted the same bright red as the fingernails and the lips, but the feet were pretty good-sized. It was dark under there, but there was no mistaking the sight. It wasn't a girl at all. It was a boy dressed like a girl!

From the corner, I heard a strangled whisper from Terry, "It's my brother."

My heart started to pound, and my breath came quick and shallow. Everything went strange. Even the light was strange, too yellow. I lifted the nightie at the backside. On the buns was a tattoo, d-a-d.

We didn't bother to crawl; we just ran out of the cabin, scampered along the side of the boat, and almost fell off the ladder into the dinghy. I rowed back to the River Rats, as Terry hugged himself, shivering even though the air was warm.

"Tell the Rats I freaked out, and I'll kill you," he said, and I respected Terry again.

When we reached shore, he made an announcement: "The River Rats are declaring war against the sugar daddies and their kind."

"What are you talking about, Terry?" Ronnie said.

"I'm talking about revenge!"

"Revenge!" shouted Ronnie, liking the sound of the word.

"Revenge!" yelled Dunc. All together, the Rats shouted, the word. "Revenge! Revenge! Revenge!"

Later that night, we built a bonfire down by the river and marked our faces with war paint like the Indians in old Westerns. Terry led us in a chant, "We the River Rats swear to rid the world of the evil black race. Swear!" he ordered.

We boys answered, "We the River Rats swear to rid the world of the evil black race."

This went on for a while, and then as the fire died down the frenzy wore out. After all, what could a few boys armed with paint guns do? And then Ronnie said something that recharged the group. "Look at Web's skin. He's darker than the rest of us." The Rats' eyes glowed as they glared at me.

I backed up a step. "I'm a spy for the sugar daddies." I didn't speak those words; Xiphi did, and laughed hysterically.

"I knew it," Chuck snarled. He was still holding a grudge from the day I stared him down.

Xiphi went phttt! in Chuck's face, and turned on Terry. "Coward, chicken liver. My great-great grandfather was an African king."

Terry doubled his fists.

"Give him room, he's going crazy," Aristotle said.

"The sugar daddies are coming for you. They're going to drag you below decks. Suffocate you. Drown you. Drown you. . . ."

"Get him!" ordered Terry.

Chuck swung wildly, and Xiphi backed away, screaming, running, Rats on his heels. He got to the dingy, pushed off from shore into the current. The Rats threw stones, but Xiphi just laughed at them and pretty soon the boat was out of range. The current carried the boat downstream and Xiphi lit the cigarette I had snitched from the dead boy/girl. It was fresh and good and strong, and with the shock of it Xiphi withdrew into his dark world and I took his place in the boat. I lay on the bottom, staring at the stars.

The next thing I remember is waking up to a roaring sound. The air was chilly, the wind had picked up, and the little boat bobbed up and down. Beyond I could see open water, the ocean. The sound I'd heard was breakers far way. I didn't want any part of an ocean, so I rowed to shore and jumped out of the boat, tripped, fell, and got soaked. I staggered along a road until I reached a bridge over a small stream. I went under the bridge, curled up, and fell sleep.

DALI STREET

Dawn.

At about the moment when I believed myself fully awake, I thought I saw a family of masked Indians with flattened heads loping on all fours by the stream bed. I waved to them. A second later a figure appeared in front of me. It was the Director from my imagination. "Look again," he said. I blinked and looked again. Something about the morning light and my own imagination had tricked me. These were not Indians, but raccoons heading home after an evening outing.

The raccoons marched in single file with drooping heads and skulking airs. "Like altar boys in a religious procession," said the Director. As the raccoons were almost past me one of the parents turned toward me and sniffed. I aimed an imaginary rifle at its head. "Breakfast!" I whispered to myself, and wished I'd had a real gun. At the motion, the Director said to the raccoons, "That's your cue, Mother!" The mother raccoon said, "You don't have to be sarcastic," and turned to her young. "Don't speak to that dirty boy; just ignore him." The masked family members raised their noses and hurried off in an orderly huff. "Okay, cut. Print that one," the Director said and sank back into the depths of my mind.

I holstered my imaginary weapon and headed into the light of the dawn. I walked in the road, which was blacktopped but very narrow, without even a yellow line down the middle. I don't know how much time passed; blankness came over me. The road blended into another wider road, and another, wider still. Cars passed by. The road was suddenly very busy.

Dumpsters in a shopping center drew my attention. Food. I climbed one of the dumpsters and looked inside. I must have arrived on the day the trash collectors made a stop because it was empty.

Beside the entry doors to a department store, a glass dome on a three-foot pedestal attracted my notice. Someone had forgotten to bring the gum-ball machine inside. A sticker on the dome held a photograph of Jerry Lewis; Jerry said, "Help These Kids. Muscular Dystrophy Association. *Chickalets.*"

I dragged the machine to the rear of the shopping center, where I found a discarded concrete building block. And bombs away!

Chickalets spilled out. I reached in with both hands and stuffed gum into my mouth until my cheeks bulged. I sucked and sucked, chewed and chewed. Sugared flavors sent shock waves through my arteries, to my brain and back again. Orange, butterscotch, cherry, mint, raspberry, lemon—I tasted them all.

The booster shot from the sugar was starting to wear off when about fifteen minutes later, trudging down the service avenue, I saw a Mrs. McIntosh's Kitchen—*Graphic Food for Graphic Folks.*

I went inside and grabbed the mouse, clicked the breakfast drop-down menu, moved the pointer to "orange juice," clicked, moved the pointer to "English muffin," clicked, and released the mouse. Thirty seconds later the juice and the muffin slid along a conveyer belt. I grabbed the food, gave the robot behind the counter one of the bills I'd stolen from Father's wallet, and collected my change. I sat by the window, staring at the statue of Mrs. McIntosh. She was plump, with white hair and spectacles. While I sipped my juice, I played the free video that came with my booth. It showed Mrs. McIntosh in a parade float throwing chicken doubloons to the homeless, and then there was a commercial with Mrs. McIntosh's voice-over: "Wholesome food. Nutritious. Tasty. Good-looking. The look and feel of graphic food for graphic folks. National governments as franchises of Mrs. McIntosh's."

Afterward I filled out the "How do we measure up?" card.

Food Quantity: Okay.

Food Taste: Can't remember.

Friendliness of Service: Excellent.

Speed of Service: Excellent.

Order Accuracy: (This one threw me. I couldn't understand why they wanted to know whether I had ordered accurately, but

I didn't want Mrs. McIntosh to know I was confused, so I wrote "Good.")

Cleanliness of Seating Area: Excellent.

Rest Room: Liked the blower.

Outside Appearance: Can't remember.

Additional Comments: Liked the statue of Mrs. McIntosh.

Name and Address: Secret, can't tell you. Am spy for foreign power.

I left the restaurant and resumed my wanderings. Half an hour later, I found a train station. Good thing I still had the money I stole from Father.

The ticket seller said, "Where to?"

"Where's the train go?" I said.

"Two trains. One goes north, one south."

"I want to go to South Bronx, New York, Dali Street," I said.

"That's rough territory," he said.

"Not for me. My family lives there. My father's chief homicide inspector for the police department, and my mother's a singer. Thousands of people from all over come to hear her sing. I've been staying with my brother from a previous marriage. You see my mother used to be married to. . . ." Aygand saygo faygorth.

The ticket seller gave me directions. Take this train, get off at this stop, take that train, don't get off at that that stop, get off at this stop. I didn't understand a word of what he said, and I took four or five wrong trains and subways and asked directions half a dozen times before I finally found my way to the South Bronx.

I looked up at the high-rises in the lee of the expressway that cut through the city. Each apartment had a balcony sticking out. It occurred to me that the balconies would make terrific launching pads for bungee leaps. I walked on and found myself in a different world. Nearly empty streets. Abandoned, crumbling brick buildings, five to ten stories high. Some with not a single unbroken window. And everywhere messages written on the walls in spray paint, so apparently this was a very literate borough of New York.

I soon came out of this district. The buildings were still grimy, but they showed evidence of habitation, with curtains on the windows and laundry hanging on rope lines. Vehicle traffic was heavy and slow moving. The sidewalks were crowded with pedestrians of varying shades of skin color, brown, red, yellow, black, blue-black. I even saw orange-brown people with freckles. Something dawned on me. Most black people weren't really black, but red-brown, yellow-brown, or blue-brown; most white people weren't really white, but beige, red-beige, yellow-beige, or blue-beige. Sometimes gray. It was only when they were like Terry's brother/sister, dead, that they were really white.

In between decrepit buildings were vacant lots. Weeds and grass pushed up through cracks in the hardtop. I thought it was kind of romantic, flowers growing out of bomb craters. Music played from kitchen radios, and TV sounds blared from living rooms. An old man with tootsie-roll colored skin sitting on a porch stoop played the harmonica, but no noise came from it. I strained to listen. The old man stood, gestured for me to come forward, and disappeared.

I went into an alley, curled up on a piece of cardboard like a cat-erpillar lit by a match, and in two seconds I was out cold. When I woke up it was dark. I started walking the streets again. A home-less man, off-white but with kinky black hair and with a patch over one eye and carrying a sack over his shoulder, gave me directions to Dali Street. "Off of Lafeyette Avenue. Follow me," he said.

Hungry but refreshed from my nap, I didn't have any trouble keeping up with the trudging homeless man. He sang to himself as if I wasn't there. We passed stores closed up in cages of steel; apartments with people on the steps singing and drinking and scolding, or sometimes quiet and playing checkers under the light of street lamps; night clubs from which came the sounds of laugh-ing, conversing people and occasional shouts of adult joy, such as hey-yoop, and ee-oo and ah-ah. I kept looking for kids, but I didn't see any. I did see some very well-dressed people disappear into a restaurant, a blue-black old guy about forty and a lady about twenty with chocolate-colored skin and dyed-blond hair. He must have been a gangster, and she was his moll.

Finally, I reached Dali Street. I stopped for a minute to watch the homeless man. He walked into a vacant lot clogged with junk and garbage bags and started picking through the stuff. The sound of the expressway overhead was a like a strained sigh. My attention wandered to spray-painted walls. They were everywhere, but especially numerous on Dali Street. Guys with stiffies. Women's body parts. Crooked crosses. But mostly words. Initials and names. Some of the words were written in foreign languages which made no sense to me. Some of the American words were swears I'd never heard before or whose meaning escaped me.

I liked looking at the words on the walls, though. Not just the swears but the love declarations, the agonies, and even the hates. Hurt, hate, love, and politics: what the stories written on the walls were about. I liked the way the spray-paint writers used colors, and I liked the mystery: who were these painter-writers? I enjoyed imagining how a creative writer, in the dead of night with his spray can, might suddenly appear like a wounded bird fallen to earth and write the words that were in his soul and then, taking strength from his actions, soar like a hawk. I was thinking these thoughts, observing how dirty words on dirty walls left a feeling in me of clean, when I saw three letters that made me swallow my Adams apple double, A-Y-G.

I went a little farther. Another A-Y-G. Then a sign over a door in spray paint, "Gayguns Faygor Saygale." The door was ajar, and I pushed it open. It was dark inside, but I went in anyway. I was in a hallway. I could smell pee, vomit, mildew, dog shit. I started up a rickety staircase. When I got to the top, I paused, listening. The only sound I heard was the rush of the expressway outside.

I was beginning to think that nothing of importance was going to happen when suddenly two guys jumped me, knocked me down, wrestled around with me, and stood me against the wall. The next thing I knew the lights were on, and I was gawking at two black boys about my own age.

"No scars, no club colors—you're a ways from home," said a tall, skinny chestnut-brown guy with big lips, big eyes, and a receding chin.

"Let's shoot him," said the other, waving a 9-mm pistol under my nose. He was short but heavily muscled, head shaved bald. His skin was dull brown, like a scuffed shoe. I looked at his gun, and then I looked at his eyes; he was serious.

"Go ahead, I don't mind dying," I snickered.

The bald boy, a little taken aback by my bravery, said, "Don't get too close to him—he's appears to have a disease of the *haid*."

Actually, I was too stunned to be afraid and too interested to act stunned. A second later I heard a familiar voice.

"Of course he has a disease of the head, he's Langdon Webster." It was Royal Durocher, ambling bow-legged down the hall. He was wearing a black cowboy hat, sunglasses, orange jeans, and a shoulder holster with a pistol. He seemed to have grown another couple of inches. He was almost six feet tall. He punched me in the belly out of friendship, and when I got my breath back he introduced me to the dark-skinned guys. They were members of the Shadows. The taller fellow was Bik, the stocky one with the gun was Nox.

"It took you long enough to get here," Royal said.

"You were expecting me?"

"Of course," he said, then turned to the other boys and said, "See you later. I want to get reacquainted with my associate."

Bik and Nox nodded to me, then left.

Royal took me to his clubhouse, a two-room apartment in the ruined building. The furnishings included lamps, a PC, fax machine, telephone, television set, but no chairs, beds, or couches. Snarls of extension cords ran all over the place and out a window to somewhere that provided a source of electricity. Just as the Autodidact's trailer had been jammed with books, so Royal's rooms were jammed with guns. In boxes, piled on the floor and hanging from nails driven into walls and ceilings, were rifles, shotguns, machine guns and handguns of every kind and caliber. I recognized a couple of the weapons that Father and I had lifted in burglaries.

I was a little fidgety, and Royal knew right away what I needed. "Have a cigarette?" he said. That was Royal, real sensitive.

"Thanks," I said, lighting up, taking a drag.

Royal had suffered some business reversals but had bounced

back, and he was in an especially good mood. Royal's moods tended to run that way—good, very good, especially good, out of this world, terrific, and taygerraygifaygic. As far as I knew Royal had never had a mood below the good range, unless you count the time he thought I'd betrayed him.

"Selling steroids to high school athletes is still a hot business, but everybody's getting into it," he said. "At the moment, I'm facing serious competition from down-and-out yuppies looking to diversify their portfolios. The yuppies have direct contact to the drug companies, and they undercut my sales. I was afraid I was going to have to go back to selling hard drugs on the streets. But I have a moral problem with that. So I did a little black mail. And then I discovered a gold mine in the cities: wars down here between rival boy gangs. Somebody has to supply the combatants with arms. They used to make do with knives, chains, home-made zip guns and hand-me-down iron from the older felons. Is that any way to conduct a war?"

I shook my head no.

"The secret to my success is providing a good product at a reasonable price and to treat everybody fair and square. The gangs respect me because I'm even-steven. Race, religion, national origin: I don't play favorites. You got the buck, I got the bang. I'm already on my way to a fortune."

Royal explained that he catered to bands of roving boys in the twelve-to-fifteen age bracket who had not yet graduated to the regular gangs. Two of these boy gangs dominated this area, the Shadows, consisting of poor black boys, and the Souvz, a bunch with ethnic origins on the island nation of Souvien. The two gangs were at war.

"What are they fighting over? Drug turf?" I asked.

"Naw, that's the older guys," said Royal. "These kids just fight for the hell of it and out of habit. That's the problem with this neighborhood, too many ingrained bad habits."

Royal paused, paced, and then he spoke, only this time there was something different in his voice. It took me a while to figure out what that thing in his voice was: it was concern. "You know what's going to happen to most of these boys?"

"I don't know. Grow up?" I said.

"They're not cut out to grow up. The lucky ones are going to die young. They're going to die in alleys. They're going to die in their own puke. They're going to die alone. They're going to die making their mothers unhappy. The unlucky ones are going to take years and years to die, years and years of useless walking back and forth before they just cave in from their ambling." He turned his back on me, whirled around, and aimed his index finger at me. "You're as bad off as they are."

"I don't care. I want to die young."

"We all want to die young, but it's got to be a glorious death. That's why I'm doing them a favor by selling them guns. Guns are their tickets to glorious deaths. Web, I have plans for millions of glorious deaths." He grabbed my T-shirt. "Soon I'll be moving my operations south and west. Do you want to be my associate?"

I wasn't sure what I wanted anymore. Life with Royal would be exciting, but short: ideal. I guess what scared me was that I didn't want to die Royal's glorious death; I wanted to die my own death, glorious or not. Still, he was my friend, the only true friend I had. What's more, he was a genius, so he'd know more than dumb me.

"I don't know," I said.

Royal socked me in the belly, and I fell to my knees. "Be strong," he said, "be sincere, be forthright, be for sure. The maybes will kill you."

After I recovered, I spent the next hour telling Royal about my adventures so far. I told him about my fight with Father, about meeting the Autodidact, about the River Rats and their hatred of blacks. Royal pretended not to pay attention. He even made a couple of phone calls, but I just kept talking until finally I could talk no more.

"Done?" Royal said.

"Done."

"I'm grateful to you, Web. You've already earned your keep."

"Huh?" I couldn't imagine what he was talking about.

"You've opened up a new market, suburban gangs of white

boys. If, as you say, the River Rats are carrying around a world of hurt, wanting to take it out on blacks, they'll want to trade their paint guns for the real thing. There's probably hundreds of other boy gangs out there in the suburbs just dying to die glorious deaths."

"I don't know," I said.

"Forget it," Royal said. "You look ready to get some sleep."

"Sure am," I said.

I found a piece of floor I liked, circled it like a dog, and lay on my side for the night. I wondered how I was going to keep warm. I looked up at Royal. "Where do you sleep?" I said.

"A leader never tells where he sleeps." He opened a closet, rummaged about, and came up with a sleeping bag and a pillow, which he tossed to me. "Make yourself at home," he said.

I yawned.

"I'll tell you a secret," Royal said. "A kid short on brains can't have too many guns. If he's smart like me he doesn't need a weapon of any kind. But smart or dumb, gun or not, a kid ought to have a pillow."

"Is this one yours?" I asked.

"It's a spare. You'll never see loneliness in Royal Durocher's posture. You'll never smell fear from Royal Durocher. And you'll never see the pillow he lays his head down upon."

Royal left his clubhouse. I was alone. It was suddenly quiet, and then I heard ticking. Tick-tick, no tick, then tick-tick-tick. It sounded to me like a clock that had forgotten how to tell time. Two seconds later I was dreaming of a gunfight, and the rest of the night went by without incident. I slept soundly and late into the morning. But I woke to the ticking I'd heard going to sleep. It took a minute of tracing down the sound before I located its source: the crumbling ceiling; bits of plaster fell in a tiny but constant rain on a radiator.

I stayed with Royal in his clubhouse for a couple days, just resting and lounging around, watching television, playing with guns. I didn't see much of Royal. He was on the telephone a lot, and there were times when he'd disappear for three or four hours. When he'd come back, he'd always bring me food—burgers, fries, pizza, cokes. But he never spent the night in the clubhouse.

Just about when I was getting bored and feeling cooped up, Royal announced that he wanted me to join the Shadows.

"You think they'd take me in?" I asked, suddenly full of the anticipation of new adventures.

"I'll vouch for you." Royal called Bik and Nox on a walkie-talkie. A minute later, they were in Royal's clubhouse looking me up and down.

Nox brandished his gun when he spoke to Royal, "He's dark but not dark enough to be a Shadow."

"Take him on as a spy," Royal said.

"A spy?" said Bik, interested.

"Sure," Royal said. "He can join the Souvz and then report back everything going on in their gang."

"What if he's already working for the Souvz and spying on us?" said Nox.

"Then kill him," said Royal.

"Great idea," said Bik, but he was being sarcastic.

"Let's save ourselves the aggravation and do it now," said Nox, no sarcasm in his voice at all. I liked him, he came right to the point; you knew where you stood with Nox.

"I don't know. He looks like a Souv," said Bik.

"I swear on my mother's love that the only language I speak is English," I said.

"Liars swear like candy rots teeth." Nox opened his mouth and flashed his cavities. His mouth was shot full of holes. His breath smelled like dead animals.

"If you boys make me mad I'll put the d-a-d hex on you," I hissed.

Bik backed up a step. "The d-a-d hex, what's that?"

"It's the brand of Cain. It sears through your skin all the way to your soul."

Nox looked at Bik. "He's got the mad boy power." Nox was definitely confused. I was making some headway, but not much.

"He's a liar." Bik spat in his hand for emphasis.

"Naturally he's a liar, but you have to admit he's a good one," Royal said.

"The d-a-d hex is the forked tongue of a snake licking your eyeballs." I was thinking about the Alien.

"He's bad, real bad," Nox said in admiration.

There it was again, Nurse Wilder's philosophy: good is bad; bad is good.

"Maybe." Bik was relenting a little, and he was the real leader, although Nox was tougher.

"I've seen Web lie so good, even *he* thought he was telling the truth," Royal said. "When Web finally is killed and saunters up to the pearly gates, St. Peter and Satan won't know which place he belongs."

Bik said he'd take my request to be a member of the Shadows "under advisement." Some of the Shadows had already been hauled into court a few times and they had picked up lawyer words such as "under advisement." Bik and Nox said they would conditionally sponsor me with the gang, but that I would have to plead my case at a special initiation rite. Then the Shadows would vote on whether to accept me in the gang. Or.

"Or what?" I said.

"Death," said Nox.

"I don't care," I said, and I meant it, and they could tell I meant it, and we all knew I was in. Bik and Nox left, and I was alone with Royal.

"Faygantaygastaygic," Royal said. "You'll report back to me everything that the Shadows do."

"I don't want to be a squealer," I said.

"It's not being a squealer. It's being on the right side, the strong side, the side of destiny. You owe me. I saved your life. Those boys would have killed you."

"I wouldn't have cared."

"Listen, Web, I love the boy gangs as if they were my own brothers. They're closer than brothers; they're clients. I just need to be kept informed as to their activities, so that I can better serve them."

That made sense to me. I hung around the clubhouse playing

with Royal's stockpile of guns, but he wouldn't let me fire them.

"You shoot a gun, you have to clean it, or else it'll rust and then it's harder to sell," he said. That's the main reason I don't participate in gunfights. You have to clean the piece afterward, and I'll do anything to avoid work. Work is not wholesome or comfortable or fitting for a boy. Work is the opposite of play, and that's what boys are supposed to do—play."

Royal didn't even look like a boy anymore. He looked like a teenager. And while he talked play, he worked hard. He made telephone calls, added figures, wrote memos, cursed to himself. I was really a lot better at playing than he was. I'd grab a gun off the shelf, and I'd look out the window, aiming at this pedestrian or that and pretend I was picking 'em off. Big-shouldered men, slow-moving old ladies, and mothers pushing baby carriages—all made good targets, because they moved at a steady rate and didn't make any sudden turns. For opposite reasons, kids were harder to hit. Mainly though I pretended to shoot at cars. I imagined their killed drivers losing control of their vehicles, which would careen into walls, roll over, and burst into flames. Actually, the way some of these people drove, you'd think they were already shot. Pretty soon Royal got sick of seeing me drumming around and making k-pshh noises, and he told me to saygit staygill and shaygut aygup.

"I can shut up, but I can't sit still," I said. "I mean I've tried, but if there's one thing I can't do it's sit still. I twitch, I jerk, I wince, I quiver."

"Web, you're what is known as restless, and the reason you're restless is TV deprivation."

One thing about Royal, he could take any idea and put some sense into it, so I watched his television. I stood and paced and growled and would have thrown up if I had had any food in my belly. I wasn't in front of the set fifteen minutes, when Royal said my viewing technique was all wrong.

"You're getting steamed up over what's on," he said. "You're hollering and jumping up and down, and acting like what you think and feel matters. It doesn't. You need to learn zentensity."

"Zentensity?" I didn't know what Royal meant.

So he demonstrated. He sprawled, dropped his jaw, zeroed in his vision to the screen, and went into a trance. After a minute he jumped up and said, "That's how it's done. Now you try it."

I sprawled, dropped my jaw, screwed my eyeballs to the screen. After a while, I went into a TV trance. It was sort of like sleeping with your eyes open, your ears listening. Without even knowing it, I was soon in a state of relaxed forgetfulness. I had mastered zentensity. Pretty soon I didn't care what was on the tube.

When I was relaxed and Royal had completed his business for the day, he asked me a question: "Want your memory back?"

"I suppose so," I said, taken off guard.

"Want the door opened to your brain cells? Want you to be you? Want total access to the uncanny?" He changed the tone of his voice, sounding like a hysterical cartoon character on Saturday morning television. "Switch back, switch back, switch back."

"You hit me on the head, I had a psychotherapist, Father threatened to turn me over to a pervert. Nothing has worked."

"That's because nobody tried hypnosis."

"Hypnosis." I was fascinated.

"Listen, Web, I've got big plans, a lot bigger than guns and steroids. And I need you."

I didn't understand how having me hypnotized was going to help Royal, but I knew he had his reasons.

"Well, okay," I said.

"Do you know what Artificial Experience is?" he asked.

"Like a movie?" I guessed.

"Close," he said. "In a movie, you get the experience of killing or getting killed without pulling the trigger or falling dead yourself. But a movie is only a movie, two dimensions. Imagine yourself coming out of the screen, going back in the screen. Living the movie in multi-dimensions."

"I don't have to imagine it," I said. "I lived it. I was born, falling out of a movie screen, landing in a swamp."

"I know, you told me," Royal said sarcastically. "That's your reality. You can make your reality someone else's reality; I'm talking about Artificial Experience. It's the ultimate, the front stoop to doomsday." He grabbed me by my shirt, his breath came in excited pants. "Soon the parents will be dead, soon the grown-ups will be enslaved, soon the girls will be our cheerleaders. We, the boys of America, will rule with weapons of Artificial Experience, Synthetic Encounters, and the Exposition of the Uncanny."

Royal was completely mad, much crazier than myself, and he had taken my ideas for his own (I had invented the categories he'd mentioned), but he was the only friend I had.

"Okay," I said.

"Congratulations. Let's go to the Catacombs of Manhattan, for your trial by hypnosis."

CATACOMBS OF MANHATTAN

Royal and I headed downtown in Royal's limo. Thanks to profits from gun running, Royal could afford a driver these days. While Royal rode in the back making business calls from his cellular phone, he made me sit in the front with the driver. Royal, separated by a glass divider, wheeling and dealing over the phone, seemed far away; watching him was like watching a TV with the sound turned down.

The driver, in a chauffeur's uniform, was a girl sixteen or seventeen years old. Her name was Siena. Her skin was dark, and she was lean, almost slinky. She had fierce black eyes, and a twist of anger in her lips. From her features, she might have passed for any race, or none of the known races, or all of them. We had the same skin color and features; we could have been brother and sister. She didn't belong to the Souvz gang, but she was a Souvien native. As we traveled down the brightly lit streets of the city, we talked and smoked cigarettes. I liked the way she blew the smoke the way you'd spit out a kiss for a demon. Her English was good, because she'd been studying it since she was five.

"Where'd Royal find you? On the streets?" she asked.

"No, back in the woods."

"Really, I'm surprised. There's no profit in the woods, and Royal's only motive is profit." .

"What about you? Where'd he find you?" I asked.

"I found him. I'm an illegal alien. My country is in the middle of a civil war, and I landed here to earn money for my family and get an education. I needed work. Royal said, 'You'll be my whore, right?' I said, 'No way.' He said, 'Then you'll be my maid.' I said, 'I'll be your whore before I'll be your maid, and I've already told you I won't be your whore.' I thought then he'd throw me out, but he laughed. Next thing I knew, he'd hired me as his driver. I still don't know why."

"I figure you're in love with him."

"I'm in love with no man."

"You don't get the feeling?"

She stared at me so hard I thought she'd crash the car. "The feeling," she said.

"Yah, what do you do when you get the feeling?"

"None of your business. And, you—I suppose you sexually harass yourself to get the feeling."

"Me, I don't get the feeling," I said.

"Never?"

"Xiphi gets the feeling for me," I said.

"Who's Xiphi?"

"My demon. He gets the feeling, but I don't."

"Because you don't want it."

"Maybe. I don't know."

"Poor little flower," she said. "Where do you live, back in the woods?"

"Used to. Right now I don't live anywhere. Yourself?"

"I stay with the women in the Catacombs, but in my heart I'm still in Souvien with my family."

"If you like it so much there, what are doing here?"

"I'm going to night school. I dream of bringing good government to my country. With good government, good cigarettes will follow."

"You'll have to fight in the civil war, won't you."

"All my people do is make war. I'm looking for a better way."

After Royal had finished his private phone conversations, he called over the intercom for me to join him in the back. Siena pushed a button and the glass divider slid open and I crawled through into the back seat. The divider closed, and Siena seemed to have retreated into another world.

"I like Siena. She's like a guy," I said.

"She's an ignorant savage," Royal said.

I blinked, stung, as if it were I who had been insulted. "She's serious-minded," I said.

"Do you know what her people do when they're desperate?" Royal said.

"How should I know? I've never been to Souvien."

"They kill a chicken and drink its blood."

"I'd like to try that," I said.

"That's because you're a savage, too." Royal flicked my lip with his forefinger. It hurt. I wanted to kill him. "See," Royal chuckled. "I've unleashed your anger."

I grabbed him, and we wrestled briefly on the seat until he pinned me. Then he said, "Siena doesn't know it, but I've got big plans for her. Once we unleash *her* anger, she will do great harm on our behalf."

A few minutes later, Siena pulled off the street and right up on the curb. We were in mid-town Manhattan. We stepped out of the car.

"Stand by," Royal said to Siena. "I'll beep you when I need you again." The limo roared off, and Royal turned to me. "It costs me more to keep my car in a safe place than to rent that hole where I'm staying now."

"With the money you make, you could live like a king," I said.

"And I will. But not yet." Royal looked at his watch.

"Where are we going?" I asked.

"Down," Royal said.

A man who smelled like throw-up sat in the sidewalk selling scarfs. Another sold argyle socks. I bumped into a woman dressed in black, and she said something to me in a foreign language. An old man, standing on a street corner and tottering like a watchtower in an earthquake, gave us the hairy eyeball, but Royal went by him as if he didn't exist. The streets were full of people like that; they didn't look seriously human, they looked like unemployed clowns.

"There's a couple of important rules in this city," Royal said. "Never look anybody in the eye, and even more important, never run away. These people around here, they see you running and they act like crazed dogs after a rabbit." Royal paused for a second and then, in an accent that reminded me of the way that Bik and Nox talked, he added, "You understand what I'm saying?"

"Sure," I said, wondering whether I was a rabbit or a dog. And then I howled like a coyote. It felt good to howl. Not a soul in the city seemed to notice.

We went into a place full of weird little booths and pictures of naked women and guys wandering around.

"What's this?" I asked.

"Peep shows," Royal said.

Royal strode up to a scowling black man and whispered something in his ear. The black man gave him a token.

Royal and I got into one of the booths. It smelled like pee; I thought, maybe instead of a peep show they ought to call it a pee show. Royal put the token in a slot and a picture came on the screen. It showed a man on top of a woman. I felt myself blush. I couldn't stop looking, but I didn't get the feeling either. I wished Doctor Thatcher was here.

"You brought me here to watch this?" I said.

"Just to see the look on your face," Royal laughed. "That look is going to be worth money to both of us."

The booth began to shake.

"We're moving," I said.

"Of course. We're going down."

I couldn't unscrew my eyes from the monitor. "Are they really doing it?"

"Of course they're really doing it. Don't you know the facts of life?"

"More or less." I didn't sound very convincing.

"Didn't anybody take you aside and give you the word?"

"I got the basics from Dirty Joe."

"I wish I'd been there for the laugh."

The booth/elevator came to a stop. The door slid open. I stepped out, although I kept watching the monitor. Now the woman was on top of the man. They both seemed to have the feeling. The door closed, and I looked around. Dark, grimy concrete. Light bulbs in wire cages. Train tracks.

"Subway tunnel?" I said.

"Watch out for the third rail," Royal said.

We walked along the tracks about a hundred feet when I heard a train coming. I thought it was going to flatten us, but we ducked into one of the many concrete recesses built into the tunnel. The train screamed past.

We walked another couple hundred feet until we came to a grate. Royal bent down, grabbed the handle, and lifted. The grate came up with creak, a crick, and a come-on-in. We climbed down a metal ladder to a narrow, concrete cave no more than four or five feet wide. Royal had brought a flashlight. Good thing, because soon the cave was pitch black.

"You're not afraid of the dark, are you?"

"No, I like the dark. Where's this go?" I asked.

"Corkscrews to the bottom of hell," Royal said, and added one of those fake bru-ha-ha laughs. He was trying to scare me, but after all I'd been through there wasn't much scare left in me.

We didn't get very far when a flashlight beam blinded us. I heard a boy's voice yell, "Secret password, or die!"

"Je me souviens," Royal said. "Counter-password?"

"Meet me at the border. Code name?"

"DoubleZero. Your code name?"

"Grand-Pre."

After that there was a reunion. Royal and the kid did a secret handshake, and I was introduced to Islands. He was about my age, very slight, even smaller than I was. He had brown hair, dark skin but blue eyes and a big grin.

"Okay, where's your personal bodyguard?" Royal said.

Islands made a clicking noise with his tongue, and another boy stepped out of the dark. His name was the Pope of Death, tall, skinny, gray-pink skin full of pimples, and he never smiled. A look of hurt feelings never left his face. Islands and Pope were members of the Souvz boy gang.

Royal held a short meeting with the boys, making a deal to sell them some guns. While Royal and Islands discussed business, I passed the time talking with Pope. He was serious-minded, and unlike Siena he talked with a thick accent.

"Tell me how bad you hate the Shadows," I said, expecting he'd say bad enough to torture them to death and flush their body parts down the toilet. But he surprised me.

"The Shadows are brave." He sounded tired and old for a boy. "You can shoot them or knife them or whip them with chains; they yell and scream and cry their eyes out, but they never complain."

"So you'd like to make peace between the gangs."

"No way, I want war. I want to kill as many Shadows as I can. I want to kill them all." He meant every word, I could tell. The same thing that had impressed me about Nox impressed me about Pope: he was sincere.

Royal and Islands finished up, and then the two Souv boys disappeared into the darkness. Royal and I continued down the tunnel. I told Royal that after having met the Souvz, I didn't want to kill them.

"You better get used to the idea. You'll probably have to kill a Shadow too."

"A Shadow? I'm going to be a Shadow. Shadows don't kill each other," I said.

"No, but Souvz kill Shadows."

"But I'm not a Souv."

"You will be."

"How can I be a Souv and a Shadow?" I said.

"Politics. It's in your complexion. You can go either way with skin color like that. If I work it right, you'll join both gangs. The truth is you'll be my spy. Secretly you'll still belong to my A-Y-G organization. You'll have to learn the Souvien language. Think you could do it?"

"I don't know. I'll try, as long as I don't have to go to school."

"Say hick, hike, hock."

"Hick, hike, hock. What does it mean?"

"Nothing, it's just practice for learning foreign languages."

Ten minutes later, I saw a purple glow ahead; Royal clicked off the flashlight. The cave opened up into a spectacular cavern amazingly well lit. Dozens of women stood at easels furiously brushing oil paints. A portrait of Juan Valdez on his burro. A burgerscape featuring Big Macs. Jesus carrying his cross. A tractor-trailer truck. A three-foot-high DOS cursor. In the background, some boring der-der-der music played.

"Mass-production art, for banks and boardrooms," Royal said.

"The walls shine," I marveled.

"These are the Catacombs of Manhattan. There's some kind of naturally occurring luminescent crystal in the rocks, and they augment it with electric lighting."

"It's like the mother ship." I could see the Alien in my mind's eye, clearer than ever, his long, thick, snakelike body, smooth scales in place of skin, his face like that of a man, resembling somewhat (I realized now for the first time) Doctor Hitchcock.

"What are all these women doing painting?" I said.

"They're raising money for their cause."

"What cause?"

"Feminism," Royal said. "Feminists live down here."

"Who?"

"Females that are pee-ohed."

"I get it," I said, but actually I didn't.

A minute later a middle-aged woman wearing a blue dress appeared. She was tall with Italian features in her face, auburn-colored hair, and a pleasant orange complexion, which I later found out was the result of eating too many carrots.

"Hello, Web," she said, as if we were old friends.

I felt a little shy in front of her, and I could barely mumble a soft hello.

"Web, this is Marla, a great sculptor. But she has other talents, not the least of which is hypnosis."

Some of the women painters set up their easels in front of us, and they started to paint my portrait. I worked hard at acting natural. Royal stood off in the background, his eyes blazing with excitement.

Marla turned to Royal. "I came all this way to try to help Web. Why here?"

"It makes a good set. Just like home, eh, Marla?" Royal said.

"Always some hurt in your humor."

"Humor without hurt is not funny. Can we get started?" Royal barked at Marla.

"All right, stay out of the way. Web, find a place to sit where you feel comfortable." Marla wasn't afraid of Royal, but I could tell that she was at his mercy. I wondered if she was one of the people he was blackmailing.

I sat cross-legged on one of the big, glowing rocks.

"Let me see your hand." Marla's voice was soft and soothing. I held out my hand, and she took it in her own. She had long, thick fingers and callouses on her palms. With her touch, I felt a little jolt. Maybe Marla had been sent by the Alien.

"Look into my eyes," she said. I looked. "What do you see?"

"Worms. Maggots. They're all wiggling."

"Look deeper into my eyes. Tell me what is there."

I looked into the wine of her eyes, and deep inside I saw the body. "A man. Maybe he's dead, or only sleeping." I was distracted by the sound of the women painting. The scrapes of their brushes sounded like the tongues of snakes scraping eyeballs. "Where are all the men?" I asked, and I knew now that I was getting hypnotized, because my words didn't seem to come from me. A second later I was outside the chair, up on the ceiling looking down. Below, naked and dripping with black muck, tied spread-eagled to the rock was Xiphi.

Marla turned to Royal, "He has a thing for men."

"Under the circumstances, what else would you expect?" Royal said.

The voices of Royal and Marla were full of echoes, and their bodies sort of flattened out as if they were projections on a screen. I imagined that they had been run over by the subway train.

"What men do you speak of?" Marla asked Xiphi.

"The men in this cavern, I mean the men who are not in this cavern, the men who went away," Xiphi said.

"Is he under?" Royal asked.

"I think so. Hard to say," Marla said.

"Web, you under?" Royal slapped Xiphi's face, but I felt the sting.

I don't know what Xiphi said, but Royal broke out in gales of laughter. "What a sense of humor that boy has got."

"He can't reach back if you keep interrupting," Marla said to Royal.

"He's going to do important work for me, and I have to know where he stands. Will he betray me?"

"It's too early for that question," Marla said. "Web, tell us what's on your mind at this moment."

"I'm wondering . . . wondering . . . where are the men?" Xiphi said.

"He's stuck on that," Royal said.

"Shut up," Marla said to Royal.

"Okay, okay, forget it. You used to be good-natured."

"That was before *I* was betrayed, remember?"

"Don't be bitter, just exercise your powers, for us, the dear little children of the Children of the Cacti."

"Now, who's bitter?" Marla let go of Xiphi's hand and put her hands on his shoulders. "I will tell you where the men are, and you will tell me where you are. Where are you?" Another good question, in a voice that seemed to be coming out of a drainpipe.

"I'm running. I'm in the woods. He won't catch me. Not this time." Xiphi stopped talking. I watched trees in Xiphi's mind flash by. "Now I'm lying on my stomach, and there's a note pad pressed against my back, and I can feel the handwriting . . . the handwriting . . . the scratching of the handwriting."

"Who, Web? Who? Name him!"

"The Alien," Xiphi said.

"Now we're getting somewhere. Good."

"Bad equals good," Xiphi said. "Where are the men? All of

them. Where are the men?" I tried to see into Xiphi's mind, but a burning, fiery mist obscured my vision and drove me back.

A few seconds went by while I retreated from Xiphi's mind, and when I came out of it, the women painters had stood up and, gathered like a chorus of comedians, were reciting a poem.

Authorities condescend to descend,
to retrieve a murderer or a drug dealer,
one of their own, a Juan of their own.
They probe with dogs, which, like desperadoes,
go into our stew pot.

The others remain above us:
the gays, the loonies, the drunks, the druggies,
the youths, the sex perverts, the misanthropes,
the special cases: aging draft dodgers;
veterans from various foreign conflicts;
distraught tigers on the lam from their compulsions;
Wall Street tycoons who lost their dough;
savings and loan officers with no interest;
men of the cloth
who have gone homo or hetro or just plain buzzy;
humanists who have mislaid their humanity;
jilted Jacks; Jill killers; just plain Bills;
Royal Durochers, Langdon Websters, and ordinary Dicks.
A list with no end of men . . . mend . . . amen.

The men who frequent the Catacombs
like to get in and get out
and while they speak often of going deep,
in practice they stay in the medium ranges.
. . . *the medium rages . . . the medium rages.*
Nothing here for them: no profit, no bribes,
no Society to defend or to tear down.
No corruption, no eruption.
We, the permanent residents,
canvass the darkness and darken the canvass.

The painters sat down, returning to their work, and Marla began to pace in slow circles around me. "Now, Web, tell me where you are at this moment."

"I am in the muck," Xiphi said.

Marla kept firing questions off, like gunshots, although afterward Royal said that Marla didn't talk all that much, and he himself never said a word.

"Ask him if he'll betray me." Royal slapped Xiphi's face. I felt the hurt. I wanted to cry. "Stick cocaine up his nose, and watch him sneeze," Royal cackle-cried with laughter.

"Shut up, Royal! Shut up!" Marla snarled, then turned to Xiphi and said softly, "Now you must tell me about this man, the one you saw in my eyes."

Royal butted in, panting like a running dog as he spoke. "Will he betray me? Will he betray me?"

I shouted down from my perch on the ceiling, "I'd like to try some of that stew, I'm pretty hungry."

Marla snapped at Royal, "You shouldn't have cut in, you broke his train of thought. Fool! You shouldn't. . . ."

"I can hear children crying," Xiphi said.

"Wait, he's off again," said Marla. "What do you see, Web? What do you see?"

Xiphi didn't answer. Mist was closing in, a hot, white fog. I couldn't see Xiphi or Royal or Marla anymore. But I could hear their voices.

"He's a long way off," Marla said. "He's listening to the future."

"They changed the music on the tape," Royal said.

At this point one of the painters interrupted. "Yes, we do that periodically, and in between you can hear the babies. That was what the young man heard."

"What babies?" Royal said.

"The weeping of cocaine babies from the infirmary," the painter said.

I heard a series of doors being shut, and then a scratching sound, a thousand old-style fountain pens scratching at my eyes—scratch, Scratch, SCRATCH. I could not close my eyes. Through the tongue scratch of a snake bending to lick my face I could see Xiphi. He was hanging from the ceiling like a bat, watching me. I was back on the rock.

"He's blocking," Marla said. "I don't know if he'll ever come out of it."

Xiphi dropped from the ceiling, muckling onto my throat like a vampire. In that split second, we were one and the same being.

Later, out of the cave and back on the tracks, jogging, I could tell that Royal didn't want to talk.

"What did I say?" I asked.

"You ran off at the mouth."

Royal picked up the pace, and I had to pant to keep up. We passed under the harsh glare of an underground lamp, a naked bulb covered with a metal mesh.

"You're lying to me," I said.

"I know what's good for you, so don't you cross-examine me."

"I'm losing respect for you, Royal. You're scared to tell me."

"I'm not scared of anything or anybody, least of all a squish like you."

"You're scared, you're yellow, you've got chicken soup running through your veins."

Royal stopped in the middle of the tracks. A train was coming. "See that nook in the wall?"

"I see it." The train was bearing down fast.

"I'm going to yell a secret you told Marla, and then dive for the nook. If you dare to listen, you'll dive last. If you're a coward, you'll dive first and never know."

The next few seconds went by in slow motion. The train bore down at fifty miles an hour. Royal shouted in my ear, "You're a . . ." and he stopped. The train kept coming. I waited to be run over. The train loomed before me, huge as an idea. Royal shouted, "killer!" I didn't move. Royal tackled me, we both flew in the nook, and the train sped past.

"I guess you saved my life for real this time," I said. "Tell me who I killed."

"You tell me."

"Somebody before I came out the muck?" I guessed.

Royal just exploded with anger. "Listen, you didn't kill any-body. Just remember that. *I'm* the killer, *I'm* the responsible one. You . . . you're just an idiot. Stupid idiot." Royal tackled me, and we fought, only this time Royal wasn't fooling around. He smashed my face time and again with his fists.

"You can't hurt me," I wailed, "you can't hurt me, you can't hurt me."

It wasn't until the sound of the train was gone, and he'd stopped hitting me, that I realized he was crying. "Get up, frog," he said, then picked up his sunglasses, which had fallen in our fight, put them back on, and pulled me to my feet. We started walking again. My elbow was scraped. My nose was bleeding, and I'd have a black eye and a swollen lower lip in the morning.

We slept that night on a grate in a tunnel. Royal said he was punishing himself for losing his temper. It was hot and hard on the grate, and I didn't sleep well. I had a bad dream. Father was trapped in a mine. He was calling me to save him, but I couldn't get to him in time. Half a mountain fell on him. Somehow I walked right through the rubble to freedom. I woke and told Royal my dream.

"Web, never tell people your dreams. You'll just bore them." He looked at his watch. "Let's go, it's time for your initiation into the Shadows."

We took a subway back to the South Bronx. It was exhilarating to be out of the tunnels into the open air. The weather was cool, cloudy. For a second I thought I could smell the dragon's breath of the expressway, unseen above us. Down here on the local street, cars went by; people yelled swears from open windows to people with heads sticking out of other open windows who responded with swears of their own. I saw a man with a patch covering one eye and a sack over his shoulder. It took a second before I remem-bered him as the fellow who had given me directions to Dali Street. I called to him, wanting to thank him. He stopped, and turned in my direction.

But he wasn't looking at me. Behind us were Nox and Bik and

about a dozen other Shadows, guns drawn. A second later something strange caught my eye. A manhole cover in the street seemed to flip over, as if pushed from below.

"Oh-oh," Royal said.

"What's going on?" I asked.

"Gunfight." Royal pulled the pistol from his shoulder holster. "It's every boy for himself."

Suddenly River Rats started foaming out of the manhole. I spotted Terry and Aristotle, all of the Rats. Apparently Royal had found Terry and broken into the suburban market, selling the Rats guns.

"Slight miscalculation on my part," Royal said. He reached into his shirt, and pulled out a thin, black ribbon, which he fastened around my neck.

"What's this?" I said.

"It's a collar," Royal said. "Keep it on at all times."

"Why?" I asked.

"It's your destiny. Keep your head down, and I'll be right back." Before I could protest, Royal had slipped away from me and was running down an alley. I got up to follow him, but somebody fired a gun, and I instinctively dropped to the pavement. Seconds later bullets were flying everywhere, and I could smell the sweet, sickly powder. I did what Royal had ordered, I kept my head down, hiding behind a row of sixteen garbage cans. I know the number because in the lulls between the shooting, I counted them to keep myself from freaking out.

Across the street, I saw Islands and Pope and other Souv boys. Quicker than you can say make my day, somebody started firing at me. But none of the bullets came close. It's a good thing they weren't good shots, because I was exposing more of myself than I should have. I was curious. I wanted to see somebody get shot. I wondered whether a shot person would fall forward or backward or just collapse. Whether they'd holler, groan, scream, or gasp. Whether they'd get a glazed look in their eyes, as if their whole life was passing before them. Maybe if I got shot, my life would pass before me. I'd get my memory back, I would know everything about myself, and then I would drop dead and go to heaven or hell or be taken on board the mother ship or just fall into the well of Total Quiet.

An innocent bystander had gotten in the way, the one-eyed homeless man who had given me directions. One of the River Rats took a shot at him, and soon everyone from all three sides was shooting at the homeless man. Eventually, he was hit and he cried out. That invited more shots. The River Rats, the Shadows, and the Souvz just filled his body with lead, and soon he was still, lying in a clump. So I had my answer about what happens to a shot person. They look confused, they stagger, they drop down, they don't say much.

By now I had problems of my own. The Shadows had shifted position and so had the River Rats and the Souvz, and somehow yours truly found himself in the middle. It was pretty exciting, bullets thudding into the garbage cans, bullets plinking off the red brick, bullets scarring drawings on the walls, bullets ricocheting off the sidewalk, bullets breaking glass in the windows over my head. I don't think the boys in the boy gangs even knew I was there. They were looking past me and through me. Happy with their own battle. I wished I was on one side or the other, the Shadows or the River Rats. Not the Souvz. I didn't want to take the time to learn their language.

I crouched between the garbage cans, not thinking, not dreaming up a plan, just cringed up, counting the cans, counting, even, bricks. I was in that self-folded position when I heard a voice I recognized. I looked up and was looking into a familiar face—big mustache, bald head: the Autodidact. His eyes burned with rage. He grabbed me and put his hand over my mouth. My body went limp.

KIDNAPPED

He carried me like a sack over his shoulder, not running but striding quickly down the alley and away from the shooting. The alley led to a street where the trailer was parked. At first I thought it was a different rig, since the trailer was painted black and the pickup was gone, replaced by a Cadillac. Inside the trailer, though, everything looked the same as before: book litter. He sat me down in a chair, taped my hands to the chair arms, and tied up my ankles with rope. He never said a word, then left. A few seconds later he started up the Caddy and we were moving. I probably could have escaped my bounds within an hour if I'd been able to work hard, but my muscles were jellofied with fear.

I looked out the window. The glass was tinted, but it was a big window, so I got a pretty good view. We left New York, headed west on I-80. Through New Jersey and into Pennsylvania: monotony. Nothing but hills and trees, like New England, except short on stone walls, and the hills ran in long, dreary ridges. At the rim of one I saw the peep show people, wrapped up in each other like a badly made granny knot. I shut my eyes, and when I opened them a minute later the peep show people were gone. I tried to recreate the image in my head, but it would not come into focus. I thought about Siena, imagining we were twins. She sensed my danger at this moment, and she was coming to my rescue. Maybe all those times I had sensed danger, I was really feeling trouble not inside myself but inside her. Maybe I was a Souv. I tried to think of some Souv words, but none came to mind. I kept watching for Royal's limo on the highway, but it never materialized. I was starting to doze off when the rig pulled off the interstate. By the time we'd parked on a dirt turn-off on a lonely road I was hoping lightning would strike me dead. I watched the door as it opened, and the man with the black-white mustache who I knew as the Autodidact filled the space with his bulk. He came toward me.

"I'm going to give you a chance to get the blood circulating," he said. He untied my legs and pulled the tape free from my wrists. "Can you stand up?"

"Yah."

"Say, 'yes, sir,' when I speak to you."

"Yes, sir," I said.

"Stand." I stood. "Move around a little." I was a little dizzy, but I didn't say anything. "Your face is not in good shape. They'll think I did it. Do you have to go to the bathroom?"

"Yes, sir."

He led me to the bathroom. He kept the door open, watching me while I went. I barely managed to unzip and do what I had to do.

When I was finished, the Autodidact said, "Let me look at your kisser." He sat me on the toilet seat. His fingers ran across the pulpy knolls of my face. It seemed to me I'd been through all this before. I shut my eyes and tried to pretend I was far away, sitting by a cool stream. "You could probably use a couple stitches over the eye." He pushed flesh—it hurt on the bone. "You're a good coagulator. You'll be all right with a scar to remember your enemy by. What's this?" He tugged at the collar Royal had given me.

I jerked my head away. "That's mine, you can't have it."

"Let me guess. A keepsake from a loved one."

"If you take it off, the Alien will send his death squads down to kill you."

"Young man, you shouldn't make threats you can't back up." He unsnapped the collar and eyed it. "Feels like genuine leather."

I thrashed and screamed. "Mine—mine! They'll kill you."

"Okay, kid, you won that one." He put the collar back on.

"Are you going to kill me? Are you going to torture me? Why did you kidnap me?"

"It's too much for me to explain right now. Let's just say that because of you I'm wanted by the law. I'm taking you to see somebody. She's a lawyer. She's going to talk to you. We're not going to hurt you."

I'd heard him lie back in New Hampshire, so I figured I knew him well enough to know he wasn't lying now. "Okay," I said.

He washed my face, hurt me by patting alcohol swabs on my wounds. Then he made me stand. He stroked, pinched, squeezed my body. "No broken bones," he said.

He led me to the dining table. "Sit," he ordered. I sat. He brought me a tall glass of water. "Drink. All of it." I drank. All of it.

While I sat, he started constructing two giant sandwiches. I watched and drooled.

"When I was your age we used to call these Dagwood sandwiches," the Autodidact said. "Do you know who Dagwood Bumstead is?"

"No, sir," I said. "Was Mister Bumstead somebody you knew in prison?"

"What else do you know about me?"

"That you were in state prison for thirty-nine years for murder."

"That's correct." He built the sandwich very slowly and carefully, as if it was going to be displayed instead of eaten.

"You were probably unjustly convicted for a crime you did not commit," I said.

"To the contrary. I was justly convicted for a crime I did commit. I held up a filling station. The attendant went for a gun under the register, and I shot him. He was sixteen years old. Two years younger than myself. He could have been my kid brother, and I killed him."

My voice rose up in anger, and I shouted my words as an accusation. "I know something else about you. You're an autodidact. You said so yourself."

He smiled the way you would at a fly you were about to squash. "And what is an autodidact?"

"A friend."

"In a manner of speaking, you may have a point," he said, very serious now. "But in common usage an autodidact is merely a self-taught person. It is a fancy word. Self-taught persons often use fancy words to masquerade the shame they feel at their lack of formal learning. I suppose that's why I told you back in New Hampshire that I was a college professor. It was my heart's desire to be perceived as a college professor. In fact, I am an ex-convict, a collector of books, and, yes, an autodidact."

"The Autodidact." I liked the sound of the word now that I knew what it meant.

"In deference to my age and modest achievements, you will refer to me as the Autodidact, sir."

"Okay, sir. You wiled away the hours in prison reading books?" I said.

"That's correct. It paid off in more than in an academic way. I started to collect and swap books. I eventually amassed a number of rare volumes. Upon my release I sold my collection and with the profits bought this trailer."

"You didn't sell them all. This place is jammed with books."

"I sold only the valuable ones. I kept the ones that had personal meaning for me, the ones that educated me. The ones that gave me the will go on in the world. Such books are not rare. They are easily accessible to most people." He stood, grabbed a book. "Aristotle. Who taught me the pleasures of logic and common sense." I thought about my geek friend, Aristotle II. He put the Aristotle book back and removed another one. "Frederick Douglas. Suffering, freedom, triumph." He put back the Douglas and held up two others. "The Marquis de Sade, forbidden fantasy. Proust, memory as art, the sentence as art." He returned the books where he found them, so apparently he had a particular place for each one.

"And the Cadillac?" I said.

"I bought the truck you saw. I stole the Cadillac. Under stress, I discovered that the civilized veneer that I'd cloaked myself with over the years was stripped away. I reverted to juvenile behavior." He talked very carefully, measuring out each word. "I believe I am over that, in control of myself at least for the moment. Now about yourself, young man. You took something from me; I want it back."

"Are you going to torture me to get it?" I won't say I was scared, but I was breathing faster than normal.

"I would torture you if I thought it would do any good. Do you know what you took from me?"

I shook my head no.

"I didn't think so. I don't know what to do with you. That's why we're going to meet with my friend, the lawyer. She has more hands-on experience than I in the world outside prison bars. Come on. You ride in the car with me."

As the Cadillac rolled down the highway, the Autodidact told me about the state prison in Concord. The men showered together in a huge room with a pitted concrete floor, and in the winter the wind from the outside whistled through the room and the bodies turned blue with cold. The Autodidact had his own cell on the third floor. It was very small, too small to keep a lot of books in. He stored most of his collection in a warehouse, arranged through a pen pal. Her name was Sally. It was her place we were headed for, in Steeltown, Ohio, along the Ohio River.

We stayed that night at a campground. I wasn't allowed to go out because my swollen face might attract attention. After an evening meal of pork chops, boiled potatoes, and peas, the Autodidact said it was time to turn in.

"Come with me," he said, and brought me into his bedroom. Even with the light on it was dark. Besides the usual books on shelves on the wall, there was a shelf of knickknacks over the bed—a picture of a woman (his mother, now dead, I found out later), another woman (Sally), some green beadlike stones, a big knife, some pens, and a notepad. But most of this small room was dominated by the bed. It was huge with metal posts at the four corners.

"You will spend the night here," the Autodidact said. "Do you have to go to the bathroom?"

"No, sir."

"How do you sleep?"

"I don't understand, sir," I said.

"Do you sleep on your back or on your belly or on your side?"

"On my back."

"Okay. Lie down on the bed on your back."

I did as he told me, and he tied my wrists and ankles to the bedposts. I was thinking about the knife on the shelf over the bed, but he took that away.

He walked to the doorway and looked at me for the longest time. Finally, he said, "Now I can get some sleep," and he went into the other room.

We left bright and early the next morning on a two-lane road. I rode in the Caddy with the Autodidact and watched the scenery through the big windows. We passed through sweet little, rounded hills, the tops covered with hardwood forests, the narrow but flat valleys cleared and planted for corn and other vegetable-garden crops. A log house or two decorated the countryside, but mainly the road was a winding, wandering rabbit warren of small farms. The region looked like a sawed-off New Hampshire. I liked it.

I was not only delighted but surprised when we drove by a black, horse-drawn cart carrying a bearded driver, a woman with a bonnet, and a couple of kids. Down the road was their farm. Something about the place took my breath away, but it was a second or two before I figured out the source of my amazement, not what was there, but what was not there. No paved driveway. No motorized vehicles in the yard. No power lines. The Autodidact said these spreads were inhabited by the Amish, people who lived without modern conveniences because of their Christian religious beliefs. They worked hard. They minded their own business. They didn't live only for their addictions.

The Amish had what Father had angled for all his life—good land for homesteading, working farms, independence from "the system," no yuppies for neighbors. Why had the Amish succeeded and why had Father failed? The answer was as plain as the nose on your face: a dutiful attitude toward the three-headed God and good living habits. Poor Father had started down the road to self-sufficiency from the wrong end.

We reached a river—big and twisty with hills often reaching right to the shore. I was impressed. It was the Ohio River, the Autodidact said, and we were close to our destination. Minutes later we left the green countryside for a gray-brown city, drab and run down as that bum who'd gotten shot on Dali Street. We'd arrived in Steeltown. Right off, I saw church steeples, so apparently Christianity was popular in this part of the U.S.A.

The Autodidact inched the Caddy and the trailer along a street which consisted mainly of boarded up storefronts. The place had a Western look, low, wood-frame buildings, the gables covered with rectangular fronts. That got me to thinking. How did I know that a town could have a Western look? I might have read about it someplace or absorbed some information via movies and TV, but from the way the idea popped into my head, natural as picking my nose with my right index finger, it was more likely that I'd actually been West at some point. The only building that appeared to have been renovated and which was thriving and which was open after five P.M. was a video store. I saw a woman in a white pantsuit, gigantic hairdo, and lipstick bright and red enough to stop a speeding drunk driver. I had a mind to sting her to see whether she was person or one of my demons.

We drove through the city along a narrow road that hugged the river bank. Soon we were out of the city, and for a few miles we passed warehouses and junk-car lots until we reached the hulk of a giant, industrial plant surrounded by a rusty, ten-foot high fence with barbed wire at the top. Inside was a behemoth of a building with no windows and huge smokestacks. The grounds were overgrown with briars and young trees. Grass grew in cracks in the empty parking lots. I didn't see a soul.

"Steel mill—shut down," said the Autodidact.

The scenery then went from ugly to beautiful. Just past the mill was a nice-looking southern mansion with pillars on the front and a big, spacious porch. Beside it was a barn.

"Nice place," I said.

"Glad you like it," the Autodidact said, pulling into the driveway. "It's Sally's family farm, tobacco plantation."

"I don't see any crops," I said. I wanted a cigarette.

"She still calls it the farm, but actually no farming goes on. Sally's against smoking, even though tobacco is the source of the family fortune."

"I like the barn," I said.

"They used to dry the tobacco in the barn."

The rig eased to a stop in front of the house. The Autodidact's shifting had improved. "Wait here," he said.

The Autodidact stepped out of the car and approached the house. He never got there. A woman about fifty, with graying red hair, a face kind of pretty but her body on the heavy side, appeared from the porch. It was Sally. I recognized her from the picture in the Autodidact's bedroom. She hesitated on the steps of the porch for a second and then ran to the Autodidact. He picked her off her feet which, given her size, was quite an accomplishment, and they hugged and kissed for maybe an entire minute. I felt squeamish, and was relieved when they finally let go. The Autodidact whispered something to Sally.

She turned her attention to my battered face, and said to the Autodidact, "Good, Lord, what have you done to him?"

"I never laid a hand on him. Tell her," he said, as I stepped out of the car.

"I was attacked rescuing orphans from a mob of frothing drug addicts, and then. . . ." Before I could get up a head of steam with this story, the Autodidact cut me off.

"The truth. Tell Sally the truth."

"He kidnapped me and tied me, but he didn't touch me," I pointed to my face. "My best friend did this to me back in New York." And then I eyed the Autodidact, and I repeated, "He did kidnap me. That is the truth."

The woman looked at the Autodidact.

"I'm afraid so," he said.

We walked to the house and sat on the porch. I looked out at the land—fields, a screen of woods, the steel plant, the river, hills to our back and in the distance across the river. No other houses in sight.

"After all the letters we wrote, after all the books you've read over these years, you had to revert to type and abduct him." Sally badgered the Autodidact so bad that I started to feel sorry for him.

"I couldn't think of anything else to do. It was the only kind of action I thought to take under the circumstances. You have a better idea?" he said.

"You could have turned him over to the police."

"Ultimately, that was my goal. I just wanted you to talk to him first. I'm a wanted man again, and he's to blame. He's . . . he's . . . ." His face tightened as he struggled to rein in his rage.

"Settle down," Sally said. "Did you question him?"

"No. I was afraid."

"Afraid of what?"

"Afraid I might be violent with him. I don't know if I can cope outside the American prison system. Prison is all I know."

"Oh, darling." And then she put her arms around him, and he put his arms around her, and she cried, and he seemed to want to cry. It was disgusting.

I didn't know what to make of all this, and I finally yelled, "Why am I your prisoner?"

"We have to release him, we have to trust in God and in the system and in ourselves. We have to tell the truth," Sally said.

"All right," said the Autodidact.

"Young man," said Sally, "your father is dead. It's believed he was murdered."

RUN RABBIT DIE

Author Jack Kerouac didn't live a life; he wrote a life. It's logical to call fiction that derives from such a sensibility Virtual Realism. It's the Virtual Realism captured in *On the Road* that accounts for Kerouac's continuing appeal to young people, who themselves live virtual lives in which movies and television play as big a role in their lives as their experiences. — From the Journal of Henri Scratch.

Sally sat me down in a chair that was too big for King Kong, let alone a skinny kid like me. Soon I learned more details of why the Autodidact had kidnapped me. After I'd run away from him, he'd called the town constable back in New Hampshire to report me as a runaway. The constable had told the Autodidact that he himself was wanted for questioning in the murder of Joe Webster and that he should turn himself in. The Autodidact hung up the phone and immediately called lawyer Sally. She made a few phone calls and got the story. A bill collector had found Father dead, his head bashed in. A couple of local people had seen me hanging around the Autodidact's trailer. They remembered the vanity plate—"FREE." Sally advised the Autodidact to turn himself in. But he didn't do it. His criminal mind, dormant for all those years of book learning, came to life and took over his personality. He'd ditched his pickup truck, stolen the Cadillac from a long-term airport parking lot, and repainted the trailer. He'd tracked me down after reading my A-Y-G doodle on his notepad.

"Now, Web, I want you to tell me everything that happened leading up to the moment that you ran away from your father," Sally said. Her lawyer's way of talking, right at me, got my attention.

I explained everything just the way I remembered it.

"You believe that this Xiphi person murdered your father?" Sally said.

"He's not a person, he's my demon," I said.

"It may have been an accident," Sally said to the Autodidact.

The Autodidact pulled at the hair he didn't have, and said, "Web doesn't know for sure what happened. He can't testify on my behalf. If he tells the police that Xiphi story, they'll reason that he flipped out. They'll still think I did it."

Sally wanted to call the police, but the Autodidact convinced her to wait until he could come up with a plan. Sally said okay—for the time being.

She showed us around her house. The mansion reminded me of some of the New England places where Father and I delivered firewood, old and fancy, but the windows were bigger and more light poured through, and it was dirtier than big northern houses, so the place felt a little friendlier. Most of the house was closed off, because (as I found out later) Sally had no kin and because she didn't normally live in the house but in a city, where her law office was located. She had inherited the farm and put it up for sale. So far, no takers. The location, beside the junked steel mill, kept the buyers away. The tour ended when she and the Autodidact took me to my room.

"Where's the key?" the Autodidact said.

"I refuse to lock him in," Sally said. "What if there's a fire?"

"What if he escapes?"

"He's no longer frightened. You're not frightened, are you, Web?"

"No, Sally," I said.

"No ma'am," corrected the Autodidact.

"Yes, sir—no ma'am."

Sally said to the Autodidact, "Are these titles your doing?"

"Is there anything wrong with showing respect?"

"John," Sally said, gently as you'd put a worm on a hook, "children no longer refer to their elders as 'sir' and 'ma'am'."

"Things are that bad?" said the Autodidact.

Sally turned to me. "Web, promise me you won't run away."

"I promise."

"He promises," the Autodidact said sarcastically.

"We must build some trust," said Sally, then turned to me. "Promise me you won't turn in John."

"The Autodidact."

"The what?" She turned to the Autodidact.

"It's a long story," said the Autodidact.

"And that thing around his neck, I suppose that's a story, too."

"You'll have to ask him about that."

"Web?"

"Mine." I clutched my throat.

"The both of you are totally mad, you know that, don't you?" Lawyer Sally didn't wait for an answer. She said to me, "Promise me you'll be good."

In this case, I could see, "good" meant keeping my promises. Since good equaled bad, and since bad meant breaking my promises, I felt comfortable in telling a lie. "I promise," I said. I liked Lawyer Sally a little bit, because in her own way she was sincere.

They left, and I was alone. I had my own bed and my own bathroom. It was like being back in the hospital, except that I didn't have my own television.

That night when I lay down to go to sleep, I tried to think sweet thoughts about Father. It wasn't easy, but I was making some headway, remembering that he had taught me the names and habits of trees, when Xiphi showed up. I didn't see him too clearly in the darkness—he was just a silhouette sitting on the window sill—but I heard his voice clearly enough. "Now that Dirty Joe is out of the way, when you find your mother, you can have her all to yourself. Aren't you glad I killed him?" I had to admit that I was.

A week rolled by. We were into high summer. I had a lot of time to myself, because the Autodidact and Sally were getting to know each other. That was how they put it: "We're getting to know each other." Were they doing it? You bet. They spent every night in the same bedroom with the door closed.

In the morning I'd sleep late, get up, wash, and eat and eat and eat, and watch an hour of television. Reception wasn't very good, because the cable company didn't reach this far into the hinterlands and Sally was too cheap to put in a satellite dish, but I didn't care. I just used the TV for zentensity.

I spent most of the time in the fields or down by the river, hunting with a bow and arrow that I found in the barn. It had belonged to Sally's brother, who had died in the Vietnam War. I shot arrows at birds. I never hit one. I shot arrows at fish. I never hit one. I shot arrows at rabbits. I never hit one. I'd scare them up, and they would streak across the field into the brush. When I was bored with hunting, I threw stones in the river, and I collected sticks and laid them on the narrow beach in designs that pleased my eye. Every hour or so, I'd take a break from whatever I was doing to walk in the ditch between the fence of the junked steel mill and the road; I'd look for cigarette butts. I almost always found two or three, enough for a smoke.

Sally was dead set against smoking. She wanted to make amends for her tobacco-growing family. I didn't care one way or another what she believed. I was taking a vacation from caring. I just wanted to catch up on eating, sleeping, lazing around, playing, zentensing, and smoking.

Sally made a big deal of dinner. She insisted we eat together and "converse." She said civilized people enjoyed civilized meals in a civilized atmosphere. Actually, though, about the only thing she could think of saying to me was, "Well, Web, how was your day?" I wasn't interested in telling her, and I could see that she wasn't really interested in hearing about it, so I'd say, "Nothing special."

The Autodidact was better company. He'd tell me about books he'd read. "Web, gaze out at the river," he said to me one time at dessert. So I stared out through the open French doors at the river valley. "Now I want you to imagine it in winter choked with ice floes. Picture in your mind a beautiful woman. She's holding a baby. She's being chased by men." And he went on to tell me the story of *Uncle Tom's Cabin*. Naturally, in my own mind I was the baby, and Eliza was my mother, the Alien was the slave hunter, and the Autodidact was Uncle Tom. Later he made me read the book. It was pretty good. I realized that I was most like Topsy, the bad-mannered slave girl. Maybe I was part black with slaves for ancestors. Maybe that was why I was cursed. Or maybe I was part girl, and *that* was why I was cursed. I thought about Terry's murdered brother/sister.

The Autodidact read the newspaper at the table, and if he found an item he liked he'd give us a report. For example: "Hey, listen to this. Somebody robbed Henri Scratch's body from the grave."

The name rang a bell, but I couldn't put a face or a personality to it.

"Scratch? The critic who was murdered last week?" Sally said.

"He was more than a critic," the Autodidact said. "He was a former priest and the founder of a cult. He did it all."

"What happened to him?" Sally asked.

"The day after his body was laid to rest they found the casket, unearthed and empty."

"A publicity stunt, I'll bet," said Sally.

The first week the Autodidact tried to work on his book about prison life, but it wasn't going well; in fact, it wasn't going at all.

The second week the Autodidact quit on the book and started to bow-and-arrow hunt with me. At first, he wasn't any better at shooting the bow than I was, but after a couple of days, he'd learned to aim that bow better than I ever did, and he could pull the string all the way back, so the arrows went Rambo fast.

Late one afternoon we were hunting by the steel-mill fence when we saw a rabbit. It was the Autodidact's turn with the bow and he let loose an arrow. It missed by a mile, and the rabbit kept running. It disappeared at the fence and a second later reappeared on the other side, racing for some briars. We found a break in the fence and crawled through.

It was a different world behind that fence. The plants were different, the views were different, the smells and even the weather were different. The mill buildings blocked the breeze and threw off the stored heat of the sun, so it was hotter. Something in the air made our noses itch. Sounds from the world at large were muffled. Close by sounds were kind of hysterical. Birds didn't tweet, they screeched; bees droned angrily; the mill building periodically groaned and crackled from the heat, like some huge tormented thing. We'd landed on Xi.

"Do you feel it, Web?" the Autodidact said.

"I'm home," I said.

"I was going to say the same thing. Prison was like this, unreal but sharp."

We jumped the rabbit by the briars and the Autodidact shot again. Missed. The rabbit ran right at the steel-mill wall. Maybe it thought there was a hole there. Well, there wasn't. The rabbit pulled up at the wall. Instead of veering off, it stopped and posed on its hind legs for a few seconds. The Autodidact let loose with another arrow. It went right through the rabbit's throat. The rabbit tried to run, made a half circle, and keeled over. When we reached it, it was still breathing; it didn't look right to me, too relaxed. The Autodidact rapped its head on the brick side of the building. The rabbit shuddered for a second, then went limp.

"It didn't seem to be in pain," I said.

"Once the body knows it's going to die, the pain goes away," the Autodidact said. "It's Nature's way."

"I want to die like that rabbit," I said.

"It beats cancer, but you never know how the end will come. A person, like an animal, has little to say about his death. And because people are so much more aware of time, their deaths are apt to be more complicated and difficult."

"You've thought about this before."

"Yes, about the boy I murdered. How he must have felt. The best thing I can say is that because of the circumstances, he never had a chance to experience any of those complex and difficult human emotions. He died like any animal overcome by a predator. The thought brings me some comfort." The Autodidact looked off for a moment into the nowheres of could-have-beens and never-weres. "Let's see about preparing this game for the dinner table."

We scrambled through the hole in the fence, walked to the trailer to dig up a book about hunting. He fingered through the table of contents. "Here it is, 'Rabbits.'"

We brought the book and the rabbit into the house. The Autodidact stood over the kitchen sink with a big knife, and while I read from the book on how to do it, he skinned the carcass. We had a fun time, because the Autodidact kept making mistakes. Eventually though, the job got done. With bloodied hands, the Autodidact held the rabbit by its feet in front of me. It looked almost human, like an acrobat dead for a year or so hanging from his heels.

"Look up a recipe for rabbit stew," the Autodidact said. Just then, Sally came in from shopping. At the sight of the carcass, she made a small, closed-mouth, controlled-screaming sound. The Autodidact explained to her that we had hunted and killed the rabbit. He was proud.

"How could you destroy that poor, defenseless animal?" she said.

"God made rabbits to benefit the predators," the Autodidact said.

"And you're a predator." She bored holes in his head with her eyes.

"Yes," he said softly. "I was convicted of predatory behavior. Remember?"

"I thought you were rehabilitated."

"I am, Sally. I'm no longer a predator of people. I was merely hunting with a boy. Men and boys have been doing that for millennia. It's not an act requiring rehabilitation or apology."

"In a civilized society, hunting is not a necessity for survival. It is a mere amusement at the expense of living creatures who already have a hard enough time."

They went round and round on that one, and never agreed. She yelled at him—"Thug!"—and he yelled at her—"Bitch!" And then the Autodidact lost control. He grabbed Sally's wrist, wheeled her around and raised a hand to her. I knew the look in his eye—I'd seen it in Father's eye. Sally screeched as if she had been cut by a whip, but it was only from fear. The Autodidact didn't follow through. After she hollered, he let go of her, backed off, sat down, and buried his face in hands.

"I came within an inch of hurting you," he said. "And all over a foolish disagreement. I'm afraid I'm not ready for a relationship."

"I know, I know," she said, forlorn and still jittery.

We didn't eat the rabbit. The Autodidact dug a hole in the yard, and we buried it. Later, the Autodidact and Sally had a long private talk in their bedroom. I tried to listen by putting my ear to the door, but I couldn't hear anything.

The next day was tense. The Autodidact avoided me, working in his trailer. Sally smiled a lot, and she was full of polite conversation. The Director whispered in my ear, "Insincere, insincere, insincere." I didn't hunt at all. I walked by the river shore. The water was dark and gloomy. I considered jumping in, drifting down the Ohio into the Mississippi, into the Gulf of Mexico, into the ocean, across to a new world or off the edge. I left the river and went up the road and stalked cigarette butts. Wherever I went, the steel mill loomed over me.

A few minutes later, I heard Sally calling me in for dinner. She and the Autodidact were on the porch, sipping their before-dinner drinks when I arrived. The Autodidact poured me a lemonade and told me to get a load off. He didn't seem too relaxed. The Director whispered, "Insincere, insincere."

The Autodidact turned to Sally. "I told you he'd know."

They wouldn't say where he was going. I was to stay with Sally for a while. Once the Autodidact had a head start, I would be turned over to the county welfare department, where I should tell them the whole truth and nothing but the truth. The "system" would take care of me. I wasn't sure whether this was the same "system" that Father had spent his life fighting, but I thought it might be pretty close. I promised to be good. Sally put her arms around me and hugged me. The Autodidact looked me up and down. His Director was whispering in his ear that I was insincere.

We ate dinner in silence. Afterward, while the Autodidact and Sally packed some things, I stole a big bag of peanuts, a loaf of bread, and a gallon of water in a plastic milk jug, and hid these supplies in my room.

Finally, it was time to go. "I don't know what to say," the Autodidact said. All those books, and he couldn't find a word.

"I'm going to bed," I said, yawning and stretching my arms over my head.

Sally kissed me good night, but the Autodidact never got close, just backed away from me. They were glad to get rid of me; they wanted to say their own good-byes. I knew they'd take forever; in fact, I counted on it. I made my bed to appear as if I was in it and slipped out the window with my paper bag full of goods.

Outside on the grass, I eavesdropped by the open living room window for a few seconds before moving on.

"Oh, Sally, I wish you'd come with me. We can start over together," the Autodidact said.

"I already have a life."

"It's a lonely life. You said so yourself."

"Perhaps, but I'm not ready to give it up. No, that's not exactly right. I'm not ready to leave behind . . . a self."

"I guess I better get going. I'll be driving all night."

"Don't call. Don't tell me about the new identity. I don't want to know. I couldn't in all honesty lie to the authorities."

I didn't hear the rest. I hurried off to the trailer, hiding in the luggage compartment. A few minutes later I heard the Cadillac's door slam and the engine start. Soon I could feel us moving. I opened the drawer, returned to the living quarters of the trailer, and took a seat in a chair by a window. I figured that once the Autodidact was away from Sally for a while, he'd calm down. When he was in a good mood, I'd reveal myself to him. He'd be mad at first. He might even knock me around a little bit, but eventually he'd realize I was good company. We'd go look for my mother. She and the Autodidact would get married, and I'd be their son.

GRAND ISLE

We picked up Route 62 and dropped south. The road took us into the bluegrass country of Kentucky. In the night light under the moon the grass in the rolling fields actually did look blue, like snow at night in New Hampshire. Wooden fences and horse barns decorated the fields. I wondered what the life of a horse thief must be like. Sneak into barn, make friends with horse, hop on and ride off. Jump over fences, ride all night under the light of the moon. Along toward sunrise race horse back to barn, nobody the wiser. Kiss his nose, walk out of barn. Outside again, drop to knees, stick face in dew on grass and sniff the Xi.

I fell asleep, snapping to wakefulness maybe an hour after dawn. As we drove further south, the air got hotter and more humid. I didn't mind too much. Like the Autodidact and his trailer, I didn't have much room for feelings, being in that state of mind where everything is ahead or behind. The Autodidact didn't have a TV in his trailer, but he did have a radio, and I passed the time listening to Country and Western music ("All my exes are in Texas and that's why I'm living in Tennessee."), Baptist ministers ("Beware the raiments of hell.") and the news ("In the Louisiana governor's race, the Dauphin is being challenged by the Duke.").

I munched on peanuts and bread and drank from my gallon jug of water, making sure not to make a mess, because I didn't want the Autodidact to notice anything different when finally he stopped and checked his trailer.

In south Louisiana, we got off the interstate onto a narrow, two-lane black-topped road. We slammed through St. Charles, Raceland, Lockport, Larose, Cut Off, Galliano. The road ran beside a bayou, which is like a river that flows real slow both ways. The bayou wasn't very wide, but it must have been dredged pretty deep because I saw good-sized fishing boats going up and down the waterway. A faded billboard showed a goofy fat guy and a skinny minnie in a bathing suit. They were sharing beers and eating from a bucket of crawfish. Father had occasionally used crawfish for bait in trying to catch bass, but I couldn't imagine crawfish by the bucketful, and I couldn't imagine eating them.

Further into the grassy swamp we drove, through Golden Meadow and Leeyville. Traffic petered out. Which made sense since eventually the road dead-ended into the Gulf of Mexico, facts I gleaned by hauling out one of the Autodidact's maps and looking up the place names I'd seen on signs. The sun was high and bright, and beyond the bayou was tall, wavy grass and the smell of sea water and fish; this was delta land, dumped by the Mississippi River years ago; it really was like driving out into the Gulf of Mexico.

At the end of the road was Grand Isle, and I looked it up in the Autodidact's library. Hotels and fine vacation houses used to line the beaches, but hurricanes took the "grand" out of the isle, sweeping it clean every forty or fifty years. When we arrived, the place had a temporary feel to it. The Autodidact pulled in front of one of the many mobile homes that set on wooden piers about ten feet tall. There were no trees in the yard, and the uncut lawn was a little stinky from overwetness. Father would have loved this place.

Through a slit in a curtain, I watched the Autodidact walk up a rickety wooden staircase to a landing, look around, knock. A few seconds later a woman opened the door. The sight of her scared me, so that I pulled away from the window. The woman had snakes in place of hair. By the time I gathered my wits about me and looked again, the Autodidact and the woman had gone inside.

I waited by the window. The Autodidact was in there maybe half an hour, and then he came back out, carrying a big, bulging sack over his shoulder. I scurried away, ducking into my hiding place under the couch.

The Autodidact opened the trailer door, and I heard a thump. He'd tossed the sack into the trailer. He left, started the car, and drove slowly away. I came out of my hole. The sack lay by the door. It looked a lot bigger before my eyes than it had seemed on the shoulder of the Autodidact. I poked at it with my finger. I was beginning to suspect what was in the sack. A rope was wrapped around the top, and I untied it and rolled down the top of the sack. Inside was the body of a man about sixty, dead. I looked at him. His eyes were closed, but he seemed at peace. He reminded me a little of the Autodidact. He was the same complexion, about the same size and age, except he didn't have a mustache and instead of a bald head, he had sideburns and kinky brown hair on his head. "Wake up," I said, but I knew there was going to be no waking up. I retied the sack and went back into my secret compartment.

The Autodidact didn't go very far, he only drove a little ways and parked. I could hear waves breaking on the shore, so apparently we were on the beach. A minute later, the Autodidact came back into the trailer. From the way he puttered around and mumbled to himself, I could tell he was nervous. An hour or two went by. I dozed, and was awakened by the sound of somebody knocking at the door. A few minutes later I was listening to a conversation between the Autodidact and the woman with snakes for hair.

"The mustache has got to go," she said.

"I've had it for twenty years. It's become part of me."

"You're not you anymore. If you don't want to arouse suspicion, you'll have to let your hair grow in, your sideburns come down a little cockeyed, like our friend in the sack."

"The new me."

"That's right, the new you. Do as I advise and no lawman will ever mistake you for that wanted character in . . . where was it?"

"New Hampshire."

"Is that in Massachusetts?"

"More or less."

As they talked, I could hear other sounds—zzzz, snip-snip, ouch. She was working on him, cutting off his mustache, doing other things to change the way he looked.

There was a pause, and then the Autodidact said, "My word, look at me. No mustache. It's going to take some getting used to."

"Okay, here's the important stuff. Texas driver's license and a Social Security number. Completely authentic. Also, a sketch about this guy's life."

"Who was he?"

"A nobody, a drug addict."

"Where did you get this . . . this . . . identity? This man?"

"You'll figure it out some day."

"I think I'm already close. Fill me in."

"I'll tell you, but remember, you promised to pay."

"And I'll keep that promise."

"I know some gentlemen in the city of New Orleans," she said. "They cruise for the homeless. They strangle the drifters and bring them to me. Me, I have a computer and a modem. I dig up their credit records, whatever else I can."

"This fellow have a family?"

"No wife. No children. Has a mother in New Mexico that he hasn't seen since he ran away from home as a young one."

New Mexico—I thought about my own mother.

"A mother. She's still alive?" said the Autodidact.

"Over eighty."

"My own mother died, probably from a broken heart after my crime."

"Don't flatter yourself. She died because she died."

"I wonder if anybody else loved this man."

"The homeless got nobody. That's why they're homeless. Look, if it wasn't me that was buying these Social Security numbers, it would be somebody else."

"I can't accept this man's things, his identity, his very being."

"I don't care what you do with it, as long as you pay me for my troubles. Like you promised. If you don't adopt this dead man's identity as your own, you're as good as caught, cross-examined, and convicted. And besides, the only way this poor fellow gets any more mileage from his identity is through you."

"I hadn't thought of that. What's his name?"

"Look at the driver's license."

"Jim Clements."

Nobody spoke for a few minutes, but I could hear the Autodidact get up, lumber around. Finally, he said, "Now what?"

"We have to have a little fire."

"A fire?"

"Suppose there's a leak in your propane system. It catches, boom! The real Jim Clements is burned beyond recognition, but everybody thinks the body belongs to John LeFauve. Then you can be Jim Clements. Nobody will be the wiser."

"We have to make arrangements to remove and store my books."

"They'll make a better fire."

"I spent my life collecting these books. These books are my soul. My everything. You must understand."

"If John LeFauve has to die, his everything must also die. Especially the books."

"I don't care about the clothes, any of my personal effects. It's only the books. Those books are me."

"The books are the old you. All the more reason they go to the grave with him, just like some Egyptian king being buried with his things."

And then there was a lot of stomping around and angry shouts from the Autodidact. Finally, he settled down.

"You know whose fault this is?" he said.

"The law?"

"A boy. A damn boy has ruined the few years of freedom I have left. If I could get my hands on him, I would kill him."

Something happened when he spoke those words. I lost the drift of the conversation, and I was listening to the gulf breakers: crash and wash, crash and wash, crash and wash. Time passed, I don't know how much, and I don't know how he got into my hiding place, but there he was, slimier and dirtier than ever, Xiphi, lying beside me. Suddenly, the Director took Xiphi's place beside me.

"Web, I think you've misinterpreted this role," the Director said, his voice more gentle than usual; for once he wasn't yelling at me. "When you play a character such as Xiphi, to get into him you have to become him, that is true—but not really. You overplayed the role."

"He's my demon," I said.

"You're making the same mistake now that you made with Dirty Joe." The Director suddenly burst into flames and out of the Director's screams, Xiphi burst forth.

"Who's real now?" Xiphi said.

I touched his cheek, and it was hot with black, fiery slime. In just a couple of seconds the heat was more intense. I could feel it on my collar, like a signal to get out of there. I wiggled through the baggage to the side door, and groped in the dark until I found the latch. I pulled it and the outside compartment door opened, and I spilled out onto the sand. It was cool and dark out, but I'd been in pitch black for so long that I could see quite well in the night light. There was a huge expanse of water and hard-packed sand and the beach was deserted. I didn't know where the Autodidact, now Jim Clements, had gone; I didn't see anybody around.

Fog from the gulf was rolling in very fast. It was exciting to watch. It made me think about movie reels I'd seen of the atom bomb going off, a cloud rolling across the landscape and a second later: destruction. The sharp smell of butchered fish excited my nose. Breakers about the size of living room sofas made an awful racket as they slapped the beach.

The trailer burned, burned, burned. The main door flew open, and Xiphi exploded from the opening. Flames danced out of the cracks in the muck on his skin. He was coming toward me, grinning, on fire.

I waded into the water. It was very warm and caressing. "Come in," I yelled. "Come in and let the water clean and soothe you." Xiphi didn't say anything, but I could hear the echo of his voice— *the raiments of hell, the raiments of hell, the raiments of hell.* He stopped at the water's edge. He was afraid to come in, because the water would wash the muck from his body and leave him naked. I dived through the breakers and came up on the other side. A hand from below, maybe the Alien's, maybe the Director's, dragged me out to sea. The wall of fog was right in front of my eyes.

I looked toward the shore. Xiphi ran back into the trailer, now completely engulfed in flames.

HIGHWAY OF BABEL AND THIRST

I don't know how long I swam, time just let go. The salt water held me up like a great big hand. I'm a good swimmer, a good floater; it was going take a while for me to drown. I started to get cold, and that scared me a little. Slowly chilling out was a bad way to go. The fog just seemed to get denser and denser. Every once in a while, I heard noises—machinery groans, splashes, and muffled voices that sounded like someone calling, "Edna, Edna."

I had never thought about dying in the dark. I was determined to last until morning, so I stopped swimming and just treaded water. I prayed to the three-headed God. Oh, Father-head, save me; oh, son-head save me; oh, holy-ghost, save me. The three-headed God refused to appear, but I could sense Him/Her/It/Them: far out in the sky, looking down on me, arguing among Itself/Herself/Himself/Themselves about whether I deserved a break or not.

I had spells where I wanted to cry, but then I remembered that Sally had told me that self-pity was a dreadfully shameful emotion and never to feel it, so I told myself not to feel sorry for myself anymore. I was getting more and more tired. And thirsty. And cold—that was the worst of it: the cold. The gulf is warm, but after you spend hours in it you get cold anyway. Water just drains away the heat inside of you. After a while you don't even feel cold, you feel weird. I thought about Father, beating me; I thought about the Autodidact and his hatred for me. I thought about my demons—Langdon, who had left me; Xiphi, who had taken his place; the Alien, who (I suddenly figured out) had educated me; the Director, who wanted to make me a star. Soon none of them seemed to matter. For once, I was haunted by neither the remembered nor the forgotten past. In the anticipation of my death, I settled on one idea: a reunion with my mother. I prayed to the three-headed God. "Oh, Lord/Lords before I die please deliver me to my mother." God did me a favor then. For a few sweet minutes, He/She/It/Them allowed me to experience joy at the thought of seeing her beautiful face, listening to her sweet voice, feeling the warm touch of her hand.

And then I heard boat noises, the belch of an engine, the groan and ache of winches and other gears, and the shifting of a hull. Soon the noises were close by. I tried to call for help, but I was so weak I didn't have enough power for a sneer, let alone a holler. A minute passed. Another. Above me and not too far away I heard men talking. I couldn't make out what they were saying; the words didn't make any sense to me. I think they were talking some kind of Asian language. Had I swum to China?

The next thing I knew the water below me swirled crazily, and I was sent ass over tea kettle. I was upside down, but not drowning; in fact, I was no longer in the water. In the next microsecond, I experienced a feeling of weightlessness. Had I been reabducted by the Alien? Then—thud! I didn't know where I was or what had happened. I sat in a moist pile of something, numb and unthinking until the smell, the sounds, and the feel told me the story. A trawler, pulling in a catch of shrimp, had picked me up and dropped me into a dismal hole in the bottom of the boat.

The shrimp were alive, but they didn't mean me any harm and I wasn't afraid of them. The bunch of them, in their nervous squiggling like a zillion tiny, married couples doing it, made a single noise which was like the sustained purr of a cat. The hole was dark and smelly; I felt as if I were at the deathbed of creatures whose feelings I could not feel, whose demise I could not mourn. In other words, I felt the same way about the death of the shrimp as I had felt about the death of Father. With thoughts like those, I couldn't help but be depressed. But I got some strength from thinking about Nurse Wilder. She used to tell me to count my blessings and praise God. So I did. At least I was with the squiggly shrimp instead of the pinching crawfish. Okay, that was a blessing. One. Praise the Lord/Lords. I felt better. Pretty soon I was able to relax. It was cramped and muggy and hot in that dungeon of shrimp, but I needed some heat, and I was beginning to warm up. Another blessing. Two. Praise the Lord/Lords. When I was less numb and my wits had returned, I realized I was mighty thirsty.

A minute later I was bruised by a cascade of crushed ice from above. I felt like the topping for a giant slurpy. I waited for the squirt of sweet syrup—my preference was for raspberry—but of course it didn't come. I crawled my way to the top of the ice. In ten minutes, the place would be too cold for the likes of me to put up with. Subtract a blessing, but praise the Lord/Lords anyway.

Even though I was pretty weak, I managed to scramble to a trap door in the roof of the hole and push it open. This was all done in the dark and by feel, so it took some time. When I got out, I saw stars overhead. The fog had lifted. A blessing. Praise the Lord/ Lords. Three.

The boat was moving fast. Up ahead in the distance I could see lights on the shore. Apparently the boat was returning to the bayou and to port after a day's fishing. They'd worked late, and everybody was tired. I know because I almost tripped over a fellow lying on deck. At first I thought he was dead, but he was only asleep. He was wiry as a boy, with dark, reddish-brown skin, straight black hair, and sharply curved eyebrows. I figured: Chinese fisherman. If I revealed myself I might wind up as flavoring for wonton soup. I crept over to the man. Beside him was a liter bottle of club soda, half empty. I grabbed it and drank the remains.

I crawled on my hands and knees along the side of the boat until I reached a porthole, where I could hear voices, Chinese talk. The soda water I had drunk started to take hold and I could feel my blood thin, my head clear, and my muscles say, "Let's go." Now that I could think, I thought: I'm scared. Who were these people? Spies? Drug runners? Killers? Agents of the Alien? Researchers for a movie? Or just shrimp fishermen? About when I was considering (but not seriously) jumping overboard, I felt a hand on my shoulder. I jumped back; the man jumped back. I said, "Who are you!" He said something I didn't understand. That brought up the rest of the crew.

"Anybody here speak English?" I said.

The response sounded sympathetic but hard to follow, "Oika skaeaps Hsilgne, tub eh deniarps sih elkna."

They didn't kill or torture me. They gave me more fuzzy water and some kind of vegetable glop with boiled shrimp and crawfish. I ate the crawfish, which was pretty good, tasting like sawed-off lobster, but I didn't have any shrimp. I felt too friendly toward these little gulf residents in the hole to want to eat them. I was drowsy after the meal, and it crossed my mind that the fishermen had drugged me, but I didn't care. I just wanted to sleep. I lay on a bunk and dozed until we were in port.

As the boat slipped into the dock, one of the men motioned for me to go up on deck. I smiled and bowed, figuring he'd do the same, because that's what a Chinaman does in the movies, but he only looked at me like I was an idiot. It was still night, but in the light on the dock, I could see a couple of white men. I thought I'd found people who could converse in English. But as I heard them speak, I realized they weren't talking my language, but some kind of weird French. I wasn't much for *parlez-vous*, but I'd heard the language back in New England. Somebody, I think it was Father, had said that you can't trust a Frenchman any farther than you can throw a Chinaman.

In fact, as I thought about it, I realized that my story was strange and awkward enough to tell in my own language. How could I tell it to Chinamen? Or Frenchmen? As soon as the boat conked the edge of the dock, I leaped onto it and raced by those startled Frenchmen and cut through a couple of yards until I was on the road that ran beside the bayou.

Soon a guy in a pickup truck pulled over, and I hopped into the cab with him. He was drunk as a skunk. The truck just wove back and forth, almost crashing half a dozen times. Meanwhile, the driver sang in French until finally he just ran the truck into a gully and came to a stop. He wasn't hurt or even unconscious. He just sat there, eyes closed, hands on the steering wheel, mouthing French words. I slipped out of the truck and started walking along the road.

I found myself on Route 90. I remembered from the map that the road ran east-west. I walked to a café to ask for a glass of water. The waitress said I smelled funny. She called the manager, and I ran outside. I went through a dumpster and came up with couple of half-drunk drinks in go-cups. In the parking lot, I saw a truck pull in from the east to gas up. Obviously the driver would be getting back on the highway headed west. I had an idea of where I wanted to go: New Mexico, to search for my mother. I counted my blessings. Four. Praise the Lord/Lords. It was a manure truck. Subtract the blessing. Back to three. But I already stank from fish, so the manure wouldn't make much difference. Put back the blessing. Four. I climbed aboard, and off we went.

I fell asleep in the manure and woke up in the middle of the next day. It was pretty here with low wooded hills, the trees not too high or too close together as they were in the East. Rocks were craggy and made designs. A road sign advertised the Alamo. I was on the outskirts of San Antonio, Texas.

At a red light, I hopped off and started walking. It was a typical service road consisting of fast-food restaurants, convenience markets, real estate offices, video-rental stores. Aygand saygo faygorth. All these places had their own dumpsters, supplying enough food and drink to feed an army.

I kept walking until I reached a huge, grand, and new hotel. It was called Home On The Range Motel. A sign said "OPEC Convention." I saw a herd of swarthy men in long white gowns. One of them was astride a camel, and news photographers were taking his picture. I heard him say something to a cohort below in a language I did not understand. I walked among the group, and they parted, their noses twitching with disgust at the smell of me.

From a café parking lot, I sneaked a ride on the back end of a truck transporting horses. From the looks of these broken-down nags, they were headed for the glue factory. I made friends with one horse, an old girl with a swayback and cataracts in her eyes. I whispered in her ear, "I love you." She snorted sweetly in response, stamped her foot, and gave me big wet kisses. She didn't care how I smelled, and I didn't care how she smelled. I patted her head and kissed her mooshy mouth. We kissed back and forth, but after a while I got tired of kissing and tired of standing. I half-leaned and half-sat on a railing. I couldn't lie down for fear of being accidentally trampled to death.

The next thing I knew, we were in the middle of the desert someplace at another café. I kissed my horse friend good-bye and got off. I raided a dumpster for a lunch of soggy hamburg rolls, but I couldn't find anything to drink, and my mouth was dry. I tried to hitch a ride. Nobody stopped, so I just walked without sticking my thumb out. It was better to walk than to stand still. The landscape was lonely but kind of thrilling, too. The weather was hot, and my neck itched under my collar. But I kept it on. What was it Royal had said? The collar was my destiny. What could he have meant by that? I had no idea, but it was all I had to remind me of the good times in my brief past. In the distance I could see purple mountains. Up close the land was dry and beige, the plants scruffy. I saw a rabbit, lots of birds, and a rattlesnake. I wished I had a gun to kill the snake. Also the rabbit. And maybe some of the birds. Way in the distance, I saw some antelope. Kill them, too. That's what it was like walking: seeing critters, pretending I was a hunter with a high-powered rifle, shooting everything that moved, getting thirsty. Waiting, wishing I could find somebody who spoke kindly and in English.

I was so wrapped in daydreams that I hardly noticed when the land closed up as the road twisted through a canyon, and I didn't see the men coming around some rocks on foot until they were almost on top of me. They were dark with straight hair. They dressed like bums, and most carried blanket packs wrapped on sticks that rested on their shoulders, wetbacks from Mexico.

One man paused and looked at me with a crook in his neck, and then he spoke to me in his own language.

"Does anybody speak English?" I hollered. That was the wrong thing to say. The men started to hurry off, not running exactly but walking very fast.

Seconds later a tractor-trailer truck came up the road and grumbled to a stop in front of us. The driver stayed behind the wheel, but a man in the passenger seat who wore a cowboy hat and blue jeans and carried a clipboard hopped down. He went around to the back of the truck and heaved open the rear doors. He said something in Mexican, but I could tell by the gruff way he used the words that he was not one of them, but probably a Texan. He didn't notice me as I hopped in back with the rest of the men. We squatted down, the doors were shut, and it was dark inside. Somebody popped a match to light a cigarette, and that was reassuring. A minute later and we were off.

Somebody had a jug of warm water, which kept getting passed around, but it was not enough. Maybe it was the heat, maybe it was the darkness, maybe it was the getting-thirstier feeling, or maybe it was the banter in a language I did not understand, but I stopped feeling sorry for myself and started worrying about others. I worried about Father, hoping he'd lucked out and ended in heaven. I worried about Royal and his ambitions. I worried about the boy gangs. I worried about the Autodidact and Sally. I worried about Nurse Wilder and Doctor Hitchcock and Doctor Thatcher. I worried about these poor people from across the border, the wives and children back home that had to be clothed and fed, the goats and chickens that had to be cared for, and the future that had to be considered. These people were so shy. I wanted to tell them that bashfulness wouldn't get them diddly-squat in the U.S.A. I worried about humanity in general. I worried about the Alien, hoping he could somehow find a way to help humanity without violating the free-will principle. I worried about the Director, who couldn't seem to make headway in getting me to act properly in the film he was making.

I could have used more than "praise the Lord/Lords" at this minute. I could have used a real, working religion, the Amish's, Nurse Wilder's, anybody's, it didn't matter. But the fact was I didn't have a religion, so why should any of the persons in God listen to me? I tried praying without religion, but it was hard, real hard to concentrate and even harder to believe that my prayer amounted to anything; that He or She or It or Them was really out there listening to me instead of to some rich guy who, when he said "praise the Lord" knew who he was talking to. I concluded that I couldn't pray for real. I apologized to Jesus and Allah and Buddha and all the rest of the gods out there whose names I did not know. My apology became my prayer. I said, "You whose name I do not know, help me. . . . You whose name I do not know, help me. . . . You whose name I do not know, help me. . . ."

In the end, what kept my spirits from falling too far were odd things—the sight of the occasional flares of matches, the dim red glows of cigarette butts, the voices of these shy people, the smell of their sweat and anxiety. By the time we reached our destination some hours later, the water was gone, everybody was thirsty and getting sleepy from lack of air, and I was thinking: might as well die here as anyplace; at least I'm not alone. So I prayed some more, "You whose name I do not know, help me. . . ." And then the doors swung open. Fresh air poured in: hope. I thought about the mother, who was gone from my memory.

Night had fallen, so it was impossible for me to tell where we were. I could see fields and then a strip of highway. The wetbacks had been brought in to pick vegetables, and they were being checked over by the guy with the clipboard. The wetback would give his name, the guy would check him off, and the wetback would race to the water bubbler for a drink. I was in the middle of the line. We were quiet. Everybody was thinking about the water. All of us had become our thirst. I guess the word that I was an outsider must have gotten to the clipboard guy, because he stopped his work and walked down to the line to me.

First he said something to me in Mexican. When I didn't respond, he said in English, "Hey, you." I broke into a run. He went after me—and fell. Laughter, Mexican style, issued from the wetbacks.

I reached the highway and walked maybe two or three miles

to a service road. Eventually I came to a place that had a pink and purple sign that looked familiar, and yet something about it sort of misted over in my mind. It said Adult Books & Videos. A man came out of the store and caught my eye. He was heavy-built with big, hairy arms, lots of turquoise rings on his fingers, cowboy boots on his feet, and a gigantic, turquoise-decorated belt buckle. He smiled at me. I smiled back. He grabbed his belt and hoisted the belt buckle.

"Howdy, sweetsums," he said.

"Water, water," I whispered.

He came toward me. I caught a whiff of him. He used an aftershave lotion that made him smell like toilet deodorizer.

"Water," I could barely breathe the word.

At that moment, the wind must have shifted because now it was his turn to catch a whiff of me. I guess the smell of decaying shrimp, manure, horse slobber, and Mexican wetback revolted him because he got a look on his face as if somebody had dunked him in a barrel of puke.

"Water, water—please," I begged.

He backed away from me in the stiff, dignified gait of men wearing high-heel boots.

I stumbled on until, lucky me, I found a Mrs. McIntosh Restaurant. The food lines were long, and I had no money. "Water?" I gasped. I was crazy with thirst. The robot wait-help did not respond. I left the line and went for the men's room. Two teenagers stood in front of the sinks, gazing into mirrors over the washbasins as they combed their hair. I couldn't stand the waiting, so I rushed into the bathroom stall, shut the door, and locked it. The toilet was flushed and clean. I counted the blessing. Praise the Lord/Lords. Four or five? I couldn't remember. Then I knelt before the water and lapped it up like a dog.

After I'd had my fill, I was in better shape. I had a vague idea where to head next. I would keep going west until I reached New Mexico. *My mother and I walk up the ramp to the mother ship with the Children of the Cacti. The Alien trains us in his ways. We return to Xi in triumph. Peace, plenty, and fun envelop Xi.*

That thought along with the water cheered me up; I was almost optimistic when I stepped out of the toilet closet. The teenagers were gone, but some people were blocking my way, two men who looked like gangsters and a rugged boy wearing turquoise-rimmed sunglasses, black trousers, and an orange T-shirt.

"Web, you've got the worst b.o. I've ever smelled." It was Royal Durocher.

BETWEEN HERE AND THERE

I was looking forward to visiting not only with Royal but with Siena, but her family had been killed by government soldiers and she had left to fight in the Souvien civil war and Royal had a new driver. And anyway I probably wouldn't have gotten to talk with Siena because I smelled so bad that Royal made me ride in the trunk of his limo. It was dark in the trunk, but there was plenty of room and the bottom was padded. It occurred to me that maybe Royal had once knocked somebody off, and I might be lying at this moment where a murdered person had been. That was comforting.

We drove to a hotel in a city. It was fun going through the lobby, me first, then Royal and his two grown-up goons lagging behind. The stink I generated was so powerful that the crowd parted, and we walked right through. We got in the elevator, and everybody cleared out. Even the goons couldn't stand it. They waited for the next ride up. But Royal showed his loyalty to me. He put one arm around my shoulder and held his nose with the fingers of his other hand, as we rode up together. I could see that he'd begun to shave regularly.

"How did you find me?" I asked.

He tugged at the collar around my throat. "I tracked you. It sends out a signal."

"You know wherever I go?"

"Everywhere. It's the same technology used to track grizzlies, wolves, spies, and cheating lovers."

"I want to take it off."

"Go ahead."

I started to remove the collar, but then something held me back. I hesitated.

"Where are you without that collar?" Royal asked. I blinked, not sure what he meant. "I'll tell you," he went on. "You're nowhere. Alone. A speck in the dark. Nobody can see you. Keep the collar, and you can be everywhere. You'll exist in the minds of others—you'll become their thoughts. Out of the dark, in the light."

Being watched was pretty close to being watched over. "I'll leave it on," I said.

"I knew you would. Destiny. Remember that word, Web."

We got off at the thirteenth floor and walked down the hall.

"The best rooms in the hotel are on this floor." Royal stopped at number 1313. "My favorite number." Royal reached into his pocket and gave me what looked like a credit card.

"What am I supposed to do with this?" I asked.

"That's your room key. Put it in the slot, and you can open the door. Across the hall is your room, number 1314. This is my suite." He knocked on wood (actually, some kind of metal alloy). "I know you're pretty tired, and it's getting late. So clean up and get a good night's sleep." If you want anything to eat, you'll find it in the fridge in the little alcove between the bathroom and bedroom. If you have any nightmares or hallucinations of your demons, call the hotel shrink. The number's on the phone list along with yours truly's."

Royal slid his card in the slot, the door opened, and he went in. Suddenly, I was alone. I walked over to my room and stared at the number, 1314. I stood for a second, the card key in my hand. Nervous as a turkey at a Pilgrim & Indian picnic, I put the card in the slot. For a second, nothing happened. I looked down at my feet. The floor was carpeted; I could sleep there. But I didn't have to. The door opened.

My room was big, clean, and decorated with wallpaper featuring cacti in bloom, sunsets, and purpling mountains. The bed was big enough to rest the crew of a fire truck. The TV was on rollers and I pushed it into the bathroom. I channel-switched until I found a program I liked, "Best Car Chases in Movie History." I left the picture on, but turned the sound down. I stripped and soaked my filthy body in the tub, just lying there in the grips of zentensity as cars careened and crashed on the video monitor.

Soon, however, the program was interrupted. On the TV screen was the Director. He was at a construction site in the middle of the desert walking with men wearing hardhats. I watched him for a few minutes. I wondered if this qualified as a hallucination. From the tub, I reached for the white telephone on the wall and dialed the number Royal had given me for the hotel psychiatrist. A gargling voice on the other end of the line said, "This is the Director. May I help you?"

"Are you real, or is the picture on the screen of you real?" I said.

"The screen image is videotaped," the Director said. "Wash up, you'll be all right."

"Thanks," I said, then hung up and sunk back down into the bathwater. I must have dozed off because the next thing I knew the water had cooled and I was all wrinkled up. The TV screen was blank.

I stood, lathered up, and showered. Clean, I shut off the water, stepped out of the tub, and toweled off. I was so tired I never reached my bed. I curled up on the bathroom mat and was unconscious in an instant. No dreams, no sudden wakings from noise or horror—just sweet sleep.

When I woke up it was morning, and the TV was still on. The prettiest lady I had ever seen was exercising. Her name was Cynthia Kerluk. I pretended she was Mother. I joined in on the exercises, going twice as fast as I was supposed to. At about the end of the session, I realized I was naked. I felt bashful, so I shut the TV set off.

My clothes smelled so bad that even I couldn't get near them. When you're filthy, you love your own stink; when you're clean, you hate it.

I punched in Royal's number on the phone.

"Yaygo," answered Royal.

"Aygit's mayge, Waygeb. I'm hungry and I need some clothes, too."

"I'll be there in five minutes." And he hung up. I tore off the bed sheet, draped my body in it, and wrapped a towel around my head until I made a pretty fair imitation of the turban cowboy I'd seen at the OPEC convention.

Royal arrived with a waiter pushing a cart loaded with plates of ham, eggs, home fries, toast, a gallon of milk, a quart of orange juice, and a change of clothes for me.

"Nice outfit." Royal whipped out a miniature camera with flash. I posed, and he took my picture.

Royal said to the waiter, "Take his dirty clothes, put them in a plastic bag, and file them in the hotel safe under archival objects."

The waiter bowed and left.

I changed into the new outfit, and we ate like starving pigs let loose in a Dunkin' Donuts. Afterward, Royal gave me the one item to make the meal complete, a cigarette. I lit up, took a long drag, while Royal got a real serious look on his face.

"Web, do you know the price of greatness?"

"No, but you're going to tell me."

He heard the sarcasm in my voice, and cuffed me on the side of the head. I fell off my chair. On the floor, I grabbed his legs and pulled him down. We wrestled. He toyed with me for a few minutes, then flipped me over on my back and pinned me. I had to give.

He jumped up and started pacing around the room. "The price of greatness is the pain the great one feels for his not-so-great subjects. Web, I'm taking off, leaving the country for a while on business. When I come back, I'll be ready to change the world." I was about to say something, but he stopped me by muffling my mouth with his hand. "I've discovered the ticket to untold wealth and power. It's being the middleman. An end can't stand being an end. An end wants to join the other end. It's the middle that makes the connection. Don't expect to understand me. Your IQ is not as high as mine. I've been tested. I'm the smartest human being in the

United States, maybe the world. That's why I feel this awesome responsibility to put my talents to use."

I gawked at him with stars in my eyes, waiting to hear his explanation.

"I plan to blackmail my father's former business associates, all of whom committed white-collar crimes. So I'll be pretty busy. While I'm away."—he reached into his shirt pocket and gave me the picture of a man with a carrot-colored beard and a hunched back—"the Director is going to be in charge."

"He's one of my demons," I said.

"He's more or less real. He's the Director of VRN, that's Virtual Reality Network, the company my father started and that I'm in the process of taking over."

"I'm saw him on television last night."

"That's right. He was inspecting the site of our entertainment center."

"What's that?"

"A shopping mall, gambling casino, and amusement park that's going to make Disney attractions look as small-time as pinball machines in a pizza joint. We don't have a name for it, but something tells me I can find one just by going back over my Web notes."

I was confused, and, as if to soothe me, an image appeared in my mind, a picture of someone who looked like me as a girl. "I wish Siena was here," I said.

"You're in love with her," Royal said.

"Am not."

"You've got the heart feeling without the groin feeling. Right?"

"What if I do?"

"Shows how sick you are inside," Royal said.

"Sick? You sent her off to war."

"I unleashed her rage, and she is fulfilling herself. When I unleash your rage, you will fulfill yourself." Royal changed the tone of his voice, from cruel to kind. "Web, VRN and I are going to transform the entertainment industry all over the world. I need your help, but right now you're too immature."

"Look who's talking," I sneered. "You're no more than I am, a runaway."

"Not exactly, Web. You're a runaway, I'm a throwaway. My father killed himself, and my step-mother remarried to a no-good bastard and they didn't want me. They made me tough. You, you're not tough."

"Am so!" I shouted, stung.

"Let me ask you a question. Do you hate your mother?"

I almost broke down and cried when he said that.

"See, Web, you're about ready to blubber all over the place. You got too much baby love in you. Until a boy can learn to hate his mother, he can't become a man."

"Not true." I fought back the tears.

"Is true. Says so in the psychiatry books."

"You're lying to me again. You never read any psychiatry books."

"Of course I didn't read any stupid books. I saw the tapes. I don't need a father or a mother or any kind of parent. I just need flunkies. And they're always around."

"You'll get your feelings hurt one day," I said.

That stumped him for a second before he answered. He fingered the rings on his hands. "As long as there's 'more' I'll never have trouble with feelings. More money. More real estate. More admiration. More control. More to get and more ahead. I'll never look back. It's looking back where less is."

At that point, there was a knock on the door. Royal let in his two goons and the waiter, who wheeled in a birthday cake with fourteen lighted candles. Royal, the waiter, and the goons sang Happy Birthday to me.

"Blow the candles out," Royal said.

I blew. The candles went out, then flared up. I blew. Out went the candles, only to fire up again. I blew. Same deal as before. I looked at Royal, and he burst into laughter.

"Trick candles, I should have known," I said.

I had eaten about a quarter of the cake along with some candle wax mixed in with the frosting before it occurred me to ask Royal the obvious question. "How did you know it was my birthday?"

"You talk in your sleep."

"Marla—she squeezed it out of me under hypnosis, didn't she?" I said.

Royal never changed his expression of malicious mirth.

"You know all about me, don't you? Please," I begged, "Tell me."

"Things have to happen first, uncanny things," he said. "Meanwhile, relax. I have a present for you to celebrate your birthday."

"For me? What is it?" I said.

"Not an 'it,' a 'he.'" Royal turned to the goons. "Go get him."

They left and reappeared a minute later with the Autodidact. It took a few seconds before I recognized him. Black-white fuzz had grown in on his head, and the mustache was gone. The eyes were the same, except for one thing. They burned with hatred for me.

"John LeFauve—excuse me, Jim Clements," Royal said, "is going to be your guardian."

"But he hates me for ruining his life. He wants to kill me," I said.

"True, true—he does want to kill you. And for good reasons," Royal said. "But I like the idea that the problem is the solution. Especially if I can make an adult suffer. Jim's going to look after you while I'm gone. He understands that if he doesn't take care of you, I will turn him over to the police for the murder of Dirty Joe. In other words, it's apparent to him that he should be a parent to you."

Under orders from Royal, the Autodidact, now Jim Clements, and I headed for the Clements homestead in the town of Valley of Fires, New Mexico. Royal thought the country life would be a good environment for me. He guessed that Jim Clements would be welcomed as the returning prodigal son by the inhabitants of the homestead. Whoever they were, Royal wouldn't say, or maybe he didn't know.

Another thing that Royal insisted upon: from here on in, the Autodidact and I were to pretend we were father and son. He was to instruct me and to provide for me. He was not allowed to beat me, lock me up, starve me, or hurt me in any way. I was to obey him. We were to treat each other with love and respect, even if we had to fake it.

To replace the Cadillac that the Autodidact had stolen, Royal had given us the new vehicle, a three-year-old Ford pickup truck, because it would fit right in with the country folk. We drove in silence for a long time. The Autodidact and I had nothing to say to each other. He wanted to kill me, but was prevented from doing so. As for myself, I wanted to escape, but I had to stay with the Autodidact because of my loyalty to Royal. I busied my eyes by looking at the view.

I liked everything about New Mexico right away: the desert, the bright clean blue of the sky, the clay-colored rivers, the green, irrigated fruit groves, the red rocks, and the distant, purple mountains which always seemed to be far away no matter how long you drove. Another reason I liked New Mexico was the possibility that my mother was here. I had it in the back of my mind that I would stumble upon some information that would lead me to her.

"Hey, what's that?" I said, looking out at desert sand so white it was like flour.

The Autodidact frowned, as if he hated the sound of my voice, and he drawled, "I believe that's the White Sands National Monument." I kept looking and looking and looking, and at about the time that the view, like glare from the black-dime eyes of my former guardian angel, Langdon, was going to disappear, the Autodidact hit the brakes. "Let's stop in for a closer look," he said. We did a U-turn in the middle of the road, and motored to the visitor center.

We viewed the displays, listened to the audios, read the explanatory material. The Autodidact stopped brooding as he got interested in the information. The sand was made of gypsum. Wind whipped up deposits many miles away, and it collected in dunes in this locale. Normally I wouldn't have bothered even pretending to show interest, but the Autodidact was so energized by learning something new that his enthusiasm rubbed off on me, and I paid attention.

Outside, we drove a loop through the dunes. I pretended we

were in the Sahara Desert. The Autodidact stopped so I could play in the dunes, and I climbed the biggest one I could see and pranced through the sand like the Sheik of Araby. I had to come down in a few minutes, because the sun was so bright reflecting off the sand that it hurt my eyes. I wished I'd had Royal's sunglasses.

Back on the highway, the Autodidact was silent and glum again. He played the radio, listening to classical music. The first town we hit was Alamogordo, which runs beside a railroad track. I saw all kinds of different people—cowboys, Indians, Mexicans, regular people, and rocket scientists. The Autodidact said the government tested missiles in this area. Not only that, but the first atomic bomb was blown up many years ago on the federal missile range not far from here.

"Look at the map," the Autodidact said. "Note how close the town of Valley of Fires is to the bomb site. Only about fifteen miles. What's the problem, kid?"

I guess the look on my face told him that something was wrong. The truth was I was thinking about my mother again, but I wasn't about to say anything about that.

"I want to go to a town called Sorrows, New Mexico," I said.

"We'll look at the map, and if it's nearby we'll stop in," he said.

"I checked. It's not on the map," I said. A minute went by. I sat there stiff-backed, determined not to cry.

"It's obvious that this place has great meaning for you," the Autodidact said.

"So what?"

"So what, sir."

"Sorry. So what, sir?"

"I have an idea," the Autodidact said. "It's a long shot, but let's give it a try."

We went to the Alamogordo library and looked up Sorrows, New Mexico, in a state history book. No such place had ever existed. I couldn't help it, I cried.

We left Alamogordo, turning off the desert valley and starting on a road that twisted upward like a snake climbing up the pant leg of an ostrich. Pretty soon we were at an elevation of over eight thousand feet in Cloudcroft. No more desert. The temperature was cool, and the land was covered with tall pines.

Half an hour later, on a secondary but paved road, we entered the Mescalero Apache Indian lands, high up in the Sierra Blanca Mountain range, rugged and green. We didn't speak. I could see that the Autodidact was busy thinking. He didn't seem angry anymore, just occupied with deep, dark thoughts. Most of this country was rural, with occasional Indian ranch houses with full-sized pickup trucks parked in the yard. I'd hoped for tepees and horses.

On the other side of the mountains, the Autodidact took a little side trip to the town of Lincoln. It was a historical place, he said. He stopped at every historical marker. I was discovering that he couldn't resist anything that had anything to do with learning. Lincoln was in some dry hills along the Hondo River, which was blocked off here and there to irrigate fields. The green of the fields contrasted nicely with the beige hills. Lincoln was a pretty town, but very small and everything was geared for Billy the Kid, who'd had some adventures there. There was a museum and a make-believe general store from the nineteen-hundreds. Billy the Kid, an Easterner from New York, had killed twenty-one people, more or less, and they'd written books about him and made movies and did up this town in his honor. The moral was clear enough: if you want to be noticed, kill somebody, the more the better. I filed away that idea.

The Autodidact wasn't too interested in the displays or the guide talks about Billy the Kid, but he did browse in the books lying around, which were not only about Billy but about Indians (who were constantly getting themselves conquered by Spanish soldiers), priests (who always seemed to be getting themselves tortured by the Indians), and Smokey Bear (who had survived a fire in the Lincoln National Forest). Which was quite remarkable, because as near as I could see in Lincoln there was no forest to burn.

"Look at this," the Autodidact said, showing me a picture of a platoon of Union soldiers, all of them black men. "They were Indian fighters after the Civil War. They were called Buffalo Soldiers by the Indians because their kinky hair reminded the Indians of

buffalo fur." I ran my hand over the Autodidact's no longer completely bald head. The Autodidact was growing hair. He had
about a six-thirty shadow. Coming in, the hair was as easy to see
as it was to feel because it was mostly white against his shiny,
tanned head.

It was late afternoon, still plenty of daylight ahead when we
drove slowly down the mountains to the wide desert valley. We
stopped to gas up in Carrizozo, a pleasant middling town at the
base of the mountains. From the crossroads we could see a small,
Spanish-style church. The Autodidact stared at for the longest
time.

"I grew up with religion," the Autodidact said. "Somewhere
along the line, I lost the faith. You lose something like that, and
it's like somebody you love dies. You grieve."

"Oh." I was thinking about Father. He was the only person I
knew well who had died, and I didn't want to grieve for him.

"Listen, kid," the Autodidact said, "I can't play along with your
friend Royal. He's crazy and probably dangerous. I have to give
myself up. I've lost Sally, the only person who's ever meant anything to me. I can't pretend I'm Jim Clements—I'm John LeFauve.
You and I are going to look up the Clements people, and I'm going
to tell them the fate of their lost kinsman. At least then, they'll
know the truth."

"But they're not even searching for truth," I said, frantic and
frightened.

"We don't know that. I have a duty to the man's memory. Once
I've fulfilled it, I'm turning myself in."

"Maybe they'll believe that Xiphi killed Father," I said.

"You need professional help, Web. I can't do anything for you.
I'll just have to trust in the system to keep from being convicted
of Joe Webster's murder. I'll do the time that I owe the state for
the car theft and whatever else they want out of me. In the familiar
environs of jail, I'll finally be able to get going on writing my book
about prison life. That book is my calling, my destiny, and here
outside, in the land of freedom, I have been unable to work. Once
I'm finished with the book, maybe they'll parole me. Maybe Sally
and I will have one more chance at love."

We hopped in the truck and drove off. The desert spread out before us, promising in its vast emptiness as an untested idea. The tiny village of Valley of Fires was about thirty miles east. We knew the town was small, because while it was on the map, it didn't appear in the population index. A few miles down the road we approached Valley of Fires State Park.

"Those Clements people, they're probably all dead." I said. The Autodidact didn't say a word. He was thinking about his duty. I was thinking that the last thing I wanted to do was to be turned over to the system. I couldn't even expect Royal to save me, because he was leaving the country. In desperation, I asked to stop at the state park, for my learning, of course. The Autodidact hesitated, then said okay. We pulled in.

The Valley of Fires was an interesting place. It had been the site of volcanic eruptions a thousand or so years ago. The volcano didn't build a mountain, it just puked out lava. You could still see the stuff as black rock formations and black boulders. The area wasn't barren though. Cactus and weeds grew everywhere. From the park, which set on a plateau maybe eighty feet above the Valley of Fires, I could look out across to the purple mountains to the east. Between us and the mountains lay the Trinity Site, where the atomic bomb had been detonated. I imagined a gigantic mushroom-shaped cloud. I asked the Autodidact whether the bomb explosion made black rocks. The Autodidact said he'd read that the bomb had melted the sand and created green glass crystals, but the government had bulldozed dirt over the area.

"Let's go," he said, and off we drove.

Several minutes later we arrived in Valley of Fires. There wasn't much to the town. As a matter of fact, there wasn't any Valley of Fires at all. It was a ghost town, consisting of a few cellar holes, shacks, jeep trails, and, overhead, buzzards, big, beautiful soaring birds that only appeared ugly when they landed to peck at the eyes of dead road meat. We pulled in front of the only sound structure in town, a mobile home, and knocked on the door. No answer. Around the yard were a shed, some junk, and pretty rocks for sale. A sign said: "Rock Hounds, leave $5 to visit former lead mine, 6 miles on a dirt road into desert. T. & L. Leah, Proprietors." We didn't know what to do, so we just stood there.

"I guess we should have asked back in Carrizozo," the Auto-didact said. He didn't exactly looked relieved, but he wasn't down in the dumps either. I could see that he was secretly hoping there were no Clements folk around for him to do his duty to.

A minute later a sheriff's car pulled up, and a deputy wearing a .44 magnum pistol on a belt holster and ten-gallon hat on his head removed himself from the cruiser. He wasn't fat, but he had an almost perfectly round face.

"Can I help you?" The deputy looked at the Autodidact, then at me.

"Is that gun loaded?" I asked him, pointing at his hip.

"Why, sure," the deputy said.

"Officer," the Autodidact said, "I'm looking for a family with the name of Clements in the town of Valley of Fires."

The deputy suddenly got a curious look on his face, and said to the Autodidact, "What's your name?"

The Autodidact was about to speak when I blurted out, "That's Jim Clements, and I'm his only son."

"Jim Clements?" An amazed look spread across the face of the deputy. "Let me see your driver's license."

The Autodidact forked it over.

The deputy stared hard at the license, broke out into a grin, and said, "By gosh, you must be Mrs. Clements' long-lost boy. She's been talking about you since the day I was born and many years before. She'd say to anybody who would listen that her boy would come back. Some people said you didn't even exist."

"I exist," the Autodidact said, stiff and sweaty.

The deputy grabbed the Autodidact's hand and pumped it. "Welcome home, Jim. It's been, how long? Almost half a century since you've been here?"

"Seems like only yesterday," the Autodidact said.

"My dad lost his memory when he was about my age," I lied. "It's only started to come back to him. But there's still a lot he can't remember."

"You poor feller, I've heard of cases like that," said the deputy.

Deputy Sheriff Bob "Pie Crust" Gallagher talked a streak blue enough to shame the light on his cruiser, and we were able to piece together the story of the Clements family, as it was known to local people. Mrs. Clements had been raised on a small ranch, really just a homestead in the desert. Her father had been one of the Buffalo Soldiers at Fort Stanton. He was a light-skinned black who'd married a white woman from the local scab town, and they'd had one child, a daughter. She—the present Mrs. Clements—had gone to Missouri, married a white man, and had a child. But her husband had died or run off, or something, and she had come back to the family homestead with her son, Jim. The boy had vanished without a trace at age twelve. Some people said he'd run away, others that he'd been kidnapped and murdered, others that he'd been claimed by the desert. At any rate, he hadn't been heard from in forty-eight years. Old Mrs. Clements lived a subsistence life on her tiny ranch in the desert, but she'd never lost hope that her boy would return to her.

We said see you later to Deputy Pie Crust and turned onto a dirt road that seemed to go off into the forever of the desert. It was three miles of bounce, bounce driving to the Clements place.

"Are you really going to tell this old woman that her only child never amounted to anything?" I said.

"We don't know that. All we know is how he died."

"She'll draw her own conclusions," I said.

"Oh, Lord, what should I do, then?" The Autodidact, desperate with duty, wasn't talking to me. He was praying.

I put in my two cents. "Tell her he was a war hero. Tell her he wiped out half of Iraq."

"It's important for all concerned that the truth be told," the Autodidact said. "Now that's that. I don't want to hear any more. I know what you're driving toward. But you don't know me. John LeFauve seems like a good man, but he's a bad man because of his terrible temper."

"I'll be better off with Jim Clements."

"I'm not Jim Clements, and you'll be better off with the system. John LeFauve will be better off in jail, so he can have the peace and quiet to write his book. Now shut up."

"Yes, sir."

The Clements place wasn't much. In fact, it was as close to nothing as you can imagine. There was a well, a shed, and a shack. Surrounded by desert for as far as the eye could see, the spread looked small, but cozy too. I wanted to live there.

Weren't we surprised to discover that we were expected. A little old lady was waiting in the yard. She looked to be about a hundred and twenty-six. She was real rickety on her feet, and her eyes were glazed over with cataracts.

"Good day, it seems that news of our arrival has preceded us," the Autodidact said, carefully measuring his words as he stepped out of the truck and walked toward the lady.

"Oh, you talk so beautiful, just so beautiful," the woman said. "My boy is a cultivated man. Pie Crust called me on the CB. I know all about you losing your memory, so don't you worry. Welcome, welcome." She stopped and got a real serious look on her face. "You . . . you are Jim Clements, aren't you?"

"He sure is, ma'am," I said.

"Pie Crust told me about you?" She turned her blind eyes in my general direction.

"I'm Web, I'm your grandson," I said.

"I think I'm going to faint with happiness," Mrs. Clements said. "Pleased to invite you into my home. It's not much, but you can stay as long as you like."

Mrs. Clements turned toward the Autodidact, reaching out a hand to touch his arm. "I'm almost blind, but I can feel your shadow on my skin because you block the heat of the sun, and I can touch. Jim, let me touch you. She put her hands on the Autodidact's face, felt it all up and down.

"You've had a good life, no scars, no hard lines." She hugged the Autodidact fiercely, and spoke in words wet with tears of joy, "Oh, my son, my son."

Royal had been right. Jim Clements had been welcomed backed to the homestead with open arms. I thought: now the Autodidact is going to lower the big truth boom and knock her for a loop.

The Autodidact said, "It's good to be home, Ma."

BUFFALO SOLDIER RANCH

We settled in and the summer went by and then the fall and the winter and the spring. It was a glorious, wonderful time, a time to put in memory for later Total Recall. I wore the collar for a couple of months, but soon I lost interest in Royal and his crazy dreams. I no longer felt alone; I had friends, loved ones, a life. Who needs to be watched when he's watched over? I removed the collar from my neck and put it away. The Autodidact grew hair in the back and on the sides of his head. The Clements' land, like Jim's head, didn't have much on top. The soil was poor, and it was cluttered with pretty but not very useful rocks. Mr. T. and Mrs. L. Leah, whose place we'd stopped at that first day, along with several people whose ranches strung over miles of desert, were our only neighbors.

Mrs. Clements' property supported a goat for milking, chickens in the yard, and a garden of table vegetables and chili peppers. In addition, there were some really nice fruit trees planted eons ago by Mrs. Clements' Buffalo Soldier father. The secret to the homestead was not what was on the surface, but what was above (the New Mexico sunshine) and what was below (water). Mrs. Clements had one of the few year-round wells in the area. The reason that the town of Valley of Fires had gone down the drain, so to speak, was the lack of water. Mrs. Clements had hung on because she could irrigate her crops. There wasn't enough for a commercial operation, but the supply was reliable enough for the needs of a family or two.

Mrs. Clements didn't have a television set. A battery-powered CB and radio were all she had for contact with the outside world.

My life brightened when I met a boy named Ike, who was a rancher's son. Ike happened to come out to the Clements place shortly after Jim and I moved in. He was riding his horse, a pinto named ATV with brown and white spots that made me drool with excitement. Mrs. Clements hailed, hugged, and fed Ike. They were old friends. She introduced us, and we hit it off right away. Ike was rangy with a goose neck and knotty muscles, a responsible kid unconsciously looking for a wild friend like me to get him into trouble. Every time we wrestled it was a tie. Ike was real serious about horses and ranching. I didn't have a horse, but I got Jim to buy me an ATV. Naturally, I named it Pinto. Ike would come by once or twice a week, and we'd take off like crazed road runners across the desert, him on his horse, me on my machine. I wasn't allowed to go out alone. Jim and Mrs. Clements were afraid Pinto would break down and I'd be bit by a rattlesnake and die of blood poisoning and/or thirst. That sounded to me like a wonderfully romantic death.

Ike and I spent a lot of time at the lead mine. The shafts were closed off, but half a mountain of disturbed rubble lay around for the collecting. We picked rocks for the T. & L. Leahs, not only from the mine refuse but from all over the territory. They were a retired couple, supplementing their Social Security income by selling rocks and by charging rock hounds five dollars each to explore the former lead mine with hammers and educated glances. The T. & L. Leahs taught us by shape and color which ones to walk away with and which to leave behind. New Mexico has a lot of strange rocks. Near Dimmit the rocks look like porcupine quills, and near Taos like Christian crosses. And then there's trinitite, green beady sand melted to glass by the A-bomb. After rock hunting, shooting was my favorite pastime. Ike would take me to his ranch for target practice. Everybody in his family had guns—pistols, shotguns, .22s, and high-powered rifles that we weren't allowed to use. I liked shooting, and I bugged Jim about buying me a rifle and taking me hunting. He hemmed and hawed and got all squeamish. Killing came easy to John LeFauve; not so to Jim Clements.

One time Ike and I were caught in a thunderstorm. The whole sky crackled with lightning, and then it rained hard enough to drown a school of tuna. Afterward I couldn't start Pinto. Ike rode me home on ATV. We went back the next day. The points had dried out, and the machine started right up. Another time we killed a rattlesnake with sticks and rocks. (Ike's idea.) We also climbed up the side of the mountain to an eagle's nest. (My idea.) We didn't kill any of the birds, just tickled their gullets. (My idea.) One more thing: I taught Ike to smoke.

The most interesting place Ike and I went (my idea) was government land where they had dropped the A-bomb. We went looking for trinitite, in hopes of selling some to the T. & L. Leahs. Ike said some of the farmers who lived near the bomb-drop had died of cancer from the radiation. We left the horse and the ATV behind some rocks and sneaked onto the property, going under the fence like badgers digging for a meal. The area wasn't much different from the surrounding countryside. The bulldozed-over dirt had blended in with the desert, and we gave up any hope of finding any trinitite. Just when we were about to leave some glitter caught my eye. On the ground was a fist-sized chunk of green rock. Through it ran gold veins.

"Trinitite," said Ike.

I held the stuff up to the light. Gold currents swirled inside the green.

"You hold it," I said.

Ike took it. "You found it. Lucky stiff," he said.

"We both found it," I said.

"You're a true friend," Ike said.

Ike and I sat on a rock and, looking at the trinitite, tried to imagine the bomb going off, the bright flash of a short-lived sun, the great noise of the explosion, the terrible hot wind that followed. The awe I felt made me grateful to Ike. Without him, I'd be lonely and restless.

"I used to have a best friend," I said. "His name was Royal Durocher, but I went my way, he went his. Now you're my best friend."

"We're like brothers," Ike said.

"We can't be real brothers because we have different parents, but we could be blood brothers," I said.

"What if you have AIDS?" Even when he was being romantic, Ike couldn't help but be serious, too.

"What if *you* have AIDS?" I said.

"So what if I did?" he said.

"I'd still want to be your blood brother." I jumped to my feet, so that I was standing on the face of Gravestone Rock.

Ike took the trinitite from my hand. "It's got a jagged edge. I'll cut you, you cut me," he said.

I turned my hand over and offered it to him. He took it in his own hand.

"Double your fist and squeeze. I want to see where the veins are," Ike said.

"You're not going to cut a vein, are you?" I was alarmed.

"I want to see the veins so I *don't* cut one, armadillo brain."

I doubled my fist and squeezed. The veins bulged in my arm. He sliced me about an inch above the palm. It didn't hurt much, but it made me feel creepy, like you feel when someone runs their nails down a blackboard. Blood trickled around the side of my arm and onto the dry, tan rock.

Ike handed me the rock and bunched his fist. I took it in my hand. Ike shut his eyes. The veins not only bulged in his arm, but in his neck. I could have ripped out his throat. I nicked his arm. Ike opened his eyes. We were eyeball to eyeball. "You have the strangest eyes, like the stuff in the trinitite," he whispered.

"Radioactive," I said, and croaked like a frog.

Ike took my arm and pressed my wound to his. It passed through my mind that he really did have AIDS. So be it, I thought.

With a voice like a preacher's, Ike said, "I swear upon my blood that I will be your friend forever."

"Ditto," I said.

"You have to say the words."

So I said the words, "I swear upon my blood that I will be your friend forever."

We stood in the sun until the blood dried on our arms. When we pulled away, the wounds opened. And then we started back for home, feeling warm and full of joy and kind of bashful.

The T. & L. Leahs gave us each a hundred dollars for the trinitite under the condition that we didn't tell anybody.

I could have spent all day every day in disorderly conduct in the desert with Ike, but he had chores to do and so did I. In fact, I only played part-time. I was working almost full-time with the Autodidact, who needed my help in fixing up Mrs. Clements' place. The Autodidact spent most of the money he had saved up in his previous life as a convict book collector for improvements on the Clements' desert homestead. The three-room shack had been falling apart for years. We installed a new, gas-fired heating system, a generator for electricity, roofing, insulation in the walls, and sheetrock over the crumbling plaster. We also built an addition on a concrete foundation. We hired some outside help for that job.

The Autodidact and I moved into the new wing. I had my own room. The Autodidact used his room for an office as well as a bedroom. As the months passed, it filled with books. The book man that had been in John LeFauve was also in Jim Clements. But there were differences, too. Where John LeFauve was suspicious and quick-tempered, Jim Clements was trusting and slow to anger. Mrs. Clements, believing the Autodidact had lost his memory, constructed a past for him by telling him all about the boyhood of her Jim. The more that the Autodidact acted like Jim Clements, the more he became Jim Clements. I rarely heard him talking about Sally or prison or his prison book. If any of those old memories cropped up in our private conversations, he'd act as if the events had happened to somebody else. Gradually, I began to think of myself as Web Clements, the son of Jim Clements.

I decorated my room with pictures of rattlesnakes, guns, motorcycles, and, especially, demons. Every time I'd see a picture of a demon or a devil in a magazine, I'd cut it out and tack it to my bulletin board. Good thing Mrs. Clements couldn't see, or I would have had a lot of explaining to do. She was a Baptist, not only anti-devil, but anti-graven image. The Autodidact didn't much like my collection, but he didn't try to stop me. He just waited for me "to outgrow this phase in your development." My posters included drooly monsters and devils with pointed beards, fiery eyes, yellow teeth, and tails. I searched for pictures that resembled my own demons—the Director, the Alien, the three-headed God, Xiphi, and

Langdon. But I didn't find any. Maybe someday I would be an artist, and I would draw them myself. I looked high and low for a poster that resembled the mother ship, but I couldn't find one. The posters of spaceships were nothing but clever drawings of toys. The real mother ship was more complicated and serious. It was a home, an environment, a station, a meeting place, a departure point, a storage unit for thoughts, a locker for love, a theater for living—it was everything. No poster could do it justice.

The Autodidact and I never worked in silence. Even as we hammered nails and laid out sheetrock, he was teaching me. He made me read books, and he gave me quizzes. I read the books the Autodidact assigned, and I listened to him carry on, maybe remembering a quarter of what he actually said. The Autodidact taught me history, geography, and, of course, his favorite subject, literature, which he spoke in the drawn-out way of an autodidact, *litter-ah-churr.* He was getting me ready for school in the fall, which I wasn't dreading nearly as much as I thought I would. I was actually looking forward to going. For one thing, I was gaining confidence that for a change I'd be able to sit still for more than thirty seconds. For another, I knew I'd meet kids my own age.

The Autodidact's favorite story was called *On the Road,* by a Mister Langston Hughes. It's about a homeless black man during the Great Depression. His name is Sargent, and he's real tired and it's snowing out. Sargent stops at a parsonage, but the minister sends him away. Desperate for a place to rest, Sargent breaks into the church. Police come, and then the most incredible thing happens. Sargent tears down the church, and Jesus Christ comes down off his cross and hits the road with the homeless man. Eventually Christ goes off on his own, and Sargent tries to hop a freight but it's full of cops. Next thing you know, he wakes up in jail. He'd only imagined he'd wrecked that church.

The Autodidact reminded me that the original Jim Clements, like Sargent fifty years earlier, had been a homeless wanderer. It was sad that some things, such as poverty and homelessness and despair, don't change, the Autodidact said. ''The same old awful and amazing and asinine things that make us human, over and over again, that's what *litter-a-churr* is about,'' he said. I never

thought too much of that explanation. I told the Autodidact I loved
On the Road because it made my stomach do an up-see-daisy. He
said when I got older I'd do most of my reading "between the
lines." That made no sense.

What the Autodidact didn't say about *On the Road*, and what
he didn't have to say because we both knew it, was that it was important that I learn about black people. A line of descendants of
Mrs. Clements had black African blood, and as the son of Jim
Clements, I was presumed to be part black. The Autodidact said
in reality he and I may actually have had some African blood in
our veins. "Who knows where we come from? Nobody can trace
it all the way back," he said. I didn't worry about being black or
white. I worried about my green and gold eyes.

Mrs. Clements did not like *On the Road*, because she thought it
was anti-Christian. The Autodidact said, so what? And they argued. They debated politics, religion, and other things. But they
never got spiteful. In fact, they often ended up agreeing and laughing when they disagreed. They often used phrases such as, "You
might have something there." And "good point." And "I never
thought about it that way before." In other words, they weren't
much fun to listen to.

The Autodidact spent a lot of time with Mrs. Clements. They
actually became like mother and son. Sometimes he complained,
even whined if she got on his case, but no matter how he felt, he
always surrendered to her wishes. When I saw them together, full
of fun and love, I'd get an aching feeling for my own mother. I
know it sounds like I was jealous, but I really wasn't. I felt, I don't
know, left out.

Mrs. Clements was glad to tell the family history. After the
army had finally conquered the Indians in the 1880s, her father's
unit had been disbanded, and he had worked for a rancher, his
former commander, a Colonel Randolph, who had deeded him
this small plot. Later, water had been found. Colonel Randolph
tried to take back the land, but his scheme didn't work. Eventually
the old colonel died, and his son got radiation poisoning and also
died. God was punishing the son for the sins of the father, Mrs.
Clements said.

Mrs. Clements' mother had been a hostess in a scab town outpost near a military base. She was an Oklahoma woman, sometimes exuberant and full of fun, other times sad and withdrawn. Her mother's sadness was the one unsettlement of spirit in Mrs. Clements that she had never been able to calm.

She talked about her Jim as a boy. What was remarkable is that her true Jim had been a lot like her phoney Jim in his previous life as John LeFauve: wild and angry and impulsive, but smart, too, and now and then even studious. Mrs. Clements' husband had died of pneumonia after taking young Jim sledding one snowy day in the Missouri Ozarks. After his father died, young Jim had become morose. That was when Mrs. Clements had moved back to New Mexico. She'd lived with her parents and her boy, who became more and more lonely and discontented. One day he disappeared. She opined that it was the guilt Jim had felt over his father's death that had led him to run away from home. She stayed with her parents, taking care of them in their old age until they died. She never lost faith that her own Jim would come back, purified and strong, to take care of her in her old age. And so it had happened.

Mrs. Clements told stories about the Buffalo Soldiers that she'd heard from her father. About the black man who had trailed Comanches for five years after they'd stolen his bride, and how he'd rescued her from them, and how a year later he'd been killed in a fray with another band of Indians. Those family yarns gave the Autodidact an idea. He started spending time in the library in Carrizozo. He took trips up to Lincoln. He went on excursions to the university towns in Las Cruces and Albuquerque. The Autodidact started doing research on the Buffalo Soldiers. He hung around with county officials, college people, and black organizations out of El Paso and Albuquerque. In January, about the time John LeFauve's money ran out, the Autodidact wangled a grant to write a book about the Buffalo Soldiers. We would have income for two years. Convict John LeFauve had found his destiny in bringing literary honor to the name of Jim Clements.

Every Sunday, we'd pile into the pickup and go to the Baptist church in Carrizozo. The Autodidact and Mrs. Clements rode in the front seat, I sat in the bed in the rear, picked my teeth, and watched the New Mexico sky. It was the bluest sky with the whitest clouds I had ever seen. At first the Autodidact was only trying to please Mrs. Clements by attending church, but as time went on he gradually reacquired the Christian faith that John LeFauve had in his own childhood, except instead of being a Catholic he was a Protestant. I tried praying to the Jesus part of the three-headed God, but it never worked. I didn't believe, I didn't disbelieve; I was in the white space between the lines in the Good Book.

I couldn't understand why Jesus would want to have anything to do with people in general, let alone me. I couldn't understand why anyone would want to have more than a nodding acquaintance with Jesus. He didn't seem like a bad man, just boring, pigheaded, and talky. I hoped Langdon, my guardian angel, would show up and explain to me where I'd gone wrong when I tried to think about God/Gods, but he never did. Xiphi, Satan's dark angel, was also missing from my life. So, I didn't get either side of the story. As for the Director, the Alien, and the mother ship, nothing—no messages, no visions or visitations, just dim memories of the ramp rising up into a busy, metal belly infested with aliens and their captives. I pretty much lived my life for the here and now.

The Autodidact found himself a girlfriend on a church picnic. She was almost as old as he was; she had three adult children who had married and moved on. Her husband had been an alcoholic, and after her kids were grown she had divorced him. Her name was Mary Jane. She reminded me a little of Nurse Wilder, except that she was a lot prettier than Nurse Wilder. She had dark skin, and her parents had been born in Mexico. Mary Jane's real name had been something else, but she'd changed it because her people had been illegal aliens and they wanted her to have a North American name.

She and the Autodidact had two things in common: they were ex-Catholics, and they were touched in the head when it came to books. She was a county librarian, who drove a bookmobile from town to town. She lived alone in a tiny mobile home in Carrizozo on a small lot. She grew flowers everywhere, in gardens, in pots, in tubs, on window sills, even in the crooks of a live oak tree, the only one on the property. The Autodidact would visit her two or three times a week. Pretty soon he started spending the night. I found the whole business irritating.

It didn't take long before I was calling Mrs. Clements Grandma. She liked to be read to aloud, and I was happy to oblige. I read books that were assigned by the Autodidact or later by my teachers in school. Speaking the words out loud to my grandma felt pleasant and helped me understand better what was being said. Grandma Clements would lie down on the couch, close her sightless eyes, and listen. Sometimes she'd burst into laughter. Other times tears came to her eyes. Now and then there'd be something she wouldn't understand. If she didn't get it, I didn't usually get it either and we'd have to ask the Autodidact. Sometimes even he didn't get it.

Because she was blind, she knew her little house by touch and smell. She cooked by touch and smell, too. I used to help her with chores. I fetched the eggs from the hens, watered the garden, and pulled weeds. The goat fed herself by browsing off the land, but she and the chickens had to be brought in the shed at night, lest the coyotes get them. The goat wouldn't allow anybody but Grandma Clements to milk her, so I didn't have to trouble myself over that job. I liked the goat's milk; it went smoothly down my throat.

My favorite chore was helping Grandma Clements murder a chicken for a meal. The Autodidact could get himself into a work frenzy over a big project, but he always seemed to have something to do when routine work had to be done. He'd rather read about hens and plan a new coop than fetch the eggs. Killing a chicken wasn't hard, but it took some strength and determination. You grabbed the victim by its long neck and did a snap-the-whip with it. The result: dead chicken. Then you cut the heads off and let the blood drain from the body. Remembering Siena and her Souvien heritage, I once drank the blood from the neck. It was warm and rich tasting, but rank. I don't recommend drinking chicken blood unless you're desperate. Plucking the chicken was no fun. I would do the main part, tearing out feathers in a mad frenzy by pretending I was tearing out the pages in the Alien's diary about me.

Grandma Clements finished the work, plucking the remaining feathers with pliers.

There were times when Grandma Clements made me nervous. The big lie that held us together as a family, her belief that we were kin, kept bothering me. I'd get these impulses to blurt out terrible truths: "Your boy was a nobody. . . . This Jim is a great man. . . . I'm not your grandson, I'm an alien. . . . You're old, you're going to die soon." But I didn't say anything. I would just sigh and ask for something to eat. She loved to feed me red beans and rice.

Once she called me over and passed her hands over my face. "I can see you're upset. I think I know why," she said. I could feel her love for me in those hands. "It's your natural mother, isn't it? You've been thinking about her." She must have felt the emotion in my face, because I could feel it myself in her fingertips.

I started eighth grade in the fall. School kept me busy. I was way ahead of my classmates in some subjects, thanks to the learning I'd received from Father (tool use), Royal (business and mischief), and the Autodidact (reading, writing), but in other subjects, such as math and science, I was behind. I caught up pretty fast. I just sucked up the knowledge.

The social life at the school was more interesting than the learning life. We had ranch kids and town kids, Anglo kids and Mexican-American kids. They used to bad-mouth each other, and sometimes there was a fight, but not very often. Sometimes it was hard to tell who disliked who. For example, ranch Anglo kids were more apt to get along with ranch Mexican-American kids than with town Anglo kids, except when it came to dating. Also, some local families of long standing might belong to the same groups, but they hated each other because of ancient feuds. I never did figure it all out, and I never did fit into any crowd. The Autodidact said I'd either be more or less accepted by all or condemned by all. As John LeFauve, raised French-Canadian in Yankee New England, he'd been in the same situation. Because of his bad personality, he'd been condemned. Because of my good personality, I was accepted. More or less. It didn't hurt that I was Ike's best friend. He was popular with everybody.

As the months passed, I grew taller, stronger, and hairier; I also found myself more and more interested in "the opposite sex," which was what the Autodidact called females. At first, girls were sort of, I don't know, in the way. I talked to them, but we didn't have much in common. Then I made a friend named Sara. She didn't get me all hot and bothered, because she was like a boy in her friendship to me. I didn't have the feelings about girls that other boys my own age had. All they talked about was a girl they called C, which was not her real name, but the cup size of her bra, which one boy claimed to have glimpsed by peeking through the air grate in the girls' gym. Every guy in my class was in love with C. Not that it mattered. She had a boyfriend who was a junior in high school. I used to try to think about C, because I wanted to be normal. But I couldn't. Instead, Xiphi appeared in my dreams. He did it with other demons, muddied fiery creatures like himself, some of them like boys, others like girls, but none of them human. They'd poke each other, crying out in pain and ecstasy. I would wake up wet.

I finished eighth grade with A's and B's. I was looking forward to the summer. Mr. T. & Mrs. L. Leah had hired Ike and me to give tours of the mine to tourists. The T. & L. Leahs planned to teach us all about how to talk to people about rocks. That got me to thinking about my future. Maybe I'd go to college and become a geologist, which Mister T. Leah described as "a rock hound with an attitude." I was also slated to help the Autodidact on another building project during the summer. We were going to install a new septic system and leaching field along with another bathroom. I couldn't understand why we needed two bathrooms in our house, and I told the Autodidact so. His answer explained everything: "Mary Jane and I are getting married."

They planned to "tie the knot" (the Autodidact's phrase) the last Saturday in June at the Baptist church in Carrizozo. I have to admit I felt a little weird about "this Blessed Event" (which was what Grandma Clements called it). All the old feelings of wanting to run away came flooding back to me. I knew that Grandma Clements and the Autodidact loved me, and that Mary Jane was a good person, but something about them "tieing the knot" left me at loose ends. I told my blood brother Ike about my feelings, and asked him what he would do. He said, "I'd be brave." I thought that was about the most noble thing I'd ever heard, so I decided to be brave and keep my anxiousness to myself.

Before the wedding, the Autodidact had a long talk with Grandma Clements. She gave her blessing to the Blessed Event. Besides the Blessed Event, they discussed the homestead. It had never had a name, because Grandma Clements' father wasn't interested in such things. The Autodidact thought the place should be called Buffalo Soldier Ranch, with the name on a new gate, to be installed at the entrance of the property. That was fine with Grandma Clements, and from that day on the Clements homestead was known as Buffalo Soldier Ranch.

Just before we left for church, I stood in the doorway of the bathroom and watched the Autodidact put on a tie. He had a collection of strange ties, but he didn't actually wear one very often. He looked handsome and squared away in a striped business suit he'd bought just for the Blessed Event. The tie was mainly blue with foamy designs that upon closer examination you could see were of surf breakers.

"Nice tie," I said.

"Thank you." The Autodidact smiled and looked wistful.

"Why do you own so many ties? You almost never wear one."

"Back in prison, John LeFauve used to fantasize that he and his beloved would get all dressed up for dinner at a fancy restaurant. One aspect of this mental game was imagining tie designs—gaudy ties, grotesque ties, stately ties. Ties celebrating ocean waves, dolphins, hurricane eyes, not to mention African totems. Later, in Grand Isle, when I was going through Jim Clements' things, I found half a dozen ties. The man had been homeless. He'd only owned one change of underwear, and yet he lugged around neckties. In this way he hung onto a little dignity."

I asked the Autodidact to teach me to make the knot. It was pretty obvious the Autodidact wanted to get going, but he didn't complain and he spent a few minutes showing me how to make a Windsor knot and a half-Windsor knot.

The wedding was a grander affair than I would have predicted.

Grandma Clements knew a lot of people in the county; Mary Jane had family galore and friends up the yin-yang; the Autodidact had some friends that he'd met through his research on the Buffalo Soldiers. Ike and his parents came, too. All those people, dressed up, happy, together, celebrating. And me? Alone in himself. After the ceremony, there was a reception at Buffalo Soldier Ranch under a rented tent awning. The wedding party (that's what they called themselves) poured wine and other drinks down their throats, danced to country and western music, and then ate like pigs. They called it fun.

I became more and more morose. I didn't even want to play with Ike. It wasn't until 2 A.M. the next morning that the whole crew packed it in and went home.

The Autodidact and Mary Jane were up first thing in the morning, getting ready to take off on a week-long honeymoon. They were driving to Santa Fe to go to a couple of art shows, and the Autodidact was going to stop at the library at the university in Albuquerque. I put up a little bit of a stink at the breakfast table.

"Why bother with this farce?" I said. "You've been honeymooning for months."

"It's only going to be for a week, and we'll be coming back," the Autodidact said, patiently. "Quit your complaining."

"Why can't I go? I'd like to see Santa Fe and Albuquerque and get away from this stinking desert valley."

That sent Grandma Clements into gales of laughter. She wasn't usually sarcastic, but she knew I was putting on a show.

"Web," the Autodidact said, "I'll take you to Santa Fe, but not now. This next week belongs to Mary Jane and me."

"I'll run away." I don't know why I said that. I knew it would upset everybody, and I was sorry. I didn't back down though. I set my jaw and screwed up my face to look stubborn.

"Jim?" Mary Jane said. "Maybe we better postpone the honeymoon."

"You aren't postponing anything," Grandma Clements said. "Web's just a little scared. But even he knows better, don't you, boy?" She didn't wait for my sassy answer. "You folks need some time to yourself. And I need somebody here to take care of things.

That's you, Web Clements." She aimed her finger at me. Of course, because she was blind she missed by a couple of feet, but it didn't matter. Everybody knew she'd hit the mark.

I was willing to let bygones be bygones, and when the Autodidact and Mary Jane left in the pickup truck I gave them big hugs and kisses and wished them a happy honeymoon. I'm afraid, though, that my good intentions were interrupted by a thought from Xiphi: there's an accident, the Autodidact's okay, but Mary Jane's killed. Luckily, she's taken out a huge insurance policy, and we're left filthy rich.

After they left, Mrs. Clements called me, "Come over here." She gave me a hug in her ancient arms. "I love you because you're my own flesh and blood." I suddenly felt a flood of love for Grandma Clements, and I hugged her fiercely.

That night before going to bed I put the collar around my neck. I was sending signals again. It was like I wasn't here anymore. Part of me, maybe the best part, was someplace else, in somebody else's mind. I thought about Father and his last words to me, "Far out." Those two words, words to live by, were all he ever gave me. Maybe they were all I could expect of a father.

The next day, late in the afternoon, driving my ATV, on our private road, in the middle of a lava field of black rock formations, almost near the highway, I was surprised by the sight of a parked vehicle, half blocking the road, a green van. Where had I seen that van before? I couldn't remember.

I got off my vehicle and walked over to the van. The driver was wearing a tight-fitting silvery uniform just like my guardian angel's. But it wasn't Langdon behind the wheel; it was Siena.

"I don't know if I want to go. I've been happy here," I said.

"My orders are to take you to your mother, if you so choose," Siena said.

What English-speaking peoples have in common is isolation. The original speakers shaped their language on an island. Their successful colonists in North America, Australia, and New Zealand were all, in their own way, islanders, peoples cut off from the rest of the world by ocean.
— From the Journal of Henri Scratch.

My mother! I couldn't think; I couldn't speak; I couldn't even feel exactly—I was a zombie. I left Pinto with the key in the ignition, running on idle, and slipped into the passenger side of the van. Before I'd even shut the door, Siena stomped the accelerator to the floorboards, and we tore through the twisting dirt road in reverse. I watched Buffalo Soldier Ranch through the windshield disappear in a dust cloud kicked up by the spinning tires. Maybe I'd never again see the ranch or the Autodidact or Grandma Clements. I didn't care—I was going to be delivered to the person I loved!

"Have you seen my mother? What does she look like?" I shouted over the roar of tires digging up dirt.

"I don't know her. I'm supposed to take you the Children of the Cacti. I was told that's where she is."

We reached the end of the drive, and the van squealed rubber as we hit the blacktop. Siena braked, shifted into first, and gunned the engine. I felt myself pressed back in the seat by the G-forces. I looked at Siena's face, like a beardless boy's, like Langdon's, so plain in comparison to her silvery uniform; I looked at her hands gripping the steering wheel. Long steely fingers, dirty, stubby chewed nails. Between the hands, through the steering wheel, the speedometer needle climbed to 50, 60, 70, 80, 90, 100, 110 miles per hour. And holding steady. The shuttle to the mother ship had escaped Earth's gravity. In the harmonizing hums of engine and tires, it was quieter now.

"Where we headed?" I asked.

"Xi," said Siena.

"The Xi of my mind?"

"The what?"

"The home of the Alien. Is my mother his captive?"

"I don't know what you're talking about. Xi is a shopping mall and entertainment complex."

Siena had been to Xi only once, when she'd been called in to go after me. Xi was being built on the California-Mexico border, a massive structure that included Spree, the largest shopping mall in the world; Luck, a gambling casino operated by the Native-American tribe which had leased its reservation to Xi developers; Phi, a holographic entertainment center; Third World Theater, which provided live-action warfare on video; and the Exposition of the Uncanny, whose purpose was unknown to Siena. Xi was owned by an investment group headed by VRN (Virtual Reality Network). Although Xi was not yet fully operational, parts of the complex—Spree and Luck—had been opened to the public on a limited basis. Even without publicity or advertising, business was already brisk.

Siena gave me a cigarette, and we lit up. I stared at her uniform. Colored lights danced in the pores of the fabric.

"It shines, I like it," I said.

"I hate it," Siena said. "I'll take my field uniform any day. But the VRN Director made me put it on when he gave me my assignment."

"The Director? Did he have a red beard and a hump on his back?"

"Yes, how did you know?"

I mulled things over for a second before I answered her question. Maybe Aristotle had been right about the powers of concentration. I'd thought so hard that my demons had come to life. Langdon had taken over Siena; the Director had spontaneously materialized. Or maybe Nurse Wilder had been right. The demons had been there all along; they had just latched onto me because

I was the Devil's child. Either way the Director had come into being, and he was going to tell me what to do next.

"Royal told me about the Director when he sent me to the Clements place. He's another one of my demons."

"You're so strange," she said.

"It's because I was on the Alien's ship for so long. Can I touch your suit?" I asked.

"No!" Siena snapped. Apparently she thought over her answer, because a few seconds later she said, "Why?"

"Never mind—I'm sorry," I said.

She glanced over at me long and hard, trying to determine my sincerity. Finally, she said, "Go ahead, touch it."

I looked for a fold, for a wrinkle, for a pucker, someplace where the fabric didn't come in direct contact with skin. I was afraid her flesh would react to my touch like gunpowder to a match. Boom! The two of us blown to smithereens. The uniform clung close to her all over. No wrinkles. No puckers. Smooth. Shimmering. I put the flat of my hand about an inch from her shoulder, and stopped at an invisible shield—solid, warm, slightly electrified. My hand started to vibrate, and I withdrew it. She cocked her head in curiosity and watched me shake.

After I'd calmed down, I asked Siena if she thought we'd see Royal in Xi.

"I doubt it. Nobody knows where he is. The Director's in charge."

"Do you miss Royal?" I asked.

"No."

"Well, I do," I said.

We drove on. A sheriff's car jumped us near the New Mexico-Arizona state line. He couldn't call ahead, because the van was equipped with a device that scrambled police radio signals. Siena pushed the van to a 160 miles per hour. The landscape flew by. The metal around us shook. In ten minutes we'd left the sheriff's car far behind.

As the sun started to go down, Siena pulled off the highway and parked. We got out, stretched, then sat cross-legged on the ground and watched the sun set as we ate C-rations, cold out of the can.

VRN had bought the food from US Army surplus left over from the Korean War and donated it to the Souvien rebels. I had tuna and noodles, and Siena had ham and rice. After we ate, we each took a turn behind a rock to go to the bathroom.

The stars were out when Siena said it was time to turn in for the night. She slid open the side door to the van, and I got in. She followed, closing the door behind her and switching on the overhead light. The living space included a small closet, sink, propane stove, bookshelf, TV, and mattress with two black pillows and black sheets. The interior, top to bottom, was carpeted in black. Siena switched on the TV and fiddled with the channel selector trying to find a station.

"This your van?" I asked. It wasn't a sincere question. I could tell it wasn't hers.

"It's VRN's. The Director loaned it to me for the mission."

"It's the transfer shuttle." I could feel Xiphi speaking through me.

Siena switched off the TV. "Nothing on—we're too far out. What do you mean . . . shuttle?"

"The mother ship is too big to land on earth. That's why you need a shuttle," Xiphi said.

Xiphi wondered whether Siena would take her uniform off and burst into flames. But she made no move to strip, and Xiphi lost interest and withdrew within the darkness. Siena and I both looked at the mattress.

"Which side do you want?" I asked.

"The driver's side," Siena said.

"Okay, I'll take the passenger side," I said.

Siena switched off the light and we lay down, a one-foot gap between us. It was pitch black in the van, but I could just make out a few dim stars through the tinted window. I was comfortable. Everything smelled familiar. But I couldn't smell Siena.

"Can I touch your uniform now? I won't be scared this time," I said.

"If you try anything, I'll have to mace you."

"I won't try anything," I said. "I don't have the feeling."

"What feeling?"

"You know, the *feeling*. We talked about it back in New York."

"Oh, that. I'd forgotten."

"Not me. I remember everything you said that day. You said you had the feeling but not with a man."

"I gave it up."

"You had the feeling and you gave it up—that's admirable."

"It's not so hard when you have a cause."

"A what?"

"A cause. I gave up the feeling because I adopted a cause. When you have a cause, the feeling gets in the way."

"If I can't have the feeling, maybe I should go for a cause," I said.

Siena told me about her cause. Most of the people in her country were poor, but a few were very rich. The government kept the rich rich and the poor poor. Government soldiers had killed her family, and for a while she herself wanted to die. She had started to feel better when Royal had introduced her to the cause, which was simple enough. Kill the bad people, take over the government, and establish freedom and justice for all.

The conversation ended and we settled in for the night. I tossed and turned, keeping Siena awake. She figured out the problem. "Get it over with," she said.

I reached out in the dark toward her voice and I touched her face. It was warm and smooth; I wanted to cry out with hope or joy, one of those emotions I didn't have much experience with, but I held back. Below, at the throat, I touched her silvery suit. It felt like the back of a lizard, and I jerked my hand away.

Early the next afternoon, we arrived in Xi—city-sized, under one roof, in the middle of the desert, smack dab on the border with Mexico. Patrons parked a mile or so away and were taken in on trolley cars. But Siena showed her pass from the Director, and the guard at the gate let us go through to a private parking garage near the main entry. From the outside, Xi was impressive in its size but otherwise nondescript as a warehouse, just a windowless building that seemed to go on forever. An aqueduct from the Colorado River snaked through a mountain pass into Xi. I'd seen something like this image before, the supply umbilical from the mother ship to the transfer shuttle.

Inside was a different story. I'd never imagined anything like this. Glass domes let in plenty of natural light; bright color schemes brought out a feeling in me that it was peak foliage time in New England.

The sign over the front entry said.

Siena and I could have strolled with the shoppers along cobblestoned streets, but instead we chose to ride one of the many moving sidewalks. We started in Xi-Queens, based on Queens, New York. We passed a restaurant, a bar, a men's hat shop, a bowling alley, and a roller-skating rink. Overhead, projected on a low ceiling, was an image of the undersides of an elevated train track. When the illusion-train went through, a roar filled my ears and the whole area jiggled.

From Xi-Queens, we moved through Xi-Soho (art galleries, mainly), Xi-Bourbon Street of New Orleans, and Xi-River Walk of San Antonio. The places all looked like the real thing, except newer and cleaner. In addition were little touches found only on Xi. For example, although homeless people were banned in the mall, robot dummies made up to resemble the homeless begged on street corners. Mall patrons were encouraged to take out their aggressions on the homeless. Kick them, punch them, spit on them. The robots "bled" and cried out in pain. For people averse to abusing the homeless, the mall developers provided robots of other types that people hated—police officers, school superintendents, politicians, business moguls, bossy women, and biker bullies. Siena kicked a robot Souvien government official in the privates. I didn't hit any robots. I just wanted to see my mother, and I told Siena as much.

"I'll bring you to her as soon as I can," she said. "We have to go all the way through Spree to get to Luck. We're going to meet a tribal official. He'll have orders for us."

At that moment, the moving sidewalk turned, and we found ourselves approaching Central Square, based on the town common in Keene, New Hampshire. On the square were trees, park benches, a cannon, the statue of a Civil War soldier with a baby face that looked like my own, and a bandstand where robot lookalikes of living First Ladies of American Presidents sang "God Bless America."

As for shopping, Spree had something for everybody. Black market, gray market, white goods. Not just products from all over the world, not just restaurants and hotels with floor shows, video arcades, and movie theaters, but centers for psychiatric counseling, chiropracty, astrology, and geomancy, and chapels representing scores of religious faiths. Giant television monitors throughout the mall displayed bargain prices and attractions such as Round-the-Clock Divorce Court, Round-the-Clock Athletic Recruitment, and Round-the-Clock Manic Wrestling.

"Let's get something to eat," Siena said.

We stepped off the moving sidewalk and strolled down the Streets of Gód—Trinity Square, Mecca Circle, Baptist Cul de Sac, Methodist Way, Cult Corner, and Go Forth Drive. Eventually, we found our way to Christian Chapel McIntosh. The main difference between this restaurant and the standard Mrs. McIntosh's was the pulpit, located on a "desk top" above the drop-down menus. Beside food menus were worship menus for patrons. I clicked "prayers."

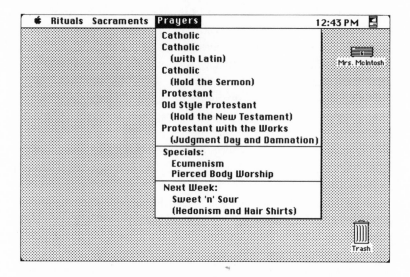

We didn't opt for a prayer, even though it came with the meal. Siena had given up religion after she'd adopted her cause. As for myself, I could have used a prayer, but I didn't think I was worthy.

After lunch, we hopped back on the moving sidewalk, which brought us to a section where the roof rose hundreds of feet from the floor, housing a hill complete with real trees, bushes, and meadows. The air felt pleasantly damp. No wonder. Water, in from the diverted Colorado River, disappeared in a swirl at the base of the hill.

"You're looking at Hydrohead Hill," Siena said. "At night when demands on the national power grid are reduced and the price of electricity is down, water is pumped to the top of the hill to a pond. In the daytime, when the price of electricity is high, the water is dropped through turbines and the electricity is sold. With the price difference in the cost of electricity, Xi not only produces its own power but also makes a profit."

The moving sidewalk passed from Spree to Luck, the Indian-run gambling casino. Lights flashed from floor to ceiling; sounds of slot machines filled my ears; a vague, metallic burnt smell tickled my nostrils. Up, down, time, and sense were irrelevant here. The patrons neither smiled nor frowned, but looked as if they'd been hit between the eyes with baseball bats. I recognized the look from when Father had a few drinks or a hit of his drug.

An Indian man, woman, twin boys about ten, and a dog walked by. The Indians, dressed in raccoon-graybrown tuxedos, were handsome and very dark. The dog was small, built like a coyote, but marked like a Dalmatian. All of them, including the dog, had dark, greasy circles painted around their eyes. I stared at them.

"They're the managers of the casino, the ones we're supposed to see," Siena said.

She showed the family her credentials.

"Phi's not open yet, and the Exposition of the Uncanny is top secret," the Indian man said.

"Read my orders. Signed by the Director," Siena said.

While the man read the orders, I said to the Indian woman, "Excuse me, but I think I remember you from a different dimension. You were raccoons under a bridge, and you snubbed me."

"Could be," said the woman.

The Indians boys said something in their language that I did not understand.

"We are descendants of the lost $$$ Indian tribe, formerly the ? ? ? Indian tribe," the Indian woman said. She went on to explain that the $$$ Indians had leased their lands to VRN for ninety-nine years. With the profits, the Indians had opened the gambling casino.

"You sold your heritage," Siena said.

"Three centuries ago, our people were converted to the white man's religion by a Spanish nun known as the Lady in Blue. Meanwhile, our Indian enemies stole the white man's horses and guns and grew strong. They almost annihilated us, took our lands and prospered. But in turn they were wiped out by the whites. Today after much study we have determined that the way to survival is to take from the white man his most valuable asset, more valuable even than his religion or his technology."

I looked at Siena, and she looked at me. We did not understand.

"My wife is trying to tell you," the Indian man said, "that we sold our homeland and built a casino to get money. Your papers are in order. Come with me, please."

We started to follow the Indian man, but the Indian woman stepped between us. "Not you," she said to me, "just her. You wait here."

The Indian man took Siena away, and the other Indians and the coyote/Dalmatian followed. They disappeared into some brightly colored lights, and I found myself alone. For the next ten minutes, I stood around and watched the gamblers. They were a preoccupied bunch. I could have stripped naked and done somersaults, and they wouldn't have noticed. When Siena came back, she was alone, and she was no longer wearing her Langdon suit. She was in a loose-fitting fatigue uniform, spotted in a tan and light green, camouflage for desert fighting. She looked like a soldier. I felt as if I'd lost her for good. Or maybe lost Langdon for good. If that was the case, Xiphi would be back worse than ever.

"I've got some things to tell you, Web," she said, a real serious look on her face. "I have to return to Third World Theater now. But there's something else. About your mother . . ."

"Listen," I interrupted, "I've been thinking. Forget that stupid war. Come and live with my mom and me. I want to be with you."

"We can never be together, Web. The cause is too important. I have to go to war. Web, do you have the faintest idea how to live?"

Her question threw me. I didn't have a clue. "Maybe we could camp in the van, travel around. You could drive. And anyway my mom will know."

"Web, your mother. . . ."

"You promised you'd take me to her."

"Web, she's dead. She's been dead for years."

"Dead! You lied to me! You betrayed me! I'll kill you." I screamed at her, but it didn't make any difference to the gamblers. The tinkling sounds of the machines rode over my tirade, and my frantic gesturing attracted no attention.

"I didn't lie to you. I only found out a minute ago that she was dead. And you *will* be taken to her. I was assured of that."

"You sure?"

"This has all been arranged. We're part of a plan. It's going to work out, Web. I have to go, I have to return to my unit. To my cause. Please understand."

I was too mad to cry, and too sad to start swinging. She took a step toward me as if she was going to touch me, maybe kiss me. Or maybe it was just wishful thinking on Xiphi's part. Anyway, she hesitated, reached into her shirt pocket, and gave me a cigarette. I put it behind my ear. The soldier in Siena took over control, and she did an about-face and walked away.

PHI

American writers of French-Canadian descent often produce drifting odysseys sounding themes of love and home. This is the "Evangeline" effect, and examples include *On the Road* by Jack Kerouac, *The Mosquito Coast* and other works by Paul Theroux, *Postcards* by E. Annie Proulx, and *Virtual Reality: The Adventures of Lotus Magellan* by . . . by . . . the name escapes me at the moment. —From the Journal of Henri Scratch.

A few minutes later the $$$ Indians reappeared, walking toward me in procession. "Come with us, young man," said the man. The boys giggled, the coyote/dalmatian barked, and the woman led the way. I followed. We walked to an elevator. The door opened and I stepped in alone.

The woman patted the coyote/dalmatian, and he got into the elevator with me. "This is $#$@!," the Indian woman said with a click. "He will be your guide."

"Is he a coyote or a Dalmatian, or what?" I asked, as the elevator door began to slide shut.

"He is what he is," said the Indian man.

The door slid closed. A soft hum and a gentle shove against the soles of my feet told me we were going up. I didn't know where. There were no numbers on the control panel. In fact, no controls on the control panel. $#$@! wagged his tail, so I relaxed some.

We stepped off the elevator into what appeared to be the outdoors. $#$@! barked, as if to say "Follow me" and then walked right through a prickly pear cactus. I bent to touch the leaves of the cactus. Nothing there but light. The entire desert vista was an elaborate holographic display. We were still inside.

The path was narrow, winding upward through rocks and thorny cacti. There was more vegetation the higher up we walked. I saw stunted cedars, pines, oaks, grasses with tufted tops, a few wild flowers, the gray cadavers of downed trees. I kept trying and failing to touch things.

We came to what appeared to be a dead end at the faces of boulders big as houses. $#$@! pressed his nose against the rocks. Some of them, I could just discern, were actual objects, even if they weren't actual rocks. Finally, $#$@!'s nose touched a pivot point, and the rock moved aside just like in a PG-rated adventure movie. We slipped through the opening, and a mazelike path wound upward through boulders to a ridge. From here I could see a hidden plateau surrounded on all sides by a steep incline. It was obvious we were in the crater of an ancient volcano.

In the distance was a tremendous pueblo built under a cliff overhang, the holograph of the precasino home of the Indians. Close to us, water poured from a rock. Not a trickle but a river, cascading down a waterfall, irrigating the two miles or so between us and the pueblo. I could hear the rushing sound. I walked right through the cataract of light. Beyond were orchards and fields of corn, beans, tomatoes, vegetables, and flower gardens. I could smell roses.

We walked to the pueblo. Everything looked as it must have when the pueblo was built nearly a thousand years ago; reddish adobe apartments were connected by patios and wooden ladders. $#$@! knew exactly where he was going. He brought me to an adobe-designed telephone booth. I punched up 911. The operator said, "For a guided tour, press one; to return to the real world, press two." I pressed two. The operator said, "Thank you for pressing two. Press one, please." I pressed one. "One moment and you will be connected to your tour guide." A couple minutes went by. I wanted to leave, but $#$@! barked for me to stay still.

"Welcome to Phi." The voice came not only out of the telephone receiver, but seemingly from everywhere, and in the deep gargle of my demon, the Director.

"My mother. . . ." I would have said more, but I didn't know myself what the question was.

"In due time," said the Director.

"You lied to me."

"You haven't been lied to. You've been deceived. Think of this distinction as the main element of human relationships. Meanwhile, enjoy the tour. Phi is not complete yet. At the moment, its holographic illusions are set only for the tastes of the Children of the Cacti. When Phi is ready for the public, hundreds of virtual worlds will be available to suit other tastes. Now hang up the phone and follow $#$@!"

I did as ordered. $#$@! brought me to a big window. Behind the glass fifty or sixty middle-aged people ate at stone picnic tables.

"Can they see me?" I asked.

"They know you're here, but they don't choose to view you," the Director said. "The Children of the Cacti exist entirely in a virtual world of their own creation. In this world there are no biting bugs, and the temperature is balmy all year-round. There is no strife."

"The strife is in Xi," I said.

"Strife *is* Xi," said the Director. "You're beginning to catch on. The trick is to transform strife into strive, Xi into Phi."

I stared hard through the window. It was the lunch hour. The Children of the Cacti seemed to be having a grand time as they ate. Dinner was strictly vegetarian, but it looked good and real—tortillas, a spicy vegetable chili, salad, all of it washed down with homemade wine served in red ceramic mugs. From their raccoon eyes, I recognized the waiters as member of the $$$ tribe. And then something struck me as odd.

"These people are all parent age, but I don't see any children. Where are the kids?"

"Think about it," said the Director. "If you were creating a world without strife, would you want any children around? There are no children of the Children of the Cacti. They finessed the kids out of their lives."

The Director droned on, telling me all about the Children of the Cacti. They lived like the Pueblo peoples you see in *National Geographic* with a few notable exceptions. Social, spiritual, recreational, even political life revolved around TV-watching in six connecting rooms. Each of the TV viewing rooms was dedicated to a certain show category—men's shows (such as sporting events), women's shows (such as soap operas), dramas, sex shows, potluck, and first-run movies. Viewers floated among the TV sets, voting every half hour by secret ballot which show or movie within the category should be selected. During off-peak hours, participants were allowed to make speeches on behalf of unpopular programs. Those shows were taped and played between 2 and 6 A.M. This was known as Minority Television.

In this society, there was no haranguing political process. Here the polls and ratings *were* the elections and the legislation. There was no competition in Phi. No goals, no sense of time but what television programming brought.

After the Director's talk about the Children of the Cacti, he told me to prepare myself for my first full-blown virtual reality experience.

$#$@! started down a ramp, and soon we were outside the pueblo and on the desert floor. Up ahead was a cliff, sixty or seventy feet up. Before my eyes, this lonely place of just rocks and tan earth began to fill with people and music, rock 'n' roll. The people were shoulder to shoulder. They danced and wiggled and sang out. A handful of people had made their way up the cliff, and one of them, a pretty woman in a flower-print dress, broke away from the group and ran to the edge. I couldn't see her face very clearly because she was far away, but I recognized her by the way she moved, dancing and lighthearted: my mother.

"Careful, Flower—the rocks are loose!" I recognized the warning voice. It was Marla, the woman who had hypnotized me in the Catacombs.

Mother laughed and started to wiggle to the beat of the music. Two seconds later, she slipped and fell. She didn't scream, just made a wheee! sound. She fell right down at me. I made as if to catch her, but she went through me. After a thump at my feet, the illusion vanished.

"That was how your mother died, in a silly accident," said the Director in a voice full of scorn and sadness. "Thereafter the Children of the Cacti called this place Sorrows."

I prayed that Xiphi or Langdon, even the Alien, would rescue me from this . . . this feeling of emptiness inside of me.

"Take me away! Please take me away," I cried out. Seconds later I was following $#$@! down a plain hallway that you might find in any office building, but I could still hear the voice of the Director.

"Most of Children of the Cacti are middle-aged, but when they first started they were rebellious youths. They found their insights through drugs. Graduated to ideas—peace and love. Flirted with Eastern religions. Tried group living—commune-ism. When their numbers declined, they sought refuge in Christianity and conventional life-styles. Invented New Age. None of if worked. The Children of the Cacti left Jesus, political ideology, and drugs. The turning point was your mother's death. Led by an excommunicated priest, they found the keys to the perfect society: trust funds, entertainment, no kids. Persons without a steady source of income, such as Dirty Joe, were banished. New people of means were recruited. Today the Children of the Cacti are learning to govern their lives and loves with entertainment as the medium and money as the method."

$#$@! barked, and we started moving again, through some pathways, down some ramps to a door that opened into a cavern, which reminded me a little of the Catacombs of Manhattan, except the air here was purer, and the views bigger and prettier. Colored rocks in the shapes of giant icicles hung from the ceiling and jutted up from the floor. The area was well lighted, but the objects themselves were real enough; at least they felt real to my touch.

"I feel like I'm in church," I said.

"You are," said the Director, his voice echoing through the cavern. It's a church, it's a cathedral, it's a mausoleum, it's an arena for the most unique statuary in the history of art. The Children of the Cacti call this place the Home of the Grateful Dead. Soon you will meet the sculptor who designed it, the Michelangelo of our time. "Everything here is her creation."

The path led around a giant boulder whose surface was the color and texture of alligator hide. On the other side, dozens of what at first glance appeared to be coffin-sized aquariums caught my attention. From among these objects appeared a woman, upright, alive. It was Marla, the hypnotist. With her painted fingernails and orange-colored skin, she looked like a witch.

"You? You're the great artist?" I said.

"I am." Marla took me by the hand. Her touch was cool. Marla talked in a whisper. "I have this special skill in the preparation of bodies after death. It is my art. After your mother was brought to me, I reconstituted her body into statuary. She was my first work, and I submitted it to the Children of the Cacti. They voted to make me artist-in-residence."

"What was my mother's name?" I asked in a whisper. The churchy atmosphere of the place commanded respect.

"I never knew her name from the outside. She gave it up. We all gave up our names. I am not Marla. We called your mother Flower."

"Flower for flower child."

"Yes. We were all flower children, but your mother was the flower of flowers."

I pictured flowers in a field, bending in the wind.

We continued to walk, and now I could see that the coffin-sized aquariums really were glass coffins, the bodies preserved in liquids that changed colors as the liquids wrapped around the bodies. Human lava lamps. The light was so dim that all I could see were vague shapes. $#$@! sniffed cautiously at the coffins. Finally, Marla stopped.

"This is the one." Even whispering, her voice echoed in the cavern, like the shadow of a wind.

"I can't see much. Can you give me some light?" I said.

"Of course." Marla touched a switch somewhere, and powerful beams from below and above shined into the glass coffin. In that split second, everything was revealed. Inside the coffin, suspended in tumbling, restless liquid, perfectly preserved, was Flower, my mother. Her face was serene, her green and gold trinitite eyes were open and staring up at heaven, mouth in a slight smile, muscles relaxed, feet bare, nails painted green and gold. She wore a flowered dress, whose folds hung down to the bottom of the casket and waved in the liquid.

"What holds her up?" I said.

"It's partly the buoyancy of the liquid, but the rest—I can't tell you. It's a secret."

There was no doubt in my mind that Mother's soul had gone to heaven. She was as beautiful and perfect as I'd imagined her, and I could do nothing more than gaze upon her. Was that what heaven was all about? Endless gazing at the face/faces of the three-headed God? You couldn't even die of boredom, since you were already dead.

"Is that all there is?" I said.

Marla laughed a little, then hummed a sad tune, which sounded with the words that I had spoken—*Is that all there is.* "It's a song from my childhood."

"Why don't you bury the dead people?"

"We wish not only to *pre*serve but to *ob*serve. The dead as art provide entertainment for the bereaved. But I can see it didn't work with you."

"I don't know what to think, what to feel. She's just there, beautiful as a sunset, but I can't touch her, I can't talk to her."

"What do you want from her? What can she do for you now that she's gone?"

"I don't know."

The Director spoke, his voice echoing against the walls of the cavern, "I know, I know, I know, I know. . . ."

"Don't show him that. He's not ready," Marla said

"He's ready," said the Director.

"He loves her, he needs to love her to remain good," Marla said. "Don't you understand? He loves her."

"I understand completely. That's the point of showing him the tape. It's already been voted upon. Do you want another poll?"

"Don't bother. You know the answer."

$#$@! barked. I followed him out of the caverns into the holographic pueblo to one of the viewing rooms. Marla stayed behind, angry and upset. The viewing room was spacious, modern in decor, well lighted, temperature-controlled, and heated. The section included a bar, a restaurant, and a lounging area. No holographs. TV monitors were everywhere. People lounged about with distant expressions on their faces; the Children of the Cacti had raised zentensity to its highest level. Nearby was a conference room where viewers met to discuss feature presentations. When we came in, a cheer went up from about twenty Children of the Cacti.

"All these people have come to see a tape on my mother?" I said, a bit confused.

"They've seen it already," the Director said. "The tape holds little interest for them. Their interest is in you, Web. This is part of your theatrical training. You see, we wish to make a performer of you. If you mind terribly being watched, if your responses are uninteresting, you will be set free, since our interest in you will wane."

"Then set me free," I said. "Let me return to Valley of Fires. I promise I won't be jealous of Mary Jane."

"Not until you view the tape of your mother." Before I had chance to reply, the Director shouted, "Roll the tape."

The monitor shimmered with an image of wild flowers. I was as captivated by the images as the audience was captivated by the expressions on my face to those images. I don't want to get into detail about what was on the tape, because, really, it was just the same thing over and over again. My mother had been a rock 'n' roll groupie. The pictures showed her at this concert and that, cheering, dancing, losing herself in the music. At one concert, some fellows hoisted her up on their shoulders, and the crowd yelled for her to show her tits, which she did. Then there was Mother backstage frolicking with the creepy band members. Mother in a bedroom with a bunch of guys. When the tape was over, the Director asked me, "How do you feel about your mother now?"

"I hate her," I said, gagging with rage.

"Good," the Director said. "We have unleashed your anger. We have removed fear and hope. Now you are ready to go to war."

A split second later something exploded in the room, not a big explosion, just a puff and some orange smoke. Out of this smoke appeared the Director. He was quite a sight. He had a carrot-colored beard and a hunched back, and he was built like so many middle-aged men, blompy. He looked very much like my demon. But in some ways he wasn't like my demon at all. His movements were herky-jerky. My demon was sluggish and bored. My demon Director always stood close to me. The real Director kept a distance between us.

"Are you real?" I said.

"Find out," said the Director.

I walked toward him, but he never seemed to get any closer than fifteen feet.

"You're just light from a holograph," I said.

"That's as real as you're going to get in Phi, kid."

While video cameras taped our conversation in the viewing room and while a couple of dozen Children of the Cacti (our audience) looked on, some watching us live on this Phi stage, others watching us live on the monitors, the Director introduced me to Third World Theater. Combatants in the government and rebel armies fought a scaled-down version of the Souvien civil war in the mountains of the former Indian reservation. The MZ (Militarized Zone) included rebel strongholds in the mountains, a government garrison on the plain, and a village in the hills on a river. VRN had brought in an entire town from Souvien, complete with civilian DCs (Designated Casualties). VRN broadcast live action of the war to a sample audience of skilled viewers, the Children of the Cacti entertainment cult. VRN was also gathering footage for later documentaries, dramatic feature films, and a TV series. Third World Theater was in the experimental stage; VRN was refining its video techniques and determining from the sample audience what viewers required in warfare to keep up their attention. Eventually, the network would broadcast round-the-clock war all over the world.

The warring factions thought that Third World Theater was a great idea. VRN supplied money and arms to keep the struggle going. More important, the TV exposure gave both sides publicity. The only thing the government and the rebels had in common was their belief that once the world knew the facts regarding the Souvien civil war, sympathy for their respective causes would follow.

"Real people. Real weapons. Real deaths. Exciting, isn't it?" said the Director. "You have been selected to participate in the war."

"Maybe I want to go back to Valley of Fires," I said, but I didn't mean it. I wanted to go to war; I just didn't like the Director forcing the idea on me.

"You're young, you're an American, you'll boost the ratings, you'll have a good time," the Director said.

I stepped toward him, but he receded a step. I stopped and snarled at him, "Why should I care about these people?"

"You don't have to care about the Souviens. You have a mission to perform."

"A mission?" Suddenly, I was interested.

"There's another American in the war zone."

"So what?"

"Web, who was your best friend in Valley of Fires?"

"Ike, my blood brother."

"Yes, the ranch boy," the Director said with a sneer. "Souvien government troops have captured him. When you turned up missing, he went looking for you on his horse and found his way into Third World Theater."

"Can't our government get him out?"

"It's not as simple as that. The leasing agreement and entertainment contract is signed by the Souvien government, the Souvien Liberation Front, VRN, the United States government, and the $$$ Indian nation. The Director paused, then called toward the control booth of the viewing room, where a raccoon-eyed Indian technician with earphones sat in front of half a dozen monitors, "*&∧%**, start the tape, please."

At this point, the war zone popped up on the monitors in the viewing rooms. I saw pine trees, fields, wild flowers. I thought of

Flower, and my heart boiled with hatred. The camera
village, located on a river. The buildings were small and p
Chickens pecked at bugs on the dusty streets. A few cows
and a couple of pigs rooted in the earth. Old women gather
ter from a well; old men sat playing cards at a table outside a   ..e
restaurant. Apparently, these were DCs. Children ran and played,
but no one seemed happy. And for obvious reasons. Government
soldiers patrolled the streets. The people spoke in a language I did
not understand.

"It was a typical, sleepy village until the war came," said the
Director. "Since the village was moved, the local people have re-
named it to fit their state of mind, which in English roughly trans-
lates as Sorrows."

Sorrows! The scene of Mother's death. A chill scurried like a
snake's tongue down my spine. All this had been arranged, but
by whom? Who *was* this Director? This agent from hell? Maybe
there was a mother ship after all, working mysterious ways upon
the Earth. Maybe the Alien was not a figment of my imagination,
but a real space doctor who had captured me for study. Oh, I felt
uncanny—uncanny and hostile. I knew this wasn't *the feeling,* but
it was as close as I was going to get.

"This is all going to be on videotape?" I asked.

"According to the contract, VRN is allowed to videotape the
war," the Director said. "We have total access, but we don't have
the right to interfere in the fighting, unless of course the ratings
are too low. That too is in the contract. That's why we can't send
a mercenary force to get your blood brother out. It would destroy
the balance of power. You, because you're a boy, will create no difficult diplomatic or legal problems." The Director hollered up to
the technician. "*&±%**, can you get us a shot of the ranch boy?"

The scene cut to a room in almost total darkness. I could just
barely tell that someone was lying in a bed. To keep his spirits up,
he was mournfully singing "where seldom is heard." Although I
couldn't see him, I knew it was Ike because I recognized his voice.

"That's enough," said the Director. The monitor went back to
regular programming. Some members of the audience stood and
stretched. Some went on to other viewing rooms. Meanwhile,

$#$@! padded off and came back a minute later dragging a back-pack in his mouth. He dropped the stuff at my feet, stuck his nose inside the pack, and came out with a waterproof map and a pack-age about the size of a paperback book.

I took the package from his jaws and looked at it, wrapped in green paper. "What's this?" I asked.

"A bomb," said the Director. "Should you choose to accept this mission, you will have to use it. Your orders." $#$@! nosed open the map on the floor and pointed with his paw, as the Director spoke. "You will return to Hydrohead Hill in Xi. We will hold back the water, and you will descend through the spillway, which emp-ties into a limestone tunnel, what the $$$ Indians call the forbidden cave. As you can see, it comes out on the side of a mountain."

"I get it," I said, following $#$@!'s wet nose.

"From this point, you will follow the river to the village, wait until dark, sneak in, place the charge against the north wall of the building where your blood brother is being held, blow out a hole, and set him free. They'll never find two fast-running boys in the darkness. Walk parallel to the river to a small cave, as yet undis-covered by the government troops, and spend the daylight hours in hiding. The following night you'll continue along this path to the border and freedom. Our infrared cameras will track you in the darkness.

"The collar," I whispered.

"Now you know why Royal gave it to you. To detonate the bomb, press the red button three times and the black button once." $#$@! nuzzled opened the pack so I could see my other treasures— food in a water-proofed container, enough for several days, a sleeping bag, and a flashlight.

"So there you have it," said the Director. "The mission: rescue your blood brother from the MZ, and get him back to America. Do you accept?"

The Director's words stirred me. My life had begun the day I'd come out of the muck. Since then my mind had filled with people-clutter—Nurse Wilder, the Doctors, Royal, Father, Mother, the Autodidact, the River Rats, the Shadows, the Souvz, Mary Jane,

Sally, Grandma, Ike, Siena, Marla, not to mention non-people such as the three-headed God, the Alien, Langdon, Xiphi, and the Director, who may or may not have been a person. At this moment, all of them lost the weight of meaning; what mattered was one thing: the mission.

"I accept," I said.

THIRD WORLD THEATER

**$**#$@! led me back to the elevator. We descended into Luck and took the moving sidewalk to Hydrohead Hill. Water poured down a long slide in sharp curves. It was a dangerous place, and Xi developers had put up a ten-foot-high chain-link fence between the rushing waters and the mall floor. My orders were to climb the fence, leap into the water, and ride the swirl right into the drain. I had to trust in the Director to reduce the water flow. I had no idea whether he was telling me the truth, or whether I'd imagined it all. Maybe I'd perish. I didn't care. My hostility toward my mother made me brave.

I had adjusted my pack on my shoulders and started to climb the fence when I suddenly remembered the cigarette Siena had given me. I stuck it in my mouth.

"Got a light?" I said to $#$@!

He left and came back a minute later with a book of matches in his mouth. He dropped it at my feet and with a good-bye bark padded off. It was the last time I saw $#$@!. I lit my cigarette and watched the smoke. It didn't make a ring or a string or a cloud. It just vanished into Xi's air-circulation system.

Cigarette between my lips, I climbed the fence and perched for a moment on top. A security guard yelled something at me. I took a last drag on the cigarette, flicked the butt into the stream, and jumped. I'm not sure exactly what happened after that. I rode down the water slide at a furious rate on the seat of my pants until I was dumped into the swirl. It was as if hands—yes, human hands—were pushing my head under water. I held my breath for the longest time. I thrashed and thrashed until I found myself free of those imaginary hands on my back. A second later I surfaced in a dark air pocket. Finally, I could take a breath. The air was dank, smelly. I may have passed out, because the next thing I knew, I was in a narrow, twisting limestone cave carved out by the river. Man-made lights high up allowed me to see; the cave it-self was no holograph. I was wet; the walls were wet and slippery, and there was an odd smell, too, like nothing else I've ever smelled, the stink of dead rocks. It was as if all the living things that went into making of this cavern, the millions and millions of wiggly creatures long extinct, had now come back to a rotting half-life as river-soaked rocks.

Some of the passages were so narrow and dark I had to crawl to get through, finding my way by flashlight. Others opened into caverns of varying sizes, although none was as big as the Home of the Grateful Dead. Lights high up sensed my presence and turned on as I passed under them. No doubt there'd be a camera up there, too, watching me.

I was going along all right, not thinking too much, just working to keep my feet on the slippery rock when I stopped short at a grisly sight. Up ahead was a bloated human body on its back, wedged between a couple of purple-gray, ice-cream-cone-shaped rocks. I dropped to my belly, as if the thing could see me. I peered at it from about fifty feet away and then inched forward. For a sec-ond, I was back on the yacht eying Terry's brother/sister with the purple strangle marks on his/her throat. The collar around my own neck seemed to get hot. The tap sound of a pebble falling from the ceiling brought me back to the world of dripping water, damp-ness, sweat, and bloated body.

The face didn't look human. It was puffed out, busted up but bloodless. It had no eyes. The teeth showed through a lipless mouth. I crept closer. It was a man dressed in an olive-drab uni-form. The feet had swollen and burst through army boots. I reasoned out what had happened. A government soldier had worked his way up the channel while it was at low water. Xi must have picked up a signal from the TV monitor, and the power-generator officials had let out water when he was in a narrow passage. Good-bye, soldier. The same thing could happen to me, and it would be good-bye, Web. But the rest of my trip was uneventful, if tiring. It took me almost three hours before I saw light at the end of the tunnel. I came out of the mountain and threw a kiss to Mister Sun, even though he hurt my eyes.

I started walking along the dry stream bed. High above, VRN camera blimps patrolled. Half an hour later, I heard a noise. I turned around and saw a trickle of water coming toward me. The water gates in Xi had been opened. I scampered up out of the stream bed and onto the land. Minutes later the river was a river again.

I reached the village of Sorrows maybe an hour before dark. Crouched in some bushes, I peeked at it across the river. The place looked shabbier in real life than than it had on the video. It was a one-dirt-street town, consisting mainly of shacks of wood and straw. Armed soldiers stood gabbing in clusters. A civilian or two would scurry from one shack to another. I saw chickens, a couple of mules, a military truck. The pigs I'd seen earlier in the video ambled to and fro as if they owned the place. Other than the milling about of soldiers and pigs, there was little activity.

I waited until nightfall before crossing the river. When I reached the hut where Ike was being held (or so my map said), I could see that I would not be able to rescue him according to the plan. Half a dozen guards were stationed around the building. They marched, they argued, they laughed. A generator supplied power for lights that lit up the area. I couldn't see any way to sneak in and plant my bomb. I stayed in the trees, watching, hoping the lights would go out and the soldiers would leave. Next thing I knew, it was dawn. I'd fallen asleep.

I started moving away from the village. Thanks to Father and my familiarity with the woods of New Hampshire, I had a pretty good sense of how to find my way in this pine forest. I noticed that some mosses grew mainly on the north sides of the pine trunks, and that the hill rose up from the west. So I knew what the directions were without a compass. I kept track of distance by counting my footsteps.

Taking a break under the shade of a pine, I asked myself the only question that came to mind: now what? I had followed the Director's plan without ever really thinking about what I'd do if it failed. I had no experience in warfare, unless you count daydreaming as experience. What kept me going was my love for Ike and my hate for my mother. I was afraid of nothing, but fearlessness wasn't going to set Ike free. I hauled out my map and pondered it. The only thing I could think of was to go to the school. Maybe Ike would be there. Maybe somehow I'd find a way to break him out.

The school was the last building in town. It was no more than a shack, kindling nailed together to form an enclosure. From my spot in the trees I could hear the teacher through the open window. I had no idea if Ike was inside or not. Stationed outside the school were a couple of guards. They both carried automatic rifles with banana clips, but they were pretty relaxed. They laughed and joked in the Souvien language. Once again, I was stymied. The soldiers didn't do anything interesting, and soon I was bored. It occurred to me to praise the Lord/Lords, but I didn't do it. Instead, I ate lunch, a veggie sandwich.

No sooner had I finished my meal than all hell broke loose. A burst of machine-gun fire mowed down the two soldiers, and a mortar shell exploded on the front steps of the school. A soldier and a boy poured out the door. The soldier and a boy were shot. I heard screams. A squeal of anguish told me one of the village pigs had been hit. At the same time, another hut in town was hit by a shell and burst into flames.

In less than a minute, the air had been filled with the sounds of gunshots, explosions, yellow-black smoke, and hollers and screams of both people and animals. I smelled fire, petroleum, gunpowder. The rebels were attacking the village. With the smoke, the fire, the noise, and the confusion, it was hard to see and impossible to figure out what was going on. I wished I were watching on a monitor so I could tell what was happening. I was beginning to understand the wisdom behind the Third World Theater and VRN. Editing of the tapes along with analysis by experts would tell more about what actually happened in the battle than the people who'd experienced it could ever know. All I knew for sure was that it was time for me to get out of here.

Moving from my position in the trees was the mistake that got me caught. If I'd stayed still, I wouldn't have been spotted. As it was, I retreated right into the lines of the rebels. I almost got shot. Bullets whistled passed me, and I hit the dirt. When I looked up, a skinny, brown-skinned man with a pointy chin beard was staring at me. I stared back, not at him but at his gun. He said something to me in the Souvien language. I had no idea what his words were, but I got the drift of his meaning. I stood and raised my hands to the sky. He frisked me, taking away my pack and my bomb.

The next few days were a blur. I was herded in with other captives, mainly boys aged eleven to fifteen, but also some women and young children and a couple of government soldiers. We were marched through the puckerbrush deep into the woods. When we finally stopped, I heard a lot of muffled Souvien talk from the rebels. A minute later, the women and children were released to find their way back. As for the government soldiers, their hands were tied behind their backs and they were forced to kneel on the ground.

Ike and I were kept away from each other. Ike tried to say something to me, but a rebel kicked his legs out from under him. Another kid started talking real fast in Souvien, and a rebel slugged him. Blood jetted from his nose. We all got the message.

My wrists were tied in front of me, and the end of the rope was wrapped around the waist of another boy. The rope from the boy behind me was tied to my own waist. A rebel soldier gave a command, and the boy in the lead started walking. And so we trudged, a string of boys. A few minutes later, I heard gunshots. The captive government soldiers had been executed.

We were given cold rice and water to be consumed as we moved. Every couple of hours we stopped for a piss, but nobody was allowed to sit or lie down. The rebel troops said practically nothing to us. Once in a while a boy would start to cry, and a rebel soldier would crack him one across the face. After a couple of those lessons, nobody cried. By late afternoon of the first day, we were all walking stiff-gaited as grown-ups. When we finally stopped to bed down, I collapsed on the ground and slept as if in a trance.

The next day was more of the same. By watching the trees, I could tell that we weren't moving all that far from the village, just snaking back and forth through the forest and moving generally west and up slope. We reached the main rebel camp around noon of the third day. The camp wasn't much—tents, a fire, a slit trench for a toilet, and a bunch of guys with guns. I liked it.

We boys were brought in a circle where we were allowed to sit Indian style and relax. All of a sudden our captors were nice to us. They laughed and joked with the village boys. Although I didn't understand what they were saying, I couldn't miss the fact that they were being especially nice to me. They brought me water, untied me, smiled, and nodded at me like tippy birds on drugs. It wasn't until days later that I figured out that my tracking collar made me special.

I finally got to talk to Ike. Which was nice for a couple of reasons, not the least of which was that he was the only one I could understand. I asked him if he'd been tortured by the government troops.

"Not really," he said. "They were only protecting me from the rebels. I made a friend, and he told me that the rebels would kill anything and anybody just for the sake of aggravation. I had to stay put until the government could find a safe way to get me back to America."

"One of your captors was your friend?"

"Oh, sure. His name was Zando. He was a captain in the Souvien army. He wanted to be president some day. In his country, the way you get to be a president is to join the army. He was good to me. He was my, I don't know how to describe him." Ike stopped to ponder for a second, and he cracked his knuckles, and I cracked mine to show I could out-crack him, and he cracked his thumbs and his toes until he had nothing left to crack, and I cracked until

I had nothing left and we calculated that he had won by two cracks except that mine were louder so I got honorable mention, and then he said, "He was my guardian angel."

I wondered if Langdon was really Zando; if maybe there was only one guardian angel and he went wherever he was needed most.

"I know this sounds incredible," Ike said, "but back home in Souvien, Zando was a rancher. He had a boy about my age. He told me all about life on the island. They believe in freedom, work, responsibility, and property. Just like here. His people have been ranching for a hundred years, just like my people. The difference is they can't ranch in peace. Some of their local folk are dirty, ignorant, mean, lazy, profane. And they shoot back."

"You're talking about the rebels," I whispered.

"They're standing in the way of progress," Ike said. He didn't exactly whisper, but he spoke real low in his soft, serious voice. "They're evil. Do you think they'll stop in Souvien?" I shook my head no. Ike went on, his voice getting softer and softer so that I could barely hear him. "There'll be another island. And another. Pretty soon, all the islands will be theirs. Pretty soon, they'll be on the mainland. Taking over our cities. Pretty soon. Pretty soon." He paused.

I couldn't bear the tension. "They'll be here," I said.

"You bet," said Ike.

"Do you think they'll kill us?" I asked.

"Not if we pray."

"You—pray?" I almost laughed. Back in Valley of Fires, Ike, like many ranch boys, had been forced to go to church, but he never gave any indication that his religious upbringing had took. Now I could see that it had.

"It can't hurt," he said.

So we held hands and prayed silently. I moved my lips but didn't actually mouth any words, because I couldn't think of anything to say. Finally, a prayer came to mind; I whisper-thought: "Well, Lord/Lords, my friend here believes in You, so maybe there is a You. Irregardless, praise the Lord/Lords."

Ike filled me in on the news from Valley of Fires. The Autodidact and Mary Jane had come back from their honeymoon early after I'd disappeared. They were feeling glum, thinking I'd run off because they'd gotten married. Good, I thought. Meanwhile, Grandma Clements was in the hospital with a stroke. Bad. But she recovered. Good.

Ike told me about coming to rescue me. He'd hopped a train with ATV, his horse, then ridden to what appeared to be a box canyon, but in fact it opened into a cave. He'd walked the horse through the cave about a quarter mile and came out under a security fence within the MZ. He didn't get very far. Some government troops were waiting for him at the end of the cave, and they'd brought him to the village.

"How did you know I'd be here?" I asked.

"The note."

"What note?"

"The note you left under my saddle."

"I didn't send any note."

"Did so. 'Help! I'm a prisoner. Come alone.' There was a map, too, and the note was signed in blood, 'Your Brother.'"

"This is news to me," I said.

"If you didn't write it, who did?" Ike was angry.

"The Director, or maybe Xiphi. Maybe even the Alien himself," I said, and I tried to explain, telling him about Xi, Spree, Luck, Phi, VRN, and the Children of the Cacti. He didn't believe a word I said.

"Web, you're sick; your brain has turned to a cow patty. You should be committed."

I got mad. "I am committed, so are you—we're committed to the rebels, or they'll kill us."

"They'll never break me, never," he said. "They killed Zando, my guardian angel. I heard his last screams."

Before we had a chance to set things straight between us, something else happened that really disturbed Ike and poisoned him forever against the rebels. Dinner was served. Turned out it was ATV, his pinto horse. They cut up steaks from a hindquarter and barbecued them over open coals. First Ike cried softly and then he started to carry on, screaming and yelling swears. The rebels soldiers took him away, tied him to a tree, and gagged him. To tell you the truth, I was hungry so I ate some of the horse. It wasn't bad. It tasted like a beef cow who had been exercising regularly with Cynthia Kerluk.

That night it rained. We slept in tents. I could hear Ike still outside tied to his tree, crying. He'd been sent to rescue me, and then I'd been sent to rescue him. Now we were both prisoners. An evil power was at work, but I was too tired at the time to think too far down the road about it.

That next day a soldier gave a speech in Souvien to all of us captives gathered in a circle around the camp fire. Just when I wished I knew what he was saying, other soldiers arrived in the camp, and were greeted with hoots and hollers and given pats on the back by the others. One of the other soldiers was Siena. She walked toward me and said, "Stand." Something about her tone, not mean but commanding, made me jump to attention. "I have been assigned to be your translator," she said in a military voice, and then her voice softened. "Have a cigarette, Web."

VRN supplied food and arms to both the rebels and the government, as per the contract between the two parties, but cigarettes, because they were not good for health, were not allowed in the MZ. But Siena had brought a suitcase full. She'd picked them up from some drug runners in the desert. For the next hour, boys and rebel soldiers sat around and smoked, except for Ike, who sulked alone.

A routine soon set in. We boys worked every morning doing all the camp details ("details" is what they call a chore in the army), so the soldiers could goof off or fight. I dug slit trenches, sewed tent tears, and washed pots and pans for Carlos and Potzo, our cooks. In the afternoon, we were brought together in a circle for classes. For a joke, Ike called our daily gatherings the circle jerk. The Souvien soldiers didn't get it. Recruits from the Souvz gang of New York got it, but they didn't laugh. Ike had to spend another night tied to a tree.

Siena became my teacher, translating the lessons taught by the rebel instructors into English. The instructors talked endlessly, but

the gist went like this. A small group of old families owned everything in Souvien, all the land, all the banks, all the businesses,
all the wealth. A few people were very rich, but most were very
poor. You were born *in* or you were born *out*. The Souviens had
a saying for this pattern: the old in or out. As the rebels saw it, the
only way to make Souvien fair for all was with a revolution.

I asked Siena about the soldiers who had been executed the day
I had been captured. That was too bad, she said. She explained that
because the rebels were on the move, captives couldn't be cared
for in POW camps. They could be converted to the cause, released,
or executed. Government soldiers could never be trusted for con-
version; if they were released, they would only come back to fight
another day; therefore they had to be executed. I followed the
logic. Siena then started to give me a lecture on government and
revolution.

At first the things she said didn't make a lot of sense to me, but
after a couple of weeks, I began to see things the rebel way. It
wasn't right that most of the people should be miserable and a few
should have everything. Since there was no way the rich were going to give up their wealth and power, the rebels had to revolt. It
was better to start over. Blow everything up and rebuild the society from the smithereens. All this appealed to my need to hate.
The rebels, in their tirades against the government, gave me a
group deserving of my hate and a good reason to hate. The rebels
also promised that the purpose of my hate was to give me strength
to kill my enemies. After the revolution, they assured me that my
hate would be turned inside out, and I could love. Another plus:
I liked the rebel life-style—sleeping outdoors, rah-rah around
camp fires, guns, irregular hours, even speech-making.

Ike was stubborn. No matter how well Siena or the other instructors or I argued, he wouldn't listen. At first he argued back,
but we just laughed at him and he got frustrated. Then he wouldn't
argue at all, but he wouldn't give in either. He would just sit there
in the circle jerk with his arms folded. Finally, he wouldn't even
look at us, and he acted as if he didn't know we were there. I
worked like a dog trying to learn the Souvien language by studying it in my spare time, but Ike didn't even try. Eventually, he re-

treated completely into his own self. It was scary to see him like that. Siena said that by accident Ike had taught himself to meditate. Which wasn't all that bad. It was just that Ike was meditating about the wrong things.

Except for those first few days when they tied him to a tree and ate his horse, Ike was treated like everyone else. He slept in the same tents, wore the same desert-camouflage uniforms, went to the same camp meetings, and pooped in the same slit trenches, so I couldn't understand why he was so full of consternation. Potzo said he was jealous, because Siena liked me more than him.

Ike and I grew so far apart that we hardly had anything to do with one another. I talked to him only when I had to, and he didn't talk to me at all. After a while, I hardly noticed he was around. The other boys and I were becoming soldiers in the rebel army, and we were pretty busy. Also, we were constantly on the move, and our units were almost never in the same area at once. Several hundred men would be spread out over many miles, keeping in touch through code calls over the radio. When you're a guerrilla army fighting a government force that depends on tanks and artillery, rule one is stay in terrain where tanks get bogged down. Rule two is never bunch up, because one artillery barrage could wipe you out. I learned these things in my military training.

Being a soldier was very interesting. I practiced shooting automatic weapons and mortars. I was issued a R.O.C.K 99 machine gun, and I studied tactics such as fields of fire, hit-and-run attacks, and night fighting. Siena taught me hand-to-hand combat; I learned how to sneak up on somebody and twist a wire around their neck to kill them so they wouldn't make a sound. I was looking for a chance to try out these new tricks, but the rebels wouldn't let me take part in actual combat. They didn't trust me, because I was an American and a boy. I had to prove myself. Siena told me to bide my time.

By keeping on the move, we could stay away from the government troops and keep from getting wiped out by them. They couldn't catch us. Because they were so heavily armed, we couldn't attack them directly. Since both sides spoiled for a fight, we fought over the village even though there was nothing there of any military value. I began to understand why VRN insisted on DCs. The village and the civilian casualties made the war more interesting for the viewers. We rebels would surprise the enemy, burn a few buildings, and leave. A couple of times we actually occupied the village for a few days until the government opened up on us with their howitzers, and we had to get out of town. Eventually most of the DCs were dead, captured, or converted into fighters. All the animals were killed off, and the buildings were burned or blown up. On the last raid, we went in and found nothing there—no people, no critters, no habitable structures. Nothing was left to fight for in Sorrows.

After Sorrows was destroyed, the government set up a garrison headquarters on the desert floor. They moved all their guns and tanks, not to mention prostitutes, to the garrison. If we'd had long-range artillery, tanks, and an air force, we could have taken the garrison in a day. But with only small arms and mortars, we couldn't get near it without being cut to pieces. Since we couldn't deliver a knock-out blow to the government, and since they couldn't even find us, at least not so they could bring their tanks and artillery into play, nothing much was going on. The war stayed a tie.

I pushed Ike into the background, thinking that he was just a stubborn boy and that soon he'd see that Siena and I were right. And then one day, I happened to find myself alone with him. There was always a space between the camp and the perimeter of defense where guards watched for enemy troops. The new recruits—which by now included more girls besides Siena, some DCs, Souvz from American city gangs as well as boy captives— were allowed to wander in that space. I was taking a walk when I spotted Ike sitting on a log, his face buried in his hands. He was so skinny and pitiful.

I sat down beside him and went into the spiel I'd learned from Siena. "You can join our troop. They'll take you on, like they took me," I said.

"I never thought much about the meaning of life before," Ike said. "I loved my parents, I loved the ranch, I loved my country. I just wanted to raise cows to feed the people. But things have changed. Web, I've become a pacifist. I have vowed before God that I will never kill."

"What if somebody was torturing your mother?"

"My pacifist cause would come first."

"Suppose there is no God. Who would you vow to then?"

"I'm vowing now before you: I will never kill."

I didn't know what to say. I'd never met a pacifist before. I thought that the breed had long ago become extinct. I offered him a cigarette. He turned it down.

"You won't eat, you won't think like everybody else, you won't even smoke. Ike, what are you living on?" I asked.

"My belief in my pacifism—it's my food, it's my be-all and end-all," he said.

For the first time, I understood. Ike was suffering for his cause. I had helped make him suffer. What good was *my* cause if it made my friend suffer? I couldn't find a way to explain my understanding to Ike, and I couldn't help him. The moment passed between us without a good word from me.

Without warning, VRN exercised its intervention clause based on low ratings and called for a cease-fire. Each side was ordered to propose a strategy for action at a meeting with VRN producers and the Director. The rebels sent four officers to represent them. Their proposal was to bring in another village from Souvien with a contingent of DCs so that the rebels and the government would have something and somebody to fight over.

The delegation was gone for two days. When they returned, they did not have happy looks on their faces. After the evening mess (which was what we called meals in the military), Siena and I sat around the camp fire smoking, and she gave me the scoop.

"Our proposal was turned down," she said.

"Why?" I asked. "It would solve VRN's problem by creating more battles."

"According to the polls of the sample audience, viewers can only be subjected to a limited number of atrocities to civilians, and then they are turned off. We're past the quota. Another thing. The polls show that most viewers want to see us lose the war. As a result, the Director ordered us to attack the main garrison in daylight so it will photograph well.

"But that whole area is mined, we won't have cover, their tanks will destroy us. It's suicide to attack," I said.

"Nonetheless, it is the wish of the Director," Siena said. "It will be a glorious death. If we take no action, our death will be slow and ignoble, because VRN is going to cut off our supplies. No food, no ammunition. The government will starve us out."

"It's hopeless. We might as well surrender and fight the real war in Souvien," I said.

"No, this is more important for the cause. We need arms and public support, and we need to spread our ideas all over the world. If we surrender, we will dishearten the folks back home. We must fight and die in glory. For the cause. It will be seen by millions on television. Our martyrdom will inspire our people on Souvien to rise up against the oppressors. We will be remembered, as we say in our country, *ad pater nauseum*."

"I want to fight, too. I want to die gloriously."

"This is not your war, Web."

"I have no father, no mother, no country anymore. All I have is the cause, the ideas you've given me." I meant those words, and yet when I spoke them, they reminded me that there was more to say. I repeated, "The ideas and. . . ." I paused. I didn't want to say any more.

Siena looked me up and down. She knew I was hiding something. "Yes, you have our ideas. They have become your ideas. They have become you. This we know. What else? What is it that we do not know?"

"Nothing," I lied. But it was a weak lie. As Father used to say, you should never lie with your pants down.

"There is something else. What is it?" Siena's voice was hard, cutting. "I can feel your concern for this other, this alien thing. What is it?"

I said nothing, but she pressed me.

"The love for your mother has returned, weakened you—is that it?

"No."

"Another cause? You've been reading the propaganda leaflets dropped by the government planes."

I shook my head. "No, nothing like that."

She grabbed my shirtfront. We were eyeball to eyeball. She was exactly the same height as myself. Her smooth face, nose, lips were all like my own. The only difference between us was in the eyes; hers were like the black dimes of Langdon. "What, then?" she asked. "What else can rank with the great idea of freedom from repression? Or equality for all? Or wealth for the many instead of the few? What?"

"Ike," I said.

She let go of me. "I should have known."

"He's my blood brother. We've parted over ideas and causes, but he's still my friend."

Siena poked at the fire. "It's normal that you should love your friend."

"It's the only kind of love in me."

"Do you believe in the rebel cause?"

"You taught me."

"But do you believe?"

"Yes," I said sincerely.

"At the same time, you love your friend and wish to see him free?"

"Yes," I said sincerely.

"You understand that the love you feel for your friend betrays the cause."

"Yes. Couldn't you just let him go? He's an American. He's not part of our fight."

"That was true until he proclaimed his principles. He is a dangerous adversary to all sides. Not only us rebels, but the government, the United States, and, most important of all, VRN."

"I don't understand," I said.

"Your friend is a professed pacifist. If he's allowed to spread his ideas, it could be the end of the world as we know it."

"I have to stick by him—he's my blood brother," I said.

"Web, I've tried to teach you about the cause. It's all I have."

She started to leave, and then she stopped. "I feel all these complicated things toward you. I couldn't begin to explain them. You and me, we're going to have to decide who we belong to, what we belong to."

"You've already decided. You just told me."

"Web, I'm as lost as you." And she walked away from me.

I sat alone by the fire, empty and weak. I wished the war would start up again. These cease-fires were confusing.

The next day the Director himself arrived, not a holograph, but in the flesh, the real thing. He didn't speak to us directly, but over an electronic bullhorn that made his voice sound even more like the Director in my imagination. And by speaking from a portable raised platform, dragged by a jeep, the real Director kept a distance between himself and the rebels.

"Siena," called the Director. "Come here." He spoke in English, and a translator put the words in Souvien.

Siena marched to the platform. "The following names have been supplied to VRN by rebel leaders. Siena, will you read them, please." A VRN assistant delivered the list to Siena, and she read it aloud.

"These boys are Good Boys," the Director said. "They will become Good Soldiers, and they will be allowed to fight in the great battle to come."

A cheer went up from the troops. I did not cheer. Two boys were not on the list, myself and Ike.

After that the Director played a videotape of my conversation with Siena the night before.

"Siena," the Director said, "You started strong, but you weakened at the end of the scene. Your loyalty to the cause has been called into question."

"I will sacrifice my life for the cause, I will do anything for the cause," Siena said.

"And you, Web," the Director said, "You've undermined Siena's resolve. You must choose between your friend Ike and the cause."

"I choose the cause," I said.

"It's not as easy as that," the Director said. "The two of you must pass a test. Siena, will you take such a test?"

"Itsyen," said Siena in Souvien. (Translation: yes.)

"You, Web. Will you the take a test?"

"Itsyen," I said.

A cheer went up from the rebel band.

The test was simple. I would be given a gun with one bullet in it. At a public execution, I would kill Ike. If I failed to pass the test, Siena would kill me.

THE EXPOSITION OF THE UNCANNY

In humans the past accumulates in the form of distorted memories that sicken us with questions. What is real? Who am I? Since the questions spring from experiences which are perceived only fleetingly and defectively, on the fly, as it were, and since the experiences are then stored in the defective database of human memory, it follows that our profound questions cannot lead to profound answers. So perhaps the cure for the malaise of memory is in the creation of an entertaining artificial profundity, an exposition of the uncanny —From the Journal of Henri Scratch.

The order came: "Move out!" I'd done it enough to know the routine: gather my sleeping bag and my few belongings, stuff them into my backpack, grab my R.O.C.K. 99 machine gun, and fall in with my squad. Today everything was different. I packed my things, but when I slung my gun over my shoulder, Siena held out her hand.

"Web, give me the piece, please," she said.

I unslung the gun and handed it to her. She took it gently. "It will be returned with one bullet in the chamber," she said. The cold in her black dime eyes told me that she had decided she would kill me if I didn't kill Ike. I respected her.

In the next moment, I got a glimpse of Ike at the end of the clearing in the woods, maybe a hundred feet away. They'd put him in a cage of alder saplings. I moved toward him, but Siena blocked my way. Four strong men lifted the cage and took Ike away. I watched them vanish in the trees.

Meanwhile, all the rebel units began to gather. It was the first time we had been brought together as a single group. I was surprised how big the force was, five or six hundred troops, including some village women and even a few children. Some of the Souvien soldiers shared cherries and apples picked from wild fruit trees. Others had adopted $$$ Indian ways, garnered from studying cave drawings created by native peoples of long ago. These soldiers painted raccoon masks around their eyes, wore Möbius strip earrings, and braided their hair. One soldier was weeping. He'd built a house of worship in the woods, but had been forced to abandon it. Another walked with his DC woman and infant, conceived and born in the mountains. I wondered what the child's citizenship status would be. A way of life had been established on this soil, not exactly Souvien or American or Indian, but a combination of the three to create something new and different.

The newcomers who captured my attention, however, were recruits from the boy gangs. I saw Islands, the leader of the Souvz boy gang back in the South Bronx. His bodyguard, the Pope of Death, had been killed before he even reached the war, run over by a drunk driver when the boys were hitchhiking to the West. I saw Terry. He wasn't fighting for the cause, but simply because he wanted to fight; he was a mercenary. Ronnie had been recruited by the Souvien government as a paid fighter, so it was possible that Terry and Ronnie might some day have to shoot each other. I saw Bik; his friend Nox had signed on with the government and been killed. Back home in America a fresh batch of boys continued the race wars among Shadows, Souvz, and River Rats.

Instead of moving by night in zig-zag lines, with our people spread out over miles of forest, we marched in daylight in a column of twos down a winding, logging road, through the big pines, through the junipers and mesquite, and into the desert all the way to Xi. For fighters who had been used to skulking, this direct approach was scary. We were sitting ducks for an attack by our mechanized enemy. After hours of walking, we reached our new camp designated by VRN, on the edge of the newest addition to Xi. To our back were hills and cliffs. To our front in the distance in the MZ was the government garrison, ringed by bunkers and barbed wire, tanks and howitzers. I half hoped they'd open fire, which would spare me the agony of killing Ike.

Waiting for us on the desert floor were a camera crew and other officials from VRN. Maintenance workers from Xi had built a bonfire heap out of wood refuse from the destroyed town of Sorrows. Surrounding us were platforms for holding lights and tracks for cameras.

In the woods, the sky had been blocked by the trees, but here under the desert floor, it was open and beautiful. It was like being back in Valley of Fires or on the deck of the mother ship, the universe spread out before me. The sky above, so immense and bright, did not seem real. It was too close. Ike flashed onto the screen of my mind. He was on his horse, galloping along the desert. The two of them, boy and pony, flew off into the sky. I trailed behind on my winged ATV.

I couldn't eat dinner. I just wandered around the campground until the sun began to set. An electronic version of Souvien folk music played over a sound system. Soldiers stood outside their tents, first keeping time with the beat, then dancing in place. It was music my mother would have loved. When the last distant glow of the sunset had faded into black night, the music stopped abruptly, and a raspy voice came over the speaker: "Will you all please gather at the bonfire set." The Director had spoken.

It took almost ten minutes for the soldiers to form a circle around the huge stack of boards and timbers from the wrecked village of Sorrows. I wasn't exactly part of the group. I was kept separated and escorted by two armed guards. The rebels gave me a round of applause as they parted and I walked through them. Huge, portable lights had been set up, and I could hear the hum of electronics. American VRN workers in blue jeans paraded around giving orders. The cameras rolled. Giant television monitors had been set up, so that no matter where anyone stood in the audience they could see what was going on at the bonfire set.

The Director stood on a wooden platform like a lifeguard stationed at a beach. Bullhorn in hand, he spoke to the audience in his gargling, drowning-man voice.

"Thank you all for coming, thank you, thank you. Because many will die in the war scenes to follow, we are holding the cast party now. I have some good news for the soldiers fighting for all these months without female company. We have brought in a contingent of professional ladies from the bordellos of Nevada and points south in neighboring Mexico." The monitors showed pretty women in their underwear. The men went crazy.

"We've had complaints that we're rigging the war in favor of the government," the Director said. "We've changed that. We're giving you rebels some limited air support and a couple of tanks for your invasion of the garrison. We've tried to make the odds even-steven. We at VRN don't care who wins. We just want action. The war resumes tomorrow, so make it a good party. We'll start now!"

The soldiers clapped and cheered. I looked around for Siena. She stood beside the Director's platform dignified as the sentry on the masthead of the Keene, New Hampshire, *Sentinel* newspaper; she did not cheer.

"Thank you, thank you," the Director said. "Have fun. The festivities will culminate at midnight with the execution of Ike, the Bad Boy pacifist. Guards, bring Web to a holding cell."

The spotlight left the Director and shined down on Ike's cage. Hoots and jeers issued from the soldiers. Then the light fell upon me, blinding me for a few seconds. When I could see again, two soldiers stood beside me. They escorted me to the new wing of Xi. A giant sign said:

Under Construction:
The Exposition of the Uncanny

Inside were walls of unfinished sheetrock, stacks of flooring tiles and lumber. The soldiers locked me in the only room that appeared to be complete. It was an ordinary enough waiting room like you'd find in any dentist's office. Small, with a single couch, magazine rack, brass lamp, and a painting on the wall. Only one thing about the room was uncanny, the painting. It showed a boy on a glowing rock. Myself. I stared hard. No doubt about it: the painting was one done of me while I was in the Catacombs of Manhattan. I paced around the room, vaguely hoping for a way out. There was none. I sat on the couch, and browsed through the reading matter to pass the time. It was the oddest collection of magazines I'd ever seen. They included the *Clean Slate Society Broadside* and the *Organ for the Institute of Original Sin,* the *Secular Humanist University Alumni Magazine,* and *Crit: an Anthology of Critical Essays of the Late 80s and Early 90s.* I picked up *Crit.* The first article was by Henri Scratch. It took a second before I remembered the name. Back at Sally's place in Steeltown, the Autodidact had read me Mister Scratch's obituary. I read the first paragraph of the essay, entitled *Defrocked, or I Think, Therefore:* "I think; therefore I am. But when I think about who I am, I am not being who I am; I am thinking. If I just do it, I don't have the satisfaction of knowing I have done it until I think about having done it, and then I am no longer doing it, and since I am no longer doing it, the understanding I have about the experience of having done it (the satisfaction) is, at best, slightly inaccurate. These, my words, constitute the impossible dream of trying to catch up with this me that was."

I yawned and put the magazine down. I glanced up at the painting on the wall. The "me" in the picture had changed; now it was Xiphi. I couldn't stand looking at the picture, and I decided to take it down. I lifted it off the nail in the wall, and was surprised to find a door where the painting had been. Well, not a door exactly. More like a hatch. I pulled the handle, and the hatch opened into a dimly lit tunnel. Maybe it was an air shaft. I climbed up into it. I crawled on my hands and knees for perhaps five minutes until I came to another hatch.

Behind the second hatch was a ramp. It hit me then: I had found my way into the mother ship. A purple light fell upon me. At that moment, I saw the Alien coiled like a cobra. He hissed at me. I took a long look at him, the last of my demons to come into being. The face could have belonged to a scholar. The scaly, snake body went back into time long before humankind had been created for the Earth.

The Alien uncoiled and slithered up the ramp. Trembling, I followed, crawling on all fours.

The ramp led to a foot-high hatch, which said "Displays." The Alien hissed, and the hatch opened. The Alien slipped in, and I bellied through. Inside it was pitch black, but the air felt more lively: I reached over my head. No ceiling. I stood, quivering with fright but determined to go on. A dim spotlight fell on me, and then on the Alien. As I walked, sensors reacted to the presence of the Alien and my body and activated the lights of the displays so I could see them.

The first display featured Pinto, my ATV. I could smell the motor oil. I wanted to hop on and ride away, but when I reached for the handlebars, the Alien snapped at my hand and I jerked back.

The lights on the ATV dimmed to black, while the next display lit up, a glass case holding the trinitite I'd found in the Trinity Site. Beside it was another glass case containing the clothes I'd worn when I'd fled from Louisiana across Texas. A tag underneath said: "Upon Completion of the Exposition, Web's clothes will be donated to the Repository of Smells, Smithsonian Institution."

After that was a bust of my head, towel wrapped around it. Under the bust was the picture Royal had taken of me in robes. Between the eyes of the bust was a button. I pushed it. Frog sounds croaked from the mouth of the bust. I jumped back in fright.

The Alien snaked to another hatch, and we went through. I touched the snake's tail just before it disappeared into darkness. It felt like Xiphi's whang in a wet dream. The next room was an art gallery. All the pictures were of me from my time in the Catacombs of Manhattan. The artists presented me in different ways. In some canvases, I looked like a lost boy. In others, I had cruel eyes and a sarcastic mouth. In others, I didn't even look like me, but was just lines, colors, and shapes.

The gallery dimmed to darkness as I walked on, following the slowly slithering Alien. I got down on my hands and knees again, as we went through a hatch. On the other side were life-size statues of myself before I'd matured. One statue wore a Langdon suit, the other was naked, covered with permanent mud: Xiphi. I touched them. Wax dummies.

The Alien and I passed through a twisting, dimly lit passage (I had to crawl) and came out in a good-sized area—I could tell by the change in the air and a slight echo of my breath. From the odd smell and from the sight that opened before me as the lights came on, I thought for a moment that I was back in the Home of the Grateful Dead.

One by one, as the Alien and I passed by, Marla's liquid-filled caskets were illuminated. I paused before each to pay my respect: Terry's brother, the murdered boy/girl with the d-a-d hex on his buns; the homeless man with a patch over one eye that the boy gangs had shot; three boys from the boy gangs—Nox, Pope, and Dunc—suspended together in one casket. On a plaque before the boy gang members were written words in poetic form of a conversation I'd had with Pope.

"The Shadows are brave."
He sounded tired and old for a boy.
"You can shoot them or knife them
Or whip them with chains;
They yell and scream and cry their eyes out,
but they never complain."
"So you'd like to make peace between the gangs."
"No way, I want war."
I want to kill as many Shadows as I can.
I want to kill them all."

Next was a casket containing a man in a business suit. Floating around in the liquid with the man were thousands of dollars in Monopoly money. I didn't recognize the man, but I recognized the person in the casket beside him. It was Mother. This time I felt neither hatred nor dream-love for her. She was just my mother, and she was gone. I got down on my knees and I wept for her, and then I wept for myself. I prayed to the persons in God for her soul. Beside Mother was Father, poor doomed, misguided revolutionary, dressed in his flannel shirt, blue jeans, and work boots, suspended in Marla's secret, preservative liquid. I had a prayer for him, too, but no tears.

I heard a hiss. The Alien lay coiled beside a hatch with a sign on it: "Danger. No Earth Atmosphere Behind This Point." The Alien slithered through and I followed. The hatch swung closed behind me. The air was musty, dirty, and smelled of puke and shit. I was in a refrigerated room with walls of ice. Encased in the ice were the polaroid pictures Father had taken of me. In the middle of the room was a block of almost clear ice. Suspended inside was an overweight, ordinary looking white man in his middle years. He was naked and his erection was pumped up to full size. A wooden stake had been driven through his heart. He had the same face as the Alien.

I heard a hiss and then a human groan from the Alien. The creature stretched out to its full length and stiffened in a death throe. The face melted to nothing before my eyes. I smelled burnt plastic. The Alien had been only a machine. I started to shiver with fear and cold.

I turned to the man in ice and stared and stared. It was Henri Scratch. We'd traveled together in his van. Someone had been on our trail. That was all I could remember. The lights dimmed behind me, a door swung open. I saw starlight, the bonfire ablaze. The warmth of outside air swept away the cold stench.

Soldiers and whores danced around the bonfire. Bright, eerie stage lights shone in my face as I walked toward the fire.

The Director stood away from me between two lights. Beside him was Siena. She carried her pistol in one hand and my R.O.C.K. 99 automatic rifle in the other. As I came toward them, Siena started toward me. When we met, she whispered to me. "You've decided?"

"Yes," I whispered back. "I'm going down in a blaze of glory. You'll kill me and I'll meet my mother in hell."

The music died away, the dancing stopped, and the cage with Ike in it was wheeled in. A soldier unlocked the cage and marched Ike toward us. He didn't seem scared, just dazed. I don't think he understood what was going on around him.

"Make him kneel," I said.

The soldiers pushed Ike to his knees, and he bowed his head. I stood behind him.

"Give me the gun, Siena," I said.

Siena put the gun in my hand, and stepped toward her stage mark.

I checked the chamber. It contained one bullet. I lifted the gun, put it to Ike's head, and I shouted at the camera, "This is what you people want. Death. Horror. Fun. Well, I'm not going to do it." Ike lifted his head.

Groans went up from the crowd of rebels. One soldier said in his native language, "The young man's noodle has cracked before it was sufficiently boiled." (Rough translation of old Souvien expression.)

I put the gun to my own head and started toward the bonfire. I felt the heat, first of the fire and then of the video lights. I dropped the gun down to my side, and turned it suddenly toward Siena. I strode toward her. She started toward her holstered pistol, changed her mind; she held her ground, but I could see her sweat.

"Are you ready to die?" I said.

"No, but maybe it's better this way."

I wheeled, and walked toward the cameraman. "This is getting out of hand," he said in English.

"Keep the cameras going," rasped the Director. "This is great stuff. He knows what he's doing."

I screamed at the Director, "You bet." And I pointed my gun at him. Siena's hand dropped to her holster. I fired. My aim was dead perfect. The bullet caught the Director right in the middle of the chest. The force kicked him backward a few feet, and he fell with a thump on his hump. I expected to die—Siena was a very good shot. But she didn't fire; she had betrayed her cause for my life. I thought it was over for the Director, but he surprised me by staggering to his feet. His black cat-burglar suit was torn up at the chest where the bullet had hit, but no blood showed. "Bullet-proof vest!" he laughed.

I knew that laugh, and I charged, tackling him like a football player. Guards rushed forward, but Royal yelled, "Stay off. This is good footage." I grabbed his carrot-colored beard and pulled it off.

"I must have told you everything under hypnosis, and you used that to haunt me," I said.

Royal ripped away the voice squack box from his chest and pulled off the rest of his makeup. "It took you long enough to figure it out."

"You sent Father the money and tempted him to take those pictures of me. You twisted the truth to make it look like I killed him in a fit of madness."

"Artistic license was necessary, since even you don't know exactly what happened, for that night you were mad."

"You put the note under Ike's saddle and tormented him."

"Yes, to make him suffer the way I made Dirty Joe suffer."

"Ike never did anything to you."

"He replaced me as your best friend."

I grabbed Royal's fake hump and twisted it. In the old days, Royal would have pinned me in nothing flat. But I'd grown stronger and quicker, and he was hampered by the hump glued to his back and bruised from the impact of my bullet. I never let go of the hump. I knew that if he could put some space between us, he'd start punching and I'd start bleeding. We rolled on the ground, getting ever nearer to the fire. He kept getting more and more tangled in his body machinery of bullet-proof mesh, padding, and wires. I finally got on top of him and picked up a rock from the ground.

"I'm going to bash your head in and throw you in the fire," I said.

"Go ahead, kill me," Royal said. He wasn't the least bit afraid. I was impressed. Royal might have his faults, but cowardice wasn't one of them. He was a noble boy.

"You'll die with my respect," I said.

"Fayguck yaygou," he said.

Just before I brought down the rock, I heard a woman's voice shout from the crowd, "Stop!"

It was Marla. I turned toward her. "Stay out of this."

"Yah, go back to your cavern of the dead," said Royal.

"You can't kill Royal. He's your brother," Marla said.

"I don't have a brother," I said.

"Royal's father was your mother's first lover. He was a producer for a rock band. You saw him in the Exposition of the Uncanny, the man with the Monopoly money."

Marla grabbed a flashlight from one of the video crew and walked toward me. I could see us both on a monitor. Marla shone the light in Royal's face. In that second, I saw Royal's green and gold eyes.

Royal made frog sounds.

I lifted the rock. I still wasn't sure whether to bash him or let him go.

Marla spoke in Royal's defense. "He designed the Exposition of the Uncanny in hopes of bringing back your memory."

"Actually, Web," Royal said, "I just wanted to see the look on your face on the monitor when you saw Scratch with a boner. Believe me, I wasn't disappointed."

"What?" I said, frowned, and lifted the rock higher over my head. Royal imitated my frown. Suddenly, I understood the humor of the situation. I started laughing. I tossed the rock away. Soon we were both rolling on the ground laughing. Ike came around, and he laughed too. Eventually all the young people were laughing. None of the adults laughed. They looked at us as if we were crazy.

Siena threw her pistol into the bonfire. The bullets in it crackled. The boy soldiers, the girl soldiers, the teen DCs, the Souvz recruits—all the young people—came forward and threw their weapons into the fire. Ike's pacifism had won out.

"Royal, did you kill Scratch?" I asked.

"I didn't have to. His wife did." Royal glanced over at Marla. "She was more of a mother to you than Flower."

Next came the uncanny, a sensation of being lifted off my feet, turned sideways, and flattened out to two dimensions, thrusted

through a black exit of hell into the eden of the silver screen to live
out the remainder of my years.

EXT. THE BONFIRE—LATER THAT NIGHT

Web drifts away from the carousing at the bonfire site until he
comes upon the green van. He stares hard at it. He recognizes
now that this vehicle was the home of Henri Scratch, his
abuser. The door slides open to reveal Siena.

                    SIENA
        I knew you'd come.

INT. THE VAN

Web and Siena grope for one other, awkward and unskilled but
full of deep feeling. The light is dim, and since they're both
about the same size, built along the same general lines, it's
difficult to tell who is Web and who is Siena. At the same time,
we see them on the van's TV monitor.

                    WEB
        This is it, isn't it? The feeling.

                    SIENA
        It's the future.

                    WEB
        Far out. Far out. Far out.

Web and Siena continue their gentle lovemaking, as we HEAR
voices from the future, Web and Royal as grown men.

                    ROYAL (Voice Over)
        Statement of purpose? Whose idea is this?
        Aristotle? Bik?

                    WEB (V.O.)
        Guess.

                    ROYAL (V.O.)
        Did my opponent put you up to this?

                    WEB (V.O.)
        Ike would never stoop to anything so low.
        I wrote it with Jim's help.

ROYAL (V.O.)
I should have known. Go ahead, read it.

WEB (V.O.)
Okay, here it is. "Statement of Purpose:
Frog Brothers Productions invites you to
live your emotional lives through us. We
will love the lovers you cannot have, cry
the tears you are too embarrassed to
shed, feel the pains you cannot bear,
spend the money you cannot make, commit
the crimes you cannot carry out; we will
kill your enemies; we will reward your
allies; we will suffer and die for you."

ROYAL (V.O.)
Sounds like something Scratch would
concoct.

WEB (V.O.)
Everything we do sounds like Scratch.
He's our inspiration.

Web and Siena sigh together in orgasm.

SIENA
I have to leave now, I have to go to war.

WEB
I'll wait.

SIENA
Don't wait. Just watch.

INT. ROYAL'S OFFICE IN THE FUTURE

The "mad boys" are now pushing forty. Royal is handsome,
heavyset, smooth, dressed in an orange and black business
suit. He sits behind a big desk. On the desk is the chunk of
trinitite Web found. In the background, visible through the
windows, is a billboard that says "Durocher for President."
Web is slender, alert, somewhat pained. He looks like the young
Jerry Brown. He's dressed in black, but we don't see him full
front. In the background is the AUTODIDACT. He's a very old
man now, but aging gracefully. As always, Royal is in command.
He's looking at the Statement of Purpose on a giant monitor.

WEB
What do you think?

                    ROYAL
              (laughs in derision)
      It's good PR. You don't believe it, do you?

Web turns toward the camera. We see now that he is dressed like a Catholic priest.

                    WEB
      Of course I believe. It's why I wear the collar.

University Press of New England publishes books under its own imprint and is the publisher for Brandeis University Press, Brown University Press, University of Connecticut, Dartmouth College, Middlebury College Press, University of New Hampshire, University of Rhode Island, Tufts University, University of Vermont, and Wesleyan University Press.

About the Author Ernest Hebert's highly acclaimed Darby series includes the novels *The Dogs of March, A Little More Than Kin, Whisper My Name, The Passion of Estelle Jordan,* and *Live Free or Die,* the second and fourth of which have recently been reprinted by University Press of New England in a joint volume entitled *The Kinship.* Hebert lives with his wife and two daughters in West Lebanon, New Hampshire, and teaches writing at Dartmouth College.

Library of Congress Cataloging-in-Publication Data

Hebert, Ernest.
Mad boys : a novel / by Ernest Hebert.
   p.   cm.
ISBN 0–87451-643-9 (hard)
I. Title.   PS3558.E277M33   1993   813'.54—dc20   93–969
∞